In the Queen's service, in the service
of the British Raj, men had to die.
It was inevitable. Over the years of
Empire, many thousands had perished
in mutiny, in open action, in riot and
pillage and fire, in drowning during
crossings of swollen river fords.
The North-West Frontier was soaked
in British blood, its lonely, terrible
mountains salted by whitened British
bones when there had been no time
to bury the dead, salted by the
mouldering corpses in the shallow,
rocky graves along the passes into
Afghanistan, corpses that had come
from almost every regiment and
corps of the British Army. The 114th
were simply following on in the
tradition, and that, really, was all . . .

Also by Duncan MacNeil

DRUMS ALONG THE KHYBER
LIEUTENANT OF THE LINE
SADHU ON THE MOUNTAIN PEAK
THE GATES OF KUNARJA
THE RED DANIEL

and published by Corgi Books

Duncan MacNeil

Subaltern's Choice

An 'Ogilvie' novel

CORGI BOOKS

A DIVISION OF TRANSWORLD PUBLISHERS LTD

SUBALTERN'S CHOICE
A CORGI BOOK 0 552 10013 7

Originally published in Great Britain by
Hodder and Stoughton Ltd.

PRINTING HISTORY
Hodder and Stoughton edition published 1974
Corgi edition published 1975

This book is set in 10-11pt Baskerville (Intertype)

Corgi Books are published by Transworld Publishers Ltd.,
Cavendish House, 57–59 Uxbridge Road,
Ealing, London. W.5.
Made and printed in Great Britain by
Hunt Barnard Printing Ltd., Aylesbury, Bucks.

Subaltern's Choice

ONE

IN THE FAR distance, they saw the figure moving towards them, slowly, staggering. In that crystal-clear air they saw it crumple, slide formlessly to the ground in a heap. They saw the Wolseley helmet roll a little way down a slope, exposing the man's head to the fierce Indian sunlight. Ogilvie's field-glasses showed the blue-green hackle of the Royal Strathspey pointing towards the high, barren hills of the Afghan border to their left.

'Mr Dewar's patrol,' he said to his colour-sergeant. 'Or what's left of it, perhaps!'

'Aye, sir.' Colour-Sergeant MacTrease wiped sweat from his face, from the heavy moustache that hung like a collision mat over a strong mouth. MacTrease was a strong man, square and tough and rugged, a Highlander from the Cairngorms. 'Will I get the men moving, then, Captain Ogilvie, sir?'

Ogilvie nodded. 'Move out, if you please, Colour-Sar'nt.'

Men climbed to their feet: there was a clatter of rifles and equipment, of side-arms and commissariat utensils. Out here on the Frontier, last outpost of the Raj, men were accompanied constantly by all life's most immediate necessities, and those of death as well. With the object of their probe now in sight, they marched the faster: but it would still take most of half an hour under a cruel sun to close the kilted heap on the ground. High overhead, circling out of range of the Highlanders' advance, vultures hung beneath a cloudless blue sky – black beastliness, watching, waiting, eagerly anticipating. Ogilvie, looking up, shook a useless fist. Pausing

7

a moment in the advance, he again put up his field-glasses to study the figure in the dust ahead, but Colour-Sergeant MacTrease beat him to it.

'It's an officer, sir. Mr Dewar himself, sir.'

Ogilvie set his teeth. 'Mr Dewar, is it! And the rest of the patrol?'

'We'll be finding that out, sir.' For a moment, the eyes of officer and N.C.O. met in a soldier's understanding: this was unpleasant business, or could prove so. However it was not the moment, nor was it Ogilvie's task, to apportion blame. They went ahead, the men running now across the rock-strewn dust of British India, not so far from the North-West Frontier, knowing that along the outer hill-crests distant Pathan eyes would be squinting down the sights of the long-barrelled rifles with their rusted snaky bayonets anxious to plunge into British stomachs. Officially at this moment, there was peace: the Queen-Empress at Windsor had no quarrel with the ruler in Kabul, nor with his hard-faced Pathans along the mountain passes. But as ever, in peace as in war, the North-West Frontier was an uneasy line between Afghanistan and the British Raj, and British regiments were still, as they had been throughout their long service to the farthest-flung jewel in Victoria's imperial crown, fine targets for the guns and steel of the border tribes.

Ahead, there was blood staining the yellow dust. Ogilvie was the first to reach Hamish Dewar. There was a furrow along the top of the head. A private retrieved the officer's helmet, brought it back smoothing the flash set into the dip of the puggaree behind the badge of the Royal Strathspey. There was a bullet-hole in the pith, at the back: a shot at a running man? An unworthy thought, no doubt; yet brag-garts could talk louder than they acted, sometimes.

Ogilvie cradled the subaltern's head in his arms, put his water-bottle to dry, cracked lips. At first there was no move-ment, no reaction at all: the face was dead white – no tan as yet, for Hamish Dewar was new to Indian service despite the star of a full lieutenant on the shoulder-straps of his khaki drill tunic. The right arm was caked with blood from a bullet wound. The eyes were closed, yet Ogilvie's feeling hand had found a heartbeat – low and uncertain, but not weak enough to suggest imminent death. They had heard no firing: the wounds were not of immediate origin. Still holding the water-bottle, Ogilvie looked up at his colour-sergeant.

'Leave him to me,' he said. 'Follow his tracks back, see what you can find.'

'It's my guess we'll no' find the patrol, sir.'

'Why's that, Colour-Sar'nt?'

MacTrease looked away above Ogilvie's head, his face stiff and suddenly formal. 'Beggin' your pardon, sir. I'd sooner not say more.'

'Whatever you'd sooner, Colour-Sar'nt, you'll say what was in your mind.'

'Sir! It was only that I fancied Mr Dewar had the look of a sole survivor, sir. I have plenty of experience along the Frontier, sir. Many and many a time I've seen this sort of thing. It's my belief the patrol has been cut up.'

Ogilvie gave an involuntary sigh. 'All right, Colour-Sar'nt, thank you.'

'I'll carry on, sir?'

'Carry on, Colour-Sarn't.'

'Sir!' Reminiscent of Bosom Cunningham, Regimental Sergeant-Major, MacTrease gave a swinging salute and turned on his heel, bringing his boot down so hard as almost to strike sparks from the rock. As though on parade at the regimental depot at Invermore in Scotland, he marched away and began roaring at the men; leaving behind two privates and a lance-corporal, who spread out as cover for the two officers, he sent the rest of the party back along the way Dewar had come, using the bush-lore of the soldier, watching for boot mark and blood drop, watching out also for what he still had no hopes of finding: signs of other British life. As he went, MacTrease sucked his teeth more than a little. He, too, had seen the bullet-hole in the back of the helmet, but for that there could be more than one explanation. Mr Dewar was not, in MacTrease's view, a coward. But he was rash, and he wouldn't be told. Rash

9

officers, however brave they might be, could be a sad and bloody drain upon a fine regiment. And MacTrease, as much as James Ogilvie, as much as R.S.M. Cunningham, as much as the Colonel, Lord Dornoch himself, felt a fierce pride in, and love for, the 114th Highlanders, the Queen's Own Royal Strathspeys, which in every sense was a family, if not a clan, regiment.

*　　*　　*

The Honourable Hamish Dewar, Ogilvie reflected as he looked down on the white, drawn face and did what he could to bandage, in a makeshift way, the bullet-torn arm and the bleeding skull, looked like being a misfit: had looked like that from the very start, from the day he had joined the regiment in cantonments at Peshawar, on transfer from an English line battalion – the 2nd Loyal North Devons. He had wanted, it seemed, action: his battalion, ever since he had joined it from Sandhurst, had served peaceably in Bermuda and had then proceeded to Colchester to undergo at least two years' home service.

'Damn boring, don't you know!' Dewar had said on that very first day. 'All social tit and poodle-faking – not my idea of soldiering!' He had lifted an arm and flexed the muscles in it: his new brother-officers stared in fascination, and a few grins were hid, as Mr Dewar next lifted both arms and sighted an imaginary rifle at the corporal of Mess servants – in full view of the Colonel, who gently and wryly remonstrated.

'Were you not taught never to point guns, my dear chap?'

'Oh, but *imaginary* – '

'Even imaginary ones?'

'Sir, I – '

'Or to bring weapons into the Mess?'

'I'm sorry, sir, but I say again – '

'Even imaginary ones, *I* say again. In any case, Corporal Thomas is not a Pathan.' Lord Dornoch laughed, looking at Dewar good-humouredly. 'Oh, you'll get your share, and more than your share, of action, and that before long, I'll promise you! In the meantime, you'll have to unlearn some of the ways of the Loyal North Devons. Here, you'll not address me as sir. Simply as Colonel, in the Mess. Also in the Mess, all other officers address each other by their first names. Clear, Hamish?'

'Clear, Colonel.' From a somewhat bovine face, the Honourable Hamish Dewar beamed around him. 'Frankly, I don't mind unlearning everything. Damn it, I *asked* for a transfer. I'm going to enjoy being with the 114th. A fellow Scot, don't you know! And the North Devons, well, they weren't up to much.'

There was a sudden silence: one of embarrassment. Lord Dornoch, who had been sipping dry sherry, set his glass down rather hard on a mahogany table beside his chair. 'Really?' he said.

'They *tried*, of course.' Dewar shrugged, and looked shrewd. 'Yokels basically, poor fellows, and softened by too much easy living in Bermuda. I felt a fish out of water, to be frank. They just weren't up to it. No – give me a good Scots regiment every time. *Scots wha hae wi' Wallace bled*. Eh, what?'

After one solitary hoot of incredulous laughter, the silence was resumed. The Colonel broke it, speaking drily. 'I'm sure we're all flattered by your opinion of *us*, my dear fellow. But you do yourself no credit by denigrating former comrades. I don't like to hear that sort of talk – but I'll say no more, for I believe on reflection you'll understand. Except this.' Dornoch tapped his knuckles on the table by his side, and there was steel and anger in his voice when he went on, 'I shall not tolerate disparaging talk of English regiments. I have seen too much bravery out here alone! It was not the Scots on their own that won and held India, remember. We've always been outnumbered by the English regiments, and I've nothing but good to say of them – and I happen to know the Loyal North Devons as a first-class fighting regiment! Is *that* clear, Hamish?'

Dewar was unbowed. He beamed again and said, 'Clear,

11

Colonel. Rebuke accepted – an apologies offered. I'm still overly proud to be a Royal Strathspey, and I'm raring for action.'

They went in to dinner. Around the table that night, after the Queen and when the cigars were lit and the port circulating around the perimeter of the gleaming Mess silver, to be followed by brandy, there was a good deal of comment, some of it chuckling, some of it caustic.

'One wonders if the man's a *Scot* at all.'

'With a name like Dewar?'

Smoke was puffed. 'Great-grandfather may have sniffed the highland breeze. *Scot wha hae!* Phaugh!'

'Damn it, his father's the Earl of Taymouth! Still – it does seem odd he didn't join a Scots regiment from Sandhurst.'

'Perhaps none of the colonels would have him.'

'Too big for his boots, is that one.'

'Likes action. He'll be getting it . . . oh, he'll be getting it, then we'll see how he likes it!'

'Nothing wrong, surely, with a man who *wants* to fight?'

'Oh, nothing indeed, but does he have to be so bloody *blatant*?'

'Well – no. Not good form really, I agree.'

A laugh. 'Let's see how he holds his brandy, h'm?'

'Now – here in the Mess?'

'No. In the anteroom, after the Colonel's gone.'

They did. Hamish Dewar did stout work on the brandy. In a corner, sitting alone, Captain Andrew Black, adjutant, did equally stout work on the whisky as was his custom: glowering the while at the antics of his brother-officers. For the 114th Highlanders, it was a memorable night. Hamish Dewar, after singing a number of Scots songs, approached Black on an unsteady course and virtually forced him to dance a Strathspey, and then a reel, giving a fair performance on a flute himself. Black, deep red in the face, with long spindly legs and whirling dress kilt, looked for all the world like a tinker at an Irish crossroads ceilidh. When Dewar passed out, Black peremptorily closed the bar and went off unsteadily to his bed, while Hamish was carried with due ceremony to his.

All in all, it was considered a fair showing – but with reservations. Next morning Hamish Dewar was up commendably early, though looking worn and disinclined for breakfast, a meal during which, by regimental custom, no one spoke. The pages of the *Times of India* formed mutual barriers, sacrosanct to all but Hamish Dewar, who remarked with extraordinary breeziness that the test of a drinker was whether or not he was capable of performing his duty the following morning.

'Which I am, as you shall see.'

Ogilvie looked round the side of his newspaper. 'Hamish, old man. At breakfast, we don't talk.'

'More fool you.' Hamish grinned and rubbed his hands, ordered strong black coffee from a servant standing attentively at his side. 'In the North Devons – '

'For God's sake put a sock in it before the Major comes in. You've changed regiments – remember?'

'I remember. My apologies, gentlemen – I'll say no more, though you'll never know what you've missed.'

Ogilvie slid the *Times of India* back into place and ate porridge, grinning to himself as he overheard the angry mutterings of the more staid officers. Regimental traditions, however odd, were prized by all formations of the Queen's services, and by none more than the Royal Strathspeys. In any case, breakfast was not a time, especially with Indian livers, to indulge in idle chatter . . . but Ogilvie was young enough to be tolerant of the newcomer. He wondered how Dewar would conduct himself during his first full day with the regiment. He soon found out. According to custom, the newly joined subaltern was taken in hand personally by the adjutant and acquainted with the 114th's cantonments. Quarters, offices, parade-ground, kitchens, barrack-rooms and bungalows, stables, harness-rooms, latrines, armoury, quartermaster's stores, sick quarters and surgery. Every officer's particular pigeon was laid open to the round-eyed stare and beaming glance of Hamish Dewar, and afterwards, in the Mess, Ogilvie heard the collated results.

'Took a real interest, I'll say that.'

'Keen?'

'Oh, very. Inexperienced naturally – but keen, yes.'

'The inexperienced shouldn't offer advice.'

A lifted eyebrow. '*Did* he?'

'He did. Guess who to?'

'Black?'

'No. As a matter of fact . . . it's odd, but he and Black seem to get on pretty well. Attraction of opposites, d'you suppose?'

'Or brother boozers. Come on now – who did he offer advice to? The Colonel?'

'Oh, much worse than that. To the R.S.M.'

'No!'

'Oh, yes! I don't know if you knew, but in the Loyal North Devons the warrant officers and N.C.Os don't stamp their feet. I don't know if they wear carpet slippers, but it's a tradition that they stamp *quietly*. I must say old Bosom was awf'lly good about it, though I notice he's still stamping like a stallion.'

Three weeks later, by which time Hamish Dewar had issued a good deal more advice to the drill-sergeants, to the Lieutenant and Quartermaster, Mr McCrum, and even, on the subject of foot comfort on the march, to Surgeon Major Corton, a message reached Lord Dornoch from Division via Brigade: Lieutenant-General Francis Fettleworth, commanding the First Division in Nowshera and Peshawar, was worried about the situation that appeared likely to develop in the town of Kalundabad, some 75 miles north of Peshawar. The General wished words with the Colonel of the 114th Highlanders. Together with Black, Lord Dornoch waited upon Division that morning. He found Bloody Francis, as the Divisional Commander was known throughout the Frontier provinces, in a state of great agitation and attended by the Brigadier-General commanding the 114th's brigade. Bidding Dornoch and Black sit, Fettleworth came straight to the point.

'That damn native bugger,' he stated.

Dornoch stared. 'Sir?'

'Oh – the ruler of Dir, Jahangir Khan. He's a shah, I believe . . . all these damn Mohammedans and Hindus – very tricky to get the style right, I find. These confounded friendly princelings are more damn trouble than they're worth, Dornoch.' Fettleworth ran a finger round inside the sweat-sticky collar of his tunic: notwithstanding the labours of the patient punkah-wallah, Division was a hot place. 'Kalundabad. I've had word through from Dir, via Army Headquarters in Murree, that trouble's brewing in the city – if you can call it that! Dismal place, all flies and stink and open drains, and God knows how many thousand damn natives all herded together. But we have to do what we can, I suppose – you'll agree there, Dornoch. What?'

Feeling like a medical man, Dornoch enquired, 'What seems to be the trouble, sir – in more precise terms, I mean?'

'I told you, my dear fellow, possible riot. I can't be more explicit at the moment. Jahangir is worried and has asked for assistance, though why his own damn little army can't cope I really don't know.' Fettleworth heaved his uniformed stomach up a notch, overlapping the magnificent desk behind which he was sitting, landing, as it were, on the buckle of his Sam Browne belt. 'Of course, it's a compliment to us – to British rule, and to the Queen. So we must co-operate.'

'What do you propose to do? Send in a column?'

Fettleworth shook his head. 'Not a column. This calls for tactful handling. I'm not going to appear panicked into pre-cipitate action. You know how things are shaping at home, Dornoch – all these damn politicians. There's a *nasty* spirit abroad in Whitehall these days – pinch-penny politics, cheese-paring clerks, and all manner of what are they, social-ists. Oh, the *people* are all right, of course they are, they still like to see the flag waving and – and the Empire, don't you know, but their leaders are so damn *paltry*.' Fettleworth waved an arm in the air, as though it carried the flag itself. 'Now where was I?'

Dornoch caught the Brigadier-General's eye and very slightly lowered a lid. 'Dir, sir,' he said. 'The Shah. Kalundabad.'

'Oh, yes, yes. Kalundabad.' A hand tapped on the desk. 'No, not a column. A patrol only. A fact-finding mission in the first place, peacefully conducted. I have no wish to stir up a hornet's-nest.'

'A patrol, sir? A patrol, some seventy-five miles from base?'

'I see no reason why not.'

'Some patrol!'

'Oh, stuff-and-nonsense! Nothing remarkable about it at all. I haven't yet specified the size of the patrol, nor its equipment and potential. Within limits, you may make it as big as you think wise – provided it is still capable of being called a patrol, provided it does not stir up the natives by its presence, and provided you do not send too senior an officer in command, thus giving it an undue importance –'

'In the eyes of Whitehall?'

'Precisely – you have it, Dornoch.'

For a moment Dornoch sat in silence, thinking his own thoughts, uncharitable ones. This was typical of Bloody Francis: always the man seemed to evade decisions, to shirk his own responsibility, to leave too much to his subordinates just so that blame, in the event of failure, could be satisfactorily opportioned. Such, however, was often part of army life and had to be endured philosophically. Dornoch made one protest. He asked, 'Why choose my regiment, sir?'

'Goodness me – why *not*? Someone has to go.'

'I agree. But my regiment is much depleted by leave, by sickness, and in the case of my officers, by absence on courses. I'm quite considerably below strength, as I'm sure Brigadier-General Johnson will have reported to you already.'

'True, true. Do I take it that you are asking to be relieved of this responsibility, Lord Dornoch?'

Again Dornoch paused, then shrugged. 'No, I'll not ask that. Elsewhere along the Frontier, things seem quiet enough.

I dare say we'll not be needed as a complete battalion in the field.'

'Quite. Good! Even had you said different, I regret that I could not have accommodated you, Colonel. I have my reasons, though I'm damned if I see why I should explain them to you.' Bloody Francis jerked up and down in a tantrum for a few moments, then subsided. 'A fine fighting regiment, with more experience of the Frontier than any others in my whole command. The very men for the job, the only ones I feel able to trust in its execution. This *needs* experience, Dornoch, needs mature judgment – and *I* need to be able to depend utterly and completely on the patrol's subsequent report. You have my decision, and shortly you will receive my detailed orders. Kindly make your arrangements with all possible despatch, and report to me personally when the patrol is ready to move out. I shall give you twenty-four hours and not a second longer.'

*   *   *

'I suppose, accepting the initial necessity, that the time limit is generous, Andrew,' the Colonel remarked as he and the Adjutant rode back to cantonments. 'No doubt you can manage in less?'

'Oh, indeed, Colonel.' Black hesitated, his long dark face solemn. 'Who would you wish to send in command, and how many rank and file?'

'Thirty men, two sergeants, four corporals. How does that sound?'

'It will meet the General's requirement, I think, Colonel. And the Officers?'

'I'd like to send Ogilvie in command, but he's only just rejoined from a patrol of his own. He'd be keen enough to go, but I'm not flogging a willing horse, Andrew. Let's say – Captain Campbell, with a subaltern. I'd suggest young Lacey. He's had a good deal of patrol experience.'

'Aye, Colonel.' Black rode on through swirling clouds of dust, past salaaming natives along the track, men who hid unworthy faces from the mounted representatives of the Queen-Empress. 'For my part, Colonel, I would put forward a third, a supernumerary if you wish. Dewar.'

'Dewar?' Dornoch sounded doubtful. 'A brash young man, more than likely to upset any native's susceptibilities, I would say, Andrew!'

'I would not entirely agree, Colonel.'

'Oh?'

'I consider him a potentially good officer – and immensely keen to see action.'

'But many corners yet to be rubbed off.'

'Certainly. Such a patrol as the General suggests may well provide the rubbing-post. I think it could do no harm.'

'Well, possibly, Andrew, possibly.'

They rode on, the decision as yet untaken. Later in the day, the detailed orders came in from Division: the officer in command of the patrol was to force-march to Kalundabad where a survey was to be made of the situation. The officer's assessment was at once to be passed down to Division by the field telegraph that ran from Dir, to which city the patrol was to march on in order to have an audience with Jahangir Khan and his advisers. After this audience a further report was to be made to Fettleworth, who, having assimilated the whole emerging situation and its possibilities for trouble, would then pronounce judgment. Simple enough – always providing events did not move too quickly in the meantime. That night Dornoch gave a full briefing to Campbell and Lacey; and agreed to the adjutant's proposal that Hamish Dewar should accompany the patrol for general experience.

Dewar was openly exultant: and his keenness commended itself to the Mess, where a party was thrown, impromptu, for the about-to-depart officers. Hamish Dewar became a little loud-mouthed, a little boastful, a little too much the leader, a little too much the usurper of Captain Alec Campbell's prerogatives: but this was taken in good enough part, and with no thought for future turns of events. And just fourteen days later news came in on the field telegraph that shortly after fording the Swat River the patrol had been ambushed

18

and eight men had died, shot to ribbons in enfilading fire from the long-barrelled jezails or cut to pieces by the bayonets. The attackers were believed to be Pathans from across the Frontier; and with the dead they had left two officers – Alec Campbell, and Lacey.

Which left Hamish Dewar in sole charge. Dewar had managed to reach Kalundabad, had detached a runner to Dir and the field telegraph, and promised his report shortly. Before he could make it, the field telegraph line to Dir had been cut. Considerable consternation at Division had resulted in orders to Lord Dornoch to prepare at once to move out the Royal Strathspeys, with a battery of mountain artillery attached. He was to hold the main body of the battalion in camp between the Swat and Panjkora Rivers, detaching in the meantime a faster but smaller force to march ahead to the relief of the original patrol. And within four hours of the receipt of orders, Captain James Ogilvie, with a subaltern, a colour-sergeant, four corporals, pipes and drums and another forty men with iron rations, was on his way to Kalundabad.

TWO

THERE WAS MOVEMENT in the face now, some returning life and awareness: there was a flutter in the eyelids. The lips worked; once again, Ogilvie gently tipped his water-bottle.

A few more minutes, and Hamish Dewar opened his eyes, stared around, not at first focusing. Then there came a puzzled look, a frown of bewilderment, as he stared at Ogilvie.

'It's all right,' Ogilvie said. 'We picked you up in time. Can you tell me what happened, Hamish?'

'It's you, James . . .'

'Yes, it's me, with an extended party from the regiment, who are going into bivouacs between the Swat and Panjkora. Your message reached Division, Hamish, then the line was cut. I have to know what happened after that. Do you understand? It's vital.'

'The regiment? What are they hanging around in bivouacs for?'

'Held in readiness –'

'Waiting to see which way the wind is blowing?'

Ogilvie nodded. 'More or less.'

'Then tell them it's an ill wind, James. Tell them that!'

'I will, just as soon as the rest of my patrol returns – and when you've told me what happened to you.'

'You've seen what happened to me. I got a bullet through the arm, then a graze on the napper . . .' Dewar's voice faded a little, and he gave a groan, his face whitening even more. Quickly Ogilvie brought up the water-bottle again, and forced some of the contents between Dewar's lips. Dewar said, 'Thanks, but I could do with something a bloody sight stronger. Got anything?'

'I don't know if you should have it – the doctor – '

'Oh, hang the bloody medicos. Give me what you've got, for God's sake, James.'

'All right, then.' Reluctantly, Ogilvie reached for his hip-flask and just wetted Dewar's lips with neat whisky. It seemed to do some good: he allowed a few drops more to pass. He glanced up, hearing the cries of the vultures: the filthy carrion birds were circling still, though he fancied with less hope. The circles were widening to the west, as though the distant Afghan hills, rearing brown and purplish into the clear sky, were calling with a voice that spoke of more death to be found in their direction.

Again Dewar said, 'Thanks. I needed that. After the wallop on the head, I went into a faint for a while, or I think I did. I'm all right now, if weak.' Tentatively, he moved his limbs. 'Nothing broken, thank God. Some more whisky, and I'll be fighting fit again.'

Ogilvie said with a touch of sharpness, 'Never mind the whisky. I want the facts, Hamish. Where's your patrol? What happened after Campbell and Lacey were killed?'

'Well, I took the patrol on for Kalundabad as ordered. It was the devil of a sweat – unaccustomed country for me – but I managed. I beat the ambush off first, of course – *and* with no more losses. After that there was another attack, and I lost seven more men – '

'What did you do with the dead?'

Dewar stared. 'Buried them, of course. I'm not that green, James. I've heard what happens even to the dead in these parts – '

'You mean you took your colour-sergeant's advice?'

'Well – yes, I suppose I did. We dug shallow graves, and made cairns of stones. Everything was done properly, you can rely on that.' For a moment, Dewar's eyes closed again and a shiver ran through his body. Then he went on, 'Well, we reached Kalundabad and things seemed quiet enough.

21

I paraded the men – showed the flag a little, you know. Some of the locals seemed to resent that – funny! In Bermuda, the North – '

'Let's keep to Kalundabad, and the 114th, Hamish.'

'All right, all right! I repeat, some of them seemed to resent my little show of strength. I decided to read the Riot Act as it were – '

'In English?'

'No. In the local lingo, as delivered by Colour MacColl. He – '

'He did this . . . willingly?'

A frown crossed Dewar's face; and he came to a sitting position. He seemed better. 'As a matter of fact he didn't. I had to argue with him – *argue* with him, in front of the men! Awf'lly bad, that. Some of you Strathspeys are bloody obstinate, James – '

'You're one of us, now, and don't you forget it. Why did Colour MacCall object?'

'Oh, said it would do no good and might do a lot of harm.'

'I see. Go on.'

'Well, I stuck to my guns. I wasn't going to climb down, though frankly, the fellow was almost insubordinate about it till I threatened him with a Court Martial – '

'*You* did that, to Colour MacColl?'

'Yes. Why?' Hamish Dewar looked astonished and hurt.

'He's just about the best we have.'

'You're taking his side, aren't you, James?'

Ogilvie said, 'I'm taking no sides, certainly not until I've heard all that happened. Let's have it quick.'

'As quick as you like, if you'll stop interrupting.' Dewar sounded ruffled. 'Well, MacColl made his speech to my orders, or I hope he did – not speaking the lingo, I couldn't check – and then these damn natives went into a huddle, looking pretty nasty while they did so. After that, they started to move towards us, with rifles and knives.'

'And?'

Dewar hesitated. 'Well, what would *you* have done?'

'I suppose,' Ogilvie said with a groan, 'the same as you

22

rather obviously did – in the circumstances. You opened fire, didn't you?'

'Yes.'

'And the result?'

This time Dewar looked away from Ogilvie's eyes. In a low voice he said, 'We were mown down to a man. Except me, as you see.'

'*All* the others?'

'I said so, didn't I?'

'Including Colour MacColl?'

'What do you mean by that, James?'

Ogilvie's fists clenched involuntarily. He said, '*Now* who do you think was right?'

'I did what I thought best. I did my duty. It's not my fault if your precious MacColl interpreted wrongly.'

'Which is something we may never know, isn't it, though personally I doubt very strongly that Colour MacColl would ever have said the wrong thing. I think your hasty action, your probably stupidly chosen words, were beyond even McColl's ability to tone down. I think you are probably responsible for the loss of many fine soldiers, Hamish. Tell me one more thing: how did *you* get out?'

'Not by cowardice, if that's the suggestion –'

'It isn't. I don't accuse you of that. A coward wouldn't have tried to read a Riot Act in a situation that was, by express order of the Divisional Commander, to be handled tactfully. A coward wouldn't – but a fool would! Now answer my question, if you please.'

Dewar glowered and said surlily, 'By quick thinking. I was doing no good by staying. I'd got on the further fringe of the mob before the slaughter started, and was giving cover fire to the others. I shot a fair number of natives down, then when I saw that all the patrol had gone I nipped down an alley. All attention was on the square where I'd paraded. I didn't have much trouble getting out of the city. I shot down the men guarding the gate – they'd slackened the guard, which was lucky for me I admit. Half of them had gone to watch the fun in the square. I got out and here I am.'

'Safe – after getting all this far from the city? How did you manage that?'

Dewar said coolly, 'I don't know if you realise, but we're not in fact all that far from Kalundabad. A day's march, perhaps. I didn't march, I ran! I had a good start, since they didn't know I'd cleared the city. Dead men can't talk –'

'But deductions can be made.'

'All right, all right!' Dewar stared. 'What's the matter with you? D'you imagine I'm in league with the natives, or something? Because I can assure you I'm not –'

'Oh, don't be so damn stupid. I want a proper report, Hamish, and a full one, that's all!'

'You're getting it,' Dewar said flatly. 'Oh, the buggers came after me, of course they did – hence the blood! I got knocked out by a close shave and when I came round they'd gone. I was in a sort of gully, a dry one, covered with bush and scrub. A pretty nasty fall, if only I'd been aware of it at the time. I suppose they couldn't find me and went home thinking I was dead. Well, I climbed out with a certain amount of difficulty – and here I am.' Dewar winced, and held a hand to his head. 'Now may I say something else, James?'

'Go on.'

Dewar said, with a gleam in his eye, 'I can't wait to get back there – to Kalundabad. As you said – I'm a Royal Strathspey. I'm desperately sorry for the deaths.'

'You don't particularly look it.'

'I think that's unfair.' Dewar got unsteadily to his feet, wincing with pain again as he made a sudden movement with his damaged arm. 'You seem to be holding me responsible. Well, if I am – if – I can take the responsibility without crying over it. But I'm still sorry it happened as it did. Perhaps I should have opened fire earlier – and not wasted time in listening to Colour MacColl's insubordination. There are some people, you know, James, who simply won't be told anything!'

Again Ogilvie's hands clenched into fists; fists that wanted nothing so much as to be planted firmly in Hamish Dewar's bovine face. But he said no more; he felt unable to trust himself to keep his temper in check if he opened his mouth. He swung away from the subaltern, wondering even as he did so if he tended to take things too much to heart, to see events too starkly black on occasions. In the Queen's service, in the service of the British Raj, men had to die. It was inevitable. Over the years of Empire, many thousands had perished in mutiny, in open action, in riot and pillage and fire, in drowning during crossings of swollen river fords. The North-West Frontier was soaked in British blood, its lonely, terrible mountains salted by whitened British bones when there had been no time to bury the dead, salted by the mouldering corpses in the shallow, rocky graves along the passes into Afghanistan, corpses that had come from almost every regiment and corps of the British Army. The 114th were simply following on in the tradition, and that, really, was all . . .

A distant splash of colour, contrasting with the land's barren brown, caught Ogilvie's attention: the kilts of the Royal Strathspey – MacTrease bringing back the rest of the party. As they marched in, the colour-sergeant detached, halted the men, and slammed a salute at Ogilvie.

'Sir!' There's nothing to be seen, beyond Mr Dewar's own tracks.' His face was grim. No sign of the patrol, sir.'

'No sign of the enemy – of any natives, I should say?'

'None, sir. Which is not to say they'll not be around somewhere.'

'But they're not showing themselves, nor attacking,' Ogilvie mused. 'Now, what do you suppose the reason for that might be, Colour-Sar'nt?'

'We're likely in stronger force than they, sir.'

'I doubt if that's it!' Ogilvie laughed.

'Sir?'

'Kalundabad,' Ogilvie said. 'There's the key, Colour-Sar'nt! They'll be expecting us to march on the city – and they don't want to deter us. The blood-lust of the tribes will have been nicely roused by now, and we're wanted in

25

Kalundabad to satisfy the local appetites – that's what I think, anyway.'

MacTrease glanced across to where Hamish Dewar was standing apart. 'Blood-lust roused, Captain Ogilvie, sir? Do I take it – '

'Mr Dewar's patrol was wiped out, Colour-Sar'nt.'

'*Wiped out!*' MacTrease's face whitened beneath its tan, his chest seemed to heave against the crimson sash crossing from shoulder to hip. 'Are you saying Charlie MacColl has gone?'

'I'm sorry – '

'He was a good friend o' mine, Captain Ogilvie – '

'I know that. I have no need to remind you, this is the Frontier. There was no blame anywhere. Every man did his duty, Colour-Sar'nt. Mr Dewar is anxious to get back to Kalundabad, and see the men revenged.' Ogilvie's eyes held those of MacTrease, whose square torso was shaking like a terrier. 'At risk of his life, he determined to rejoin the regiment and report, and this he has done. There will be no blame cast, you understand?'

'I understand, Captain Ogilvie. Sir! May I ask, what are the orders now?'

Ogilvie looked down at the N.C.O.'s face, the face that showed so clearly MacTrease's warlike desire, his wish to go in and kill, and kill again. No highlandman ever took kindly to being bested. But this was not yet to be. Ogilvie said, 'The orders are not for Kalundabad, Colour-Sar'nt. We march back to rejoin the Colonel, and report. With the General's wishes in mind, I shall not risk worsening the situation in the city. If the Colonel should decide to advance, then that is a different matter – and will be carried through at battalion strength, with the attached artillery in support.' He looked up at the sun, pulled his watch from his pocket. 'Half an hour's fall-out, Colour-Sar'nt, then we march back towards the Swat River.'

'Sir!' Saluting, MacTrease turned about and fell the men out. Except for two men detailed as pickets to watch the hills, they shrugged off equipment and fanned sweat-streaked

26

dirty faces with helmets, lay at full stretch on the ground with their rifles ready to hand. In precisely half an hour's time, MacTrease shouted them back on their feet again, and the files marched out southward with – since they were in any case well visible to any hidden eyes – the pipes and drums sounding bravely out into the still air so that the kilts swung with all the pride of a Highland regiment marching through the cheering streets of Edinburgh.

*   *   *

'Colonel?'

In the Malakand Pass Lord Dornoch, roused from his bivouac, sat up to find Andrew Black waiting with a lantern. 'Yes, Andrew?'

'The picket in the northern sangar, Colonel, reports a small column moving for us. It could be Mr Dewar, or Captain Ogilvie, or it may not. The light is not yet enough – '

'Stand the men to, Andrew, we'll take no chances here.'

'Very good, Colonel.'

Black turned away, gave an order to his attendant bugler. A moment later the call to arms rang out clear along the pass, and everywhere men scrambled up, seizing rifles and helmets, mustering under their corporals, chivvied by the harsh voices of the colour-sergeants. Bosom Cunningham, Regimental Sergeant-Major, strode down the awakening lines, eagle-eyed, fondling his ever-present pace-stick held rigidly horizontal under his left arm-pit. 'Come along there, come along there, turn out and keep your eyes skinned . . . '

Moving along, glancing up at the sky, Cunningham noted the increasing light. Soon the men became visible right down the line of bivouacs, and shortly after this the R.S.M.'s alert ear caught the sound of the pipes and drums from the north, bearing down on the Malakand from the plains of Swat. The tune was unmistakable: 'Farewell to Invermore', the march composed by Pipe-Major Ross on the battalion's leaving the depot for India so many years before. Already the word was coming down the line from the extended sangars: 'It's some of ours!'

Cunningham spied the Colonel and the Adjutant ahead, and went up at the double. 'Sir! It'll be one of our patrols. Have I permission to stand the battalion down, sir?'

Dornoch nodded. 'You have, Sar'nt-Major, you have, but see that the hillside pickets remain fully alert. I'll pass the word round the moment I have news to tell, the men may be sure of that.'

'Very good sir. Thank you, sir.' Cunningham saluted and turned about. The bugles sounded once more, and men relaxed, thought about breakfast from the field kitchens, and a pipe. At the head of his small column, James Ogilvie marched in along the pass. Men with their helmets pushed to the backs of their heads, with tunic collars unfastened, raised a cheer and a wave of welcome. But the cheering faltered and died, the returning soldiers marching into an anxious silence when it was seen that Ogilvie was accompanied by the Honourable Hamish Dewar but by only half the number who should have been with the combined patrols. Eyes looked out for friends and failed to find them.

With fresh anger burning in his heart, Ogilvie halted and dismissed the patrol.

THREE

Ogilvie was about to leave the Colonel after he and Dewar had made their reports in the presence of the Adjutant when Lord Dornoch stopped him.

'A word in your ear, Captain Ogilvie.' The Colonel nodded dismissingly at the other two, then walked a little way along the pass below the frowning hills with the pickets posted in the sangars, watchful for snipers. Ogilvie fell into step beside him. 'Now, James: what's your opinion of Dewar?'

Ogilvie hesitated. This was the kind of thing he hated, though he knew it to be inseparable from rank and seniority, knew it to be something that would grow rather than diminish through the years ahead when he won promotion to real command. He knew that a similar repugnance for honest but damning reports had dogged his own father's career in the regiment, and more so later, as he had been elevated to the General Staff and gained his position as Army Commander in Murree. But an answer had to be given, and quickly. Ogilvie found his tongue.

'I think he's basically good material, Colonel, with little thought for his own safety in action –'

'For which we have, in fact, only his own story?'

'Yes, true. But I believe what he said, Colonel.'

Dornoch laughed wryly. 'For that matter, so do I. It was too disingenuous to be otherwise than true! But go on, James.'

'He's somewhat brash, Colonel. He'll improve with added experience.'

'One hopes that experience will teach him to listen to his colour-sergeants.' Dornoch sighed: he had been saddened by the unnecessary casualties. 'Myself, I have spoken my mind to Dewar and have no further rebuke for him, but I fancy General Fettleworth's going to be far from pleased at the turn of events. Nevertheless, one must look for the bright spots: Dewar has given me a helpful inside view of Kalundabad, which may well prove of value, I suppose.'

'Yes, Colonel.'

They paced on. 'What I wanted to ask you, James, was this: you have faith in Dewar – faith enough to take him under your wing, and make an officer of him?'

'Certainly, Colonel, if you feel I can do so.'

Dornoch said at once, 'My dear fellow, there's no-one I'd sooner trust with the job, so that's settled. I'll arrange with Black for him to join your company in place of poor Lacey. And it's likely he'll be seeing further action soon enough, so go to it! The fellow's obstinate and self-assured, but you'll have to cut through that somehow – I leave it to you to find the way!'

'I'll do my best, Colonel.' Ogilvie hesitated, looking up at the surrounding hills, at the now climbing sun bringing gold and green and purple light from eastward to dapple the crests. Already the chill of the night was going, melting away before the first of the morning heat. 'Colonel, can you tell me what you intend to do with the battalion?'

'Not yet, James. Give me time! I'll have to talk to Major Hay and Captain Black first – a council of war, James! All the same, your own views wouldn't come amiss to help me clear my mind.'

'I've not been in Kalundabad myself, Colonel.'

'No. But you've enough experience to make an assessment. A patrol, a strong patrol, of British infantry has been wiped out, but an officer got away to tell the tale. The natives'll be cock-a-hoop at a bloody victory, and Jahangir Khan's position is weakened thereby. So, by Jove, is ours! If we march in, we'll enter a possible bloodbath, with all that will mean for British pride. On the other hand, if we don't go in quickly, they'll think we funk the issue.'

'Why not send a runner back to Peshawar, Colonel, and wait for reinforcements – including cavalry and more gunners?' Ogilvie asked.

Dornoch laughed. 'Oh, I shall detach a runner with a report to Division, of course. But I have no hope at all of a speedy answer – and frankly I believe the order, when it does come, is likely to be to withdraw. General Fettleworth is never anxious to disturb the politicians' serenity! He'll not want a tribal war for the sake of Jahangir Khan, or for a handful of dead Scots either.'

'He'll opt for caution, Colonel?'

Again Dornoch laughed. 'My dear fellow, knighthoods are seldom awarded for *in*caution, at least when failure follows – and General Fettleworth has a pessimistic mind at times!'

'Then – ?'

'We shall see, we shall see. I shall remember that I have an independent command here – and no *fast* means of communication with Division! I shall also remember that on the Frontier the *speed* of the retaliatory strike can be of paramount importance.' The Colonel smiled, and Ogilvie saw the gleam in his eye, the gleam of anticipation: there was little doubt in Ogilvie's mind that the battalion's movement would be northward for Kalundabad. Dornoch said, 'Thank you, James, you've been an admirable listener. Now follow Dewar's example, and see to your breakfast.'

'Very good, Colonel.' Ogilvie saluted smartly. The Colonel went on with his walk, pacing the track in deep thought. On his way towards his company's bivouacs for a word with the men, Ogilvie fell in with the Adjutant.

'Ah, James.'

'Yes, Andrew?' Ogilvie, as he answered, lifted an eyebrow: for some time past, Black had seldon used the brotherly Christian name of regimental tradition when addressing him; and when he did, the use generally indicated oiliness and favour-currying. To some extent, Black's method of address

31

could be used as a pointer to his temper – James, Ogilvie, Captain Ogilvie: fair, worsening, bad.

Currently Black's face was dark and frowning, and a small muscle twitched at one corner of his mouth. 'I wonder, would you mind telling me why the Colonel was so anxious to have your undivided attention just now?'

Ogilvie shrugged, feeling his dislike of Black mounting. He revealed what would shortly have to be known in any case. 'He's posting Hamish Dewar to my company. He wanted to know if I agreed. I'm sure he'll be telling you – '

'Captains, I think, customarily take *orders* from colonels, do they not?'

'Oh, damn it all, Andrew! It does no harm to talk about such things – '

'Hoity-toity, we are very touchy this morning! Do I take it you did in fact agree?'

'I did, yes.'

Black pursed his lips. 'I trust you'll prove a good example, James, indeed I trust that. Young Dewar is fine material . . . I shall be watching, oh yes, I shall be watching.'

'Then I hope you learn something as well!' Ogilvie snapped, his face reddening.

'That is impertinent – '

'Then I apologise.'

'I am glad to note it.' Black lifted a hand and wagged a finger in Ogilvie's face, solemnly. 'I have had words with Dewar just now. He tells me you forced the pace back to the battalion – '

'Certainly – bearing in mind that I had an urgent report to make to the Colonel – '

'Even to the extent of making a night arrival in the Malakand, a time of extreme danger to a small detached party, without the necessary numbers to extend the proper pickets? I think this was foolish, Ogilvie, very foolish. A better apportionment of your timing would have ensured an arrival when the sun was up, would it not?'

'Yes, it would, but – '

'But, but, but. But me no buts, Captain Ogilvie, please!

32

You were at fault. Your initial arrival, that is to say in the mouth of the pass, took place just as night was falling, according to Mr Dewar. Very foolish, very lacking in a proper care for planning. Bear this in mind in future.'

Black stalked off, bony, lugubrious, bristling, his kilt sagging in ungainly fashion from his skinny rump. Ogilvie fumed. The Frontier was not held in check by delays, however prudent! Ogilvie had made a conscious decision to accept the risks in the interest of speed; the decision made, he had acted upon it – despite the protests of Hamish Dewar who, even if he had never before served on the Frontier, seemed to have read some military papers on the district. Making again towards his company's bivouacs, Ogilvie gave a sudden short laugh. Galling, to be called to account by a greenhorn! Worse, though, was Captain Andrew Black, who looked like being set to give another turn to the dagger he had kept in Ogilvie ever since he had joined the 114th Highlanders. Black, lonely drinker, eaten away by jealousy, by feelings of inferiority on account of his non-landed background in a Mess composed virtually exclusively of aristocracy and landed gentry, could never prevent his consuming worm from showing in vicious back-biting and in an over-zealous attention to minute detail which seemed to allow him little time for a proper maintenance of relationships with his brother-officers. Poor Black: hated by the men for his finicky methods and his wicked tongue, tolerated by the officers, treated with a cautious reserve by the Colonel – a poor choice for Adjutant, but one that was irreversible short of his being transferred from the regiment; which the Colonel, who was a kindly and considerate man, would not inflict even upon Black's pride unless, one day, the man should leave him no alternative. His thoughts on Black, Ogilvie simmered.

*   *   *

'Sar'nt-Major!'

'Sir!' Slam, slam: Bosom Cunningham, in immaculately starched khaki drill, with the brass of his rank shining in the sunlight on his sleeve, gave a cracking salute and smote boot-leather against rock, staring the Adjutant in the eye.

'Orders from the Colonel, Mr Cunningham. See the pickets are fully alert, and have the rest of the battalion mustered at ease – but not parted from their rifles. The Colonel will speak to them.'

'Sir!' The Regimental Sergeant-Major marched away, left right left, pace-stick rigid, eyes darting. Miraculously, there was not even dust on his shining boots, Ogilvie noticed as the old soldier marched past. Ogilvie stared after Bosom Cunningham with respect and affection. The R.S.M. seemed to have been in the army for ever, even before the Royal Strathspey had been formed: in his imagination Ogilvie could see him in some previous existence – one of the dark-uniformed men of the ten independent companies of the watch over the Highlands who, in 1740 at Aberfeldy in Perthshire, had been banded together to form the first muster of the Black Watch, the Royal Highland Regiment. The old fire-eater, loyal and fair and honest as the day, seemed to forge an unbreakable iron-and-flesh link between the great days of the clan regiments and modern times. Without him, the regiment would never be the same, and when the day of his retirement came a lot of the fine spirit must surely leave with him. Meanwhile, very much in the present day, the R.S.M. was busy passing the orders to the colour-sergeants. When the muster was complete, Cunningham reported to the Adjutant, who in turn reported to the Colonel. Dornoch's talk to the battalion was concise, giving them the facts about Dewar's patrol but taking care to praise Dewar's bravery in bringing through his report at risk of his life, and casting no blame; and informing them that two independent runners would be sent through to Peshawar with a full report for the General. In the meantime the battalion would move out, advancing across the plain of Swat to ford the Panjkora and make for Kalundabad with all speed.

As he finished, cheering broke out, echoing off the rocky walls of the Malakand Pass. Revenge was a very human

34

emotion: and revenge was unmistakably present that day in the wild yells from the kilted ranks.

* * *

'No hard feelings, James?'

Ogilvie lifted an eyebrow. 'About what?'

'The night arrival,' Hamish Dewar said. 'Black rather forced that out of me, you know. Leading questions, and all that. I'm awf'lly sorry.'

'Oh, that's all right, Hamish. I'll not lose any sleep over Black and his barbed comments!'

'You don't like him, do you?'

'No,' Ogilvie said shortly. 'But I'd prefer not to discuss him – '

'Behind his back?'

'It's hardly the done thing, is it?'

Dewar gave a light laugh, and looked sideways at Ogilvie, who at once felt like a true-blue public-school prefect. But Dewar didn't pursue the conversation; they went on in silence ahead of B Company, listening to the clink and rattle of equipment, to the marching feet, the occasional singing that lasted until Black, with a face of thunder, rode down the line putting a stop to it. Ogilvie watched the pickets on the hillsides, fascinated as always by their movements on the march. Posted in front of the column, and at its rear, all the way along the pass to protect the flanks, men who kept on the jump throughout, watching for snipers, for ambushes; men who, on relief, came down the steep hillsides at the run for safety's sake, with other rifles ready behind for cover as they made that scrambling run down into the pass. It was an unpleasant experience for tall men: the short-legged Ghurkas were better fitted for hill running ...

'You're quiet, James.'

'Oh.'

'Sorry!' Dewar grinned. 'I didn't mean to intrude on your thoughts, but a little bit of conversation does help to pass the time on route marches, what?'

'In and around Colchester?'

'I say, that wasn't called for.'

'No, it wasn't,' Ogilvie said at once, 'and I'm sorry. But do remember this is the Malakand, and it can be as bad as the Khyber if the tribe decide to make it so. You need your eyes about you, Hamish.'

'It looks to me as peaceful as the Pass of Killiecrankie!'

'Well, let's hope it stays that way, Hamish.' Finding his thoughts turning back to Scotland, Ogilvie remarked, 'I tell you one thing: this land makes one homesick for the Pass of Killiecrankie. It's not so far from my own home — and it's a long while since I've been there now.'

'Yes.' Dewar marched on, wiping streaming sweat from his face. 'Ogilvie of Corriecraig . . . fine old place. I never met your people, though I believe it was your grandfather who taught my father to shoot, when the old man was a child.'

'Lord Taymouth? Yes, I believe that's so, Hamish.' On an impulse, Ogilvie asked, 'Tell me, why did you join an English regiment in the first place? With the Taymouths behind you — '

'Sheer bloody-mindedness, old man. I'd had the clan shoved down my throat ever since I could remember, and I wanted to strike out on my own.' Dewar grinned. 'In the end, blood overcame bloody-mindedness. *"Nowhere beats the hairt mair kindly, Than beneath the tartan plaid."* Or something like that. *"Gie me but one hour o' Scotland, Let me see it e'er I die."* It's all in the blood, and blood will out. I had to admit I was wrong, and here I am. And enjoying it tremendously, James. We Taymouths are the heart of Scotland.'

'Really?'

'Does that sound conceited? I'm sorry if it does, but facts are facts, and why not have pride in them? We're allied to both Menzies and MacNab — I have many forebears in the burial ground at Killin. On the MacNab side, we were standard bearers to the MacNab himself, while Menzies fought for Bruce at Bannockburn — and supported Prince Charles Edward in the Forty-Five. Have you been to Glenfinnan, and looked along Loch Shiel, where the Prince came ashore to fight?'

Ogilvie nodded, smiling. 'I have. And all this means that the poor old Loyal North Devons never really had a chance?'

Dewar laughed and relaxed. 'I suppose so. A Scot – ' He broke off, shading his eyes for a long look up the pass. 'Vultures. Couldn't that mean an ambush ahead?'

'I doubt it. More likely a meal. They're coming down, not flying high or hovering.'

'Funny how they know, isn't it?'

'About death? They – '

'Not about actual death. Possible death – an advance knowledge. I had them with me most of the way down from Kalundabad. Filthy brutes!'

'It's a savage and blood-soaked land, Hamish. The vultures epitomise it all, in a sense. The cruelty and the killing . . . they're part and parcel of the life out here, the cleaners-up, if you like.'

'Very charming housemaids, I must say.' Dewar shivered. 'God, I'd hate to end up in those beastly beaks!' He fell silent as the column advanced on the great black birds of prey: they rose hoarsely squawking, as the pipes and drums in the lead approached them. Passing by in their turn, Ogilvie and Dewar saw the half-finished meal: the gaping stomach and fleshless neck of a tribesman in tattered remnants of clothing and with a snaky-bayoneted rifle lying beneath his body. The stench was appalling.

*　　*　　*

There was no incident in the Malakand Pass: the battalion moved out of the mouth during the afternoon, emerging into the plain of Swat with the high mountains dark behind them and the pipes and drums beating out into the still air of the plain. The heat was intense: men's uniforms were so soaked with sweat and caked with dust that the sweat had turned into a layer of mud to stiffen tunics and kilts. Shortly after leaving the pass, Dornoch halted the column for a meal and a rest. Men flopped down where they stood, weary almost to the point of exhaustion in spite of the night's bivouac. Nevertheless, they were undismayed: they were that much the nearer to Kalundabad, and they were raring for action. Every man in the battalion had lost friends, and not only friends made within the regiment: in many cases, they were friendships made at home before joining the colours, childhood friendships, men whose wives or mothers would look at the survivors, when one day they would march back into barracks at Invermore, with haunted eyes, eyes that would hold a very special look of pleading.

But the talk along the resting line was not of war or revenge: these things, soldiers took for granted once the order had been given. The talk was of lighter things: currently, some ribaldry about a trumpeter of the 17th Lancers, who, before the 114th had left Peshawar, had been awarded twenty-eight days detention for having sounded Dismount instead of Reveille outside the married quarters of the officers of that excellent regiment. And of some other things that were not so light.

Andrew Black, on a soft-foot prowl among the men, happened to overhear a few comments that he was not supposed to be listening to: having heard them, he approached James Ogilvie.

'A word in your ear, Ogilvie.'

Ogilvie got to his feet, walked away with the Adjutant, smelling whisky on the latter's breath. Black said, 'There is some talk that must be stopped.'

'What talk is this?'

'To do with Dewar.' Black paused weightily. 'Reflecting on his courage.'

'At Kalundabad?'

'Yes. Wondering how he managed to get out safely – '

'I've wondered myself, but – '

'Captain Ogilvie, I shall not – '

'Allow me to finish – Captain Black. I was about to add – but not by way of questioning his courage. I'm sure there was no cowardice. No doubt he had a high degree of luck.'

38

Black nodded. 'I'm glad you agree. Now, this talk must be stopped, and *you* shall stop it.'

'Why me?'

'Because the talk I happened to hear was among your own company – that's why you.' Black, halting to face Ogilvie, prodded him in the chest with a bony, tobacco-stained finger. 'If you find the names helpful – Lance-Corporal MacLean, and privates Grant, Meldrum, Weir and MacAskill. I suggest they are put on company orders.'

'Not by me, Andrew.'

Black's eyebrows shot up. 'Do I understand you *refuse*?'

'Yes.'

'Then I shall go straight to the Colonel,' Black almost shouted at him, his face mottled with anger. 'I – '

'Go to whom you like,' Ogilvie answered coolly. 'B Company is my responsibility and I shall run it my way. I'll not put any man on orders just because you happened to eavesdrop, Andrew, and that's an end of it. What the men talk about is not my concern or yours – until it interferes in any way with discipline, of course – that, I'll grant you, warrants a check. But not till then. I – '

'Captain Ogilvie, you will – '

'Now hear me out, Andrew.' Ogilvie spoke forcefully but kept his voice down. 'What do you imagine the result would be if I were to do as you say? Would it not be increased talk – to make such an issue of an overheard conversation, in the circumstances a perfectly natural one? Do you think Dewar would thank you for giving official publicity to such gossip, or for letting him be seen as an object of your favouritism perhaps?' Ogilvie laughed. 'In any case, believe me when I say that Hamish Dewar is more than capable of looking after himself without your interference!'

For a moment it seemed that the Adjutant might strike Ogilvie: Black was trembling all over as though with some high fever, and his face was deeply flushed. A fist came up: but Black saw sense in time, and turned away and stumbled off across the rough ground. He did not, as threatened, make for Lord Dornoch: Ogilvie had been right, and inside himself Black knew this well. He had acted hastily. But Ogilvie, watching the Adjutant go, was to some extent troubled. Such talk *was* unpleasant – no doubt of that. A word in the proper ear might well help; and after the hurried meal, before the march was resumed, he caught the eye of the Regimental Sergeant-Major.

'Mr Cunningham . . . '

'Sir!' Stamp, salute. Then a fatherly smile. 'Begging your pardon, Captain Ogilvie, but you have a worried look. You wish my help?'

Ogilvie grinned. 'I do, Sar'nt-Major – as ever! We've not much time, so I'll come to it straight. I'm told there's talk in the ranks – '

'Talk, sir?'

'About Mr Dewar. Do you understand, Sar'nt-Major?'

'I understand very fully, sir. Have you the names?'

'I have.' Ogilvie passed on Black's information.

'They're trouble-makers, sir, all of them. That MacLean will be losing his stripe if he's not careful. If there is more scandalous gossip, I'll see to it myself that he's broken. Mr Dewar is not a coward, Captain Ogilvie, that I'll warrant. He's simply a . . . I'm sorry. I'll say no more. Sir!'

'Braggart?' Ogilvie suggested with another grin.

Mr Cunningham fractionally moved one eyelid. 'A young gentleman who's inclined to talk of more than he knows, sir. I shall deal with the talk, Captain Ogilvie, you may be sure.'

'Tactfully and quietly, Sar'nt-Major. But – firmly?'

'Sir!'

Ogilvie nodded. 'Thank you, Sar'nt-Major.' Cunningham saluted again, and crashed about and away. Ogilvie watched him move towards the Colonel, right arm swinging from the shoulder, huge moustache rigidly waxed despite the cruel heat. Cunningham wouldn't go straight from Ogilvie to the source of the gossip: he was far too old a hand for that. Cunningham, ramrod of the regiment in peace and war, knew when it was his role, for the good of all, to be a buffer. Very often more was achieved that way, and the hard-won insignia on his sleeve, and the Sam Browne across his broad chest, told him that the Secretary of State's warrant was enough to back his tactful strictures without support from any officer's commission.

*   *   *

After their brief rest, the men were fallen in by companies and once again formed column of route for the march. Before and behind them were detachments of section strength as advance guard and rearguard; whilst ahead again were the scouts who had replaced the pickets required for the march along the mountain passes. Captain Black, riding his horse up and down the line constantly, kept in touch with the whole battalion and with the gun batteries, exhorting, swearing, seldom praising. With halts for rest and food kept now to a minimum, the 114th Highlanders forded the Swat River, heading on for the Panjkora to make the crossing north of the river where the waters divided. As they approached the river, last natural barrier before Kalundabad, Captain Black, on a visit to the advanced scouts, now out of sight beyond some rising ground, came galloping back hell-for-leather, his Highland claymore glinting in his hand as he pulled his horse up before Lord Dornoch.

'Sir, the enemy! They're waiting across the river in some strength. I estimate four hundred men.'

'Field-guns?'

'None visible, Colonel.'

'I see.' Dornoch shaded his eyes and looked back along the column, at the khaki tunics and the colourful kilts, at the sombre grey-green guns of the mule-borne mountain battery. There was both exultancy and sadness in his voice as he turned back to the Adjutant. 'Captain Black, warn the men for action. We must assume we've been already spotted by their scouts, therefore we shall march with the pipes and drums playing. My compliments to the Pipe-Major: well-filled bags to his pipes, and he'll know the tune I want.'

41

Black saluted, and wheeled his horse. As the Colonel galloped his horse ahead, the advance of the Royal Strathspey continued towards the river bank, the pipes and drums beating out their own action tune, 'Cock o' the North'.

FOUR

SURMOUNTING THE RISING ground well ahead of the column, Lord Dornoch looked down upon the twisting Panjkora River, rocky, hostile with the native levies in view along the farther bank. The water reflected the hard blue of a metallic sky as it cut its meanders through the dun-coloured plain.

The Colonel turned to Major Hay at his side. 'They could be Jahangir's men, I suppose.'

'I'd doubt that, Colonel.'

Dornoch gave a grim smile. 'Frankly, John, so would I!' He surveyed the native horde through his field-glasses. 'They've not the look of an escort!'

'What d'you mean to do?'

'Why, make the crossing, of course –'

'We'll come under very heavy fire,' the Major pointed out. 'Caught in the middle of a ford is not the best place for a pitched battle.'

'But inevitable. And it'll not come to that, perhaps.' Dornoch looked once more through his field-glasses, then reined in his horse. Turning, and lifting a hand, he halted the column behind him. He beckoned to his runner. 'All officers and N.C.O.s to report at once,' he said crisply. 'That includes the gunners.'

'Sir!' The man doubled off. Dornoch re-examined the river bank. The flow of water was not at its full force, he believed, and the crossing itself should not prove too difficult. He cantered back towards the column. In ones and twos the officers and N.C.O.s mustered. From the guns came the Major commanding the battery, with his sergeants and bombardiers. When all were present Dornoch indicated his plans.

'I shall advance ahead of the column, gentlemen, and make an attempt at parleying. Frankly I expect little result from that, but I have to bear in mind my overall orders not to exacerbate the situation. Tact, until it proves too costly or too useless, is still the watchword. I shall be accompanied by Major Hay and my bugler. If, as I suspect, there is to be no parley, then I shall pass the order to deploy. The battalion will then form in line along the eastern river bank, spreading to left and right of the guns. Major Pilkington, I intend to use your guns as my spearhead.'

'Yes, sir.'

'When I order my battalion to deploy, you will bring your battery forward as quickly as you can and take up your firing position on the river bank, using the native centre as your point of aim. After the enemy has opened fire with rifles – I repeat, gentlemen, *after the enemy has opened fire*, and not before – I shall order the guns to open. Captain Black has reported an apparent absence of native artillery, and I confirm his observations. Your guns, Major Pilkington, will clear the way for us – indeed, the threat itself may be enough. Your fire will be supported by my rifles and Maxims, and the battalion will cross the river under cover of the combined fire. Clear, gentlemen?'

'One question, sir.' This was Major Pilkington, a lantern-jawed man with piercing blue eyes. 'What would you estimate the depth of water to be?'

'Good God, I've no idea, frankly, but I don't think the river's running full. You're anxious about your guns crossing?'

'Yes, sir – '

'I think you'll manage – the Panjkora is rocky here, which indicates no great depth. It'll be a tough job for men and mules, but we shall manage. Anything else? No?' Dornoch waited a moment longer, then nodded in dismissal. 'Keep in column of route until I give the order, then, Bugler, sound the Advance.'

As the officers and sergeants went back to their positions

44

in the march, the notes of the bugle rang out towards the river, savage, exultant, harshly sending warning that the army of the Raj was coming. Once again the pipes and drums struck up 'Cock o' the North' and the battalion moved ahead with the silk of the Queen's Colour accompanying the colours of the Royal Strathspey – for it was Dornoch's custom to turn a blind eye to the regulation forbidding the carrying of the colours into battle, and no senior officer had yet thought fit to remind him of that regulation. Coming closer, the men of the leading files could see the opposing army – lean, brown-skinned tribesmen, Pathans from Afghanistan by the look of them, men with the faces of hawks, turbaned men with knives and rifles, men ready to fight to the death. Dornoch's face set hard: young Dewar had been every kind of a bloody fool to have precipitated this! The march to Kalundabad should have been peaceful, a mere police operation rather than the advance of an army of blood and war.

When the pipes and drums were within five hundred yards of the river bank, Dornoch once again halted the column. The men stood easy, silently watching as their Colonel rode his horse forward at the walk, accompanied by the second-in-command and the one bugler. In the centre, the gunners stood by their mules, ready to advance and assemble their ten-pounder breech-loaders when the word came. There was a creak of leather, a subdued rattle of equipment along the ranks of men, Scots and English. As Lord Dornoch reached the bank and halted, even these sounds ceased. In an almost total silence, they all watched him lift a megaphone to his mouth and begin to speak in Urdu. Some of the men could understand the snatches that they heard, some could not; but all could get the drift: the Colonel's words were of a peaceful intent, of friendliness towards Jahangir Khan, ruler in Dir; but underlying them was another clear intent, one that come what may he would cross the Panjkora that day.

As Dornoch spoke, a rising murmur came from the massed tribesmen opposite. Rifles were waved in the air: the natives

45

were not in a listening mood. Dornoch paused. He had started speaking again when a white ball of smoke rose in the air across the river, and a bullet came zipping close by his right sleeve, nicking the material. At once he broke off, snapped an order to the men with him, brought his horse round on rearing legs, then rode back towards the column as the notes of the bugle rang out. In what was now a hail of bullets, the Royal Strathspeys deployed, fanning out along the bank, taking what cover they could while the mountain battery swept down in the centre, assembled its mule-borne guns, and swung to bear on the enemy. Ogilvie, making his way along his company's front, saw the gunner Major looking towards Lord Dornoch for orders, saw the latter's nod. A second later, all six guns of the battery opened, sending their ten-pounder shells flinging across the strip of water to smash into the close-packed tribesmen. Bodies were seen spiralling into the air as the shells exploded: cries and screams floated back. The slaughter was immense as the bombardment continued, added to by the battalion's Maxim guns. Ogilvie shouted at Hamish Dewar, who was on his feet and yelling.

'Get down, you bloody fool!'

Dewar took no notice: Ogilvie got up himself and dragged the excited subaltern down by force. As Dewar put his head up again a bullet tore through the front of his Wolseley helmet. He looked surprised and a little sheepish as he flattened to the ground. 'Thanks,' he said to Ogilvie. 'I should be all right now. I've had one through the back, and now one through the front!'

'There's still the two sides to go. Don't take stupid chances. Men's lives are valuable out here – even yours.'

Dewar grinned but said no more. Looking towards the Colonel, Ogilvie saw him call out to his bugler, and a moment later the Cease Fire was sounded. The din from the mountain battery died away: the smoke and the stink of explosives lingered on. The tribesmen seemed to be in a poor way, with a large number of dead and wounded, but though they had withdrawn a little way from the bank they had not fled. Dewar asked, 'What's the Colonel up to now – going to let the bastards re-form, d'you suppose?'

Ogilvie looked sideways. 'What would you do, Hamish? Carry on the bombardment?'

'Yes, I would, of course! Till they were all corpses.'

'And thereby waste ammunition on non-necessities. I dare say the Colonel prefers to conserve his shells for possible use in Kalundabad – where the supply position isn't likely to be good!'

Dewar was about to make some further remark when, in the comparative silence of the lull, the Colonel's voice was heard, and Ogilvie saw him wave his claymore above his head. 'The battalion will re-form into column and advance, B Company to remain with his battery in case of need. The remainder follow me across the river. Sar'nt-Major – fast, if you please!'

There was a roar from Cunningham, shouts from the colour-sergeants and section sergeants. At the double, the Royal Strathspeys formed column. Lord Dornoch moved down to the bank and out into the river, splashing from rock to rock, soon up to his horse's belly in water. After him went Hay and Black, and the battalion's pipes and drums. Bullets spattered the water all around as the main body of troops followed on into the river, holding rifles and equipment high and dry. Men fell in ones and twos: a piper cursed as the wind went out of his bag; he lifted his pipes and shook them at the tribesmen, swearing. Behind him a boy drummer fell screaming, going right under until a brawny private seized him and carried him bodily on with his silent drum. Ogilvie, who had deployed B Company so as to give the widest fire possible, urged his men to rapid shooting till the very bolts of the rifles became almost too hot to the touch. The aim was good: many more tribesmen were picked off as the battalion waded across the ford. When one of B Company fell dead, Hamish Dewar grabbed his rifle and blazed away, his eyes shining. When the last of the main body had crossed, Dornoch, with plenty of fire now at his disposal on the farther bank, ordered B Company and the mountain battery to cross. The guns were quickly dismantled and secured to the backs of the mules. The native drivers urged the heavily laden beasts down to the water, hauling them across, half swimming, on their bridles, with their great eyes rolling in terror. By now little more rifle-fire was coming down on the ford: the Pathans were under a close fire themselves, and were pressing back in what looked like full retreat – except for a small body of men sniping from behind a sangar some two hundred yards back from the bank. At one moment their fire came close to Dornoch, a bullet zipping up a spurt of sandy earth near his boot. Ogilvie, who with his company was just emerging from the crossing, heard an oath by his side: Hamish Dewar.

'The bastards! They're out to get the Colonel. Well, we'll see about *that*.'

Before Ogilvie could stop him, Dewar was running, charging like a lunatic for the sangar and its concealed snipers, waving his claymore about his head like a clansman of old. Bullets hummed like bees around the flying figure: at one moment he spun, halted briefly with blood running down his right leg, then charged on again, yelling in a sheerly blood-curdling manner. So sudden had been his rush that many of the men were just staring after him open-mouthed: then under a bellow from Cunningham they gave covering fire. Bullets poured into the walls of the sangar, mostly without effect except that they served to keep the snipers' heads well down. Reaching the sangar, Dewar leapt up on to the wall, then went down behind in another leap. Men ran towards him, but Dewar, it seemed, needed no help. His claymore blade was seen briefly, once, twice, three times – flashing in the sun, and red. Then his face appeared as he jumped back to the top of the sangar – his face beaming and happy, his eyes bright with the lust of killing. 'Three for the vultures!' he yelled. 'Three bodies, three separate heads. God, we'll show them who's Cock o' the North!'

Ogilvie looked across at the Colonel. Dornoch seemed to be prey to a mixture of emotions. He was not a man who cared for killing for its own sake, but Hamish Dewar's act had been an immensely brave one and had saved a good many lives. Dornoch lifted his own claymore in a kind of salute and called out, 'Well done, Mr Dewar, well done indeed.'

The tribesmen were now in full retreat; Dornoch let them run, and read prayers over his dead as they were buried. Then, after a brief rest, the battalion, with the wounded carried along in *doolies*, was on the move again, on the final leg for its encampment outside Kalundabad.

* * *

'Lance-Corporal MacLean!'

MacClean slammed to attention before the Regimental Sergeant-Major. 'Sir!'

Cunningham looked him over. 'You'll have seen, I don't doubt, what Mr Dewar did today?'

'Sir!'

'And you'll have taken due note, I trust. You understand me?'

MacLean's face was stiff. 'I saw a brave act, sir.'

'Aye, you did indeed, MacLean. A braver one you'll never see, and in my opinion it warrants the Victoria Cross. Mr Dewar is a brave man.'

'Sir!'

'And there'll be no more talk such as I've heard just recently.' Cunningham lifted his pace-stick and tapped the chevron on MacLean's tunic-sleeve. 'I'm thinking you're something of a disgrace to your stripe, Mister MacLean, and make no mistake about this, if you don't keep a still tongue in your head, and see to it that your friends Weir, Grant, MacAskill and Meldrum do the same, I'll have that stripe off your bloody arm quicker than it takes me to down a dram! Now fall out.'

'Sir!' Lance-Corporal MacLean turned about, stamping his boots. He marched away smartly, left right left, arms swinging. The R.S.M. was a hard-faced old bastard and there was nothing hidden from him, nothing at all . . . and it behoved a lance-corporal with ambitions to keep his nose clean at all times. There would be no more talk of that sort. Behind him, grinning a little, the old bastard – who could read MacClean's mind even through the back of his head – gave his moustache a tweak and also marched away with his back erect. He had promised tact, and in his book he had not broken that promise. In the British Army there was tact and tact. Some men merited one sort, some the other. MacLean understood basic English and responded better to a firm hand than he did to the easy approach.

Mr Cunningham was satisfied, though he acknowledged the good hand of Providence which, that day, had given the clear and indisputable lie to gossip.

FIVE

KALUNDABAD LAY IN the foothills of the great mountain range of the Hindu Kush, the traditional Hindu-breaker of Mahomet, natural barrier between Hindu and the followers of the Prophet, preventer of the spread of Hinduism north and west. The Hindu Kush ran into the Pamirs northward toward Turkistan; and easterly lay the Himalayas, and the mysterious land of Kashmir on more mysterious Tibet's western flank. The Royal Strathspeys marched, with the city in sight at last, very close to the world's roof as yet another night began to fall upon the great snow-topped mountains, the wail of the pipes and the drumbeats echoing back from the vast rock walls.

As they approached the city, Hamish Dewar was mostly silent and preoccupied, studying the nearer crests ahead. Along those crests would be tribesmen in plenty, men who would have sent back word of the British advance at battalion strength. Ogilvie felt Dewar's unease emanating strongly, and was not surprised: in Kalundabad, Dewar would be badly wanted. It took guts, to march back, even in company with the battalion: and here, almost in the shadow of the Pamirs, the battalion looked small enough indeed.

With the old walled city and its close-packed buildings and its minarets some two miles away, Black came down the column, walking his horse, passing orders to the company commanders. 'The Colonel intends to halt the column one mile from the city. The battalion will fall out and pitch tents by companies. Each company will detail pickets to guard its own lines, and for tonight B Company will provide the quarter-guard. Captain Ogilvie?'

'Yes?'

Black said formally, 'You will be officer of the Guard, Captain Ogilvie. See to it that a zealous watchfulness is maintained at all times. Have you any questions?'

'I'd like to know the precise orders. I imagine we're likely enough to be attacked, and if –'

'The Colonel believes an attack *not* to be likely at this stage, Captain Ogilvie, and the orders are that you shall report at once to the Colonel personally if you should see anything suspicious. There is to be no firing without his permission, is that clear?'

Ogilvie nodded. 'Clear.'

Black moved on down the column. Ogilvie, catching Dewar's eye, gave a slight shrug. He could only hope Dornoch would be proved right: he himself felt doubtful, not liking the feel of their surroundings. It was all too peaceful, too unopposed: there was the feeling of a trap. Dewar seemed to bear this out. 'If I had the say,' he announced, 'I'd go in now and give 'em hell!'

'It's what I'd like to do too,' Ogilvie said, 'but the Colonel has to have half an eye on Fettleworth, don't forget – and Fettleworth has half an eye on Whitehall!' He laughed suddenly. 'It's the old, old story, Hamish – you'll learn! We always fight with one hand tied behind our backs by the India Office.'

'Some fate, for a soldier.'

'We're not just soldiers out here. We have to be ruddy diplomats as well!' He added, 'This isn't really a war situation, remember.'

'What do you call it, then?'

'I suppose . . . civil disturbance. We're acting for Jahangir Khan.'

'You don't sound very sure yourself, James.'

'Things aren't always very clear cut, out here.'

'They were when I was last in Kalundabad. Clearer cut they couldn't be! Bullets and knives have a very decided voice as far as I'm concerned. I heard that voice almost all the way, James, till you picked me up. I was dead lucky to get out. Now I'm back, I want to make a nice, final job of it.'

'Well, you may get the chance yet,' Ogilvie said with a laugh. A few moments later the bugles sounded from the head of the column, and Ogilvie, in obedience, halted his company. The N.C.O.s fell out smartly, and Colour-Sergeant MacTrease marched up the line for orders.

'We make camp here, Colour-Sar'nt, beside the track.'

'Sir!'

'B Company's to provide the quarter-guard, so I'll want four sections under Mr Dewar, with their sections sergeants, to mount guard at once, dispersed around the perimeters – you'll have to pitch tents for all with the remainder of the company, Colour-Sar'nt, and see to it that speed's the word. It'll be full dark very soon now.'

'Sir!' MacTrease about-turned with a slam of boots, and the shouting of the sergeants and corporals began all along the column, with the Adjutant and the R.S.M. keeping sharp eyes on all movement. As the section sergeants reported, Ogilvie gave orders for the guard mounting and, under the general command of Hamish Dewar, the sections were marched to their respective areas around the camp perimeter. As the darkness increased, Ogilvie made his first round of the quarter-guard, then reported to Major Hay. Camp fires were lit, and the Scots grouped around them, taking their ease, eating a meal of bully beef and rice provided by the field kitchen, before turning into the tents. Throughout the night, Ogilvie remained constantly awake, patrolling the perimeter, visiting the pickets in the outposts, having words with the sergeants and the subalterns who took their watches turn and turn about, quartering the surrounding country through field glasses as the moon came up bright and cold to shed silver over the distant peaks of the Pamirs. There was no lack of vigilance: the Royal Strathspeys were too experienced in the ways of the Frontier to take any chances, to close any weary eyes whilst on guard, knowing too well that a moment's carelessness could lead to the knife in the back or the sudden volley from close at hand. During one of his patrols Ogilvie fell in with Bosom Cunningham, somewhat to his surprise.

'No camp-bed for you, Sar'nt-Major?'

'Not till the dawn, Captain Ogilvie, sir, not till the dawn, when I'll snatch an hour.' Cunningham heaved his chest and pointed around the hills with his pace-stick. 'I don't trust the hill tribes, sir.'

'Or the pickets, Mr Cunningham?'

'I've known pickets to have a blind side, sir.'

Ogilvie nodded. 'True enough. But you'll wear yourself out if you're not careful.'

'Awa' wi' that, sir!' Cunningham said with spirit. 'I'm no' that old yet!'

Ogilvie grinned. 'And you know very well that the men are a damn sight more wary of you than they are of any of us!'

Cunningham grinned back, his teeth gleaming in the moonlight. 'Maybe that's true, too, sir. I know this anyway: they're a sight more scared of me than they are of the enemy – which is as it should be, too.'

'Go on with you, Sar'nt-Major! It's just part of the act and you know it.'

'Aye, well.' Cunningham lifted a hand and tweaked at his moustache. 'It's a necessary act. If you're more scared of your own side, you'll never run from an enemy's fire. It's an act that saves lives – and makes empires, if you'll forgive the boast!' His eyes twinkled. 'By the way, sir. I've dealt with the rumour-mongers – you'll know what I mean?'

'I do, and thank you, Mr Cunningham.'

'We'll hear no more o' that now.' Cunningham hesitated, looking out over the hills. 'You know, sir, this place reminds me of the Pass of Brander, by Loch Awe in Lorne. That steep side there – like a wall.'

'Just the place for a last stand?'

Cunningham said, 'You took the words right out of my mouth, Captain Ogilvie. I just hope they'll not be prophetic!' The R.S.M. saluted and turned away, continuing his personally-appointed patrol. Ogilvie reflected as he moved away about his own duties that with a different man from Cunningham an officer might well have taken umbrage at the R.S.M.'s perambulating presence as an implied slight on his own vigilance: but not with Bosom Cunningham. The old Warrant Officer had no guile about him, no slyness, no officiousness even. But he was mightily concerned about the regiment and the welfare of every man in it; and had an attack come, and him in his bed, Bosom Cunningham would never have forgiven himself for not being, as it were, on parade.

In a chill wind off the mountains, Ogilvie began another round of the pickets. When the first tints of the dawn touched the eastern hills, then brought up, starkly, the lines of white tents, he was able to relax. Night had gone and there had been no attack. The hills appeared empty of life, and peaceful, as at six a.m. the bugles sounded Reveille and the men began to come out from the tents to wash in a freezingly cold stream nearby. Shaving mirrors were propped on rocks, on cleft sticks, on anything handy: and the battalion scraped its collective face clean of hair. Thus decently presentable, they formed a short-sleeves queue to take their breakfasts from the field-kitchen. Watching, Ogilvie wondered how long the commissariat would last, how long before a reaction to Dornoch's report came through from Peshawar – reaction, plus, perhaps, reinforcement and supplies. He looked along to where the gunners of the mountain battery were encamped: throughout the night men had stood by the assembled guns, ready to go into action at the drop of a hat. How long could those guns be kept in action, if fighting should start and the battalion be held between those frowning hills?

* * *

After breakfast, all company commanders were summoned to Lord Dornoch's tent. State-of-readiness reports were made: Mr McCrum, Lieutenant and Quartermaster, indicated a fortnight's supply of provisions, longer if bare subsistence were resorted to. To some limited extent, they could live off the country, though it appeared as barren as most of the Frontier lands and foraging parties would be very open to attack. Major Pilkington of the gunners reported three hundred rounds left – fifty per gun, after the action on the Panjkora. Dornoch, anxious to provoke nothing in accordance with what he knew would be Bloody Francis Fettleworth's wishes, was undecided as to his course of action. Making up his mind after some discussion not to force any issues pending the possible despatch by Fettleworth of a stronger formation, the Colonel announced that he would seek a parley, approaching the city gates himself under a flag of truce with Captain Black, a bugler, and an escort.

When the officers were dismissed Ogilvie made his way thoughtfully to B Company's lines, pondering the complexities of command, of the many factors that must sway any decision, not the least of them being the interpretation, often a curious one, placed by remote warriors and civilians in safe places upon decisions taken at the scene of action. In the company lines he found Dewar carrying out a rifle inspection with Colour-Sergeant MacTrease and a junior subaltern, MacInnes. For a moment, Ogilvie stood and watched: Dewar was making a conscientious and painstaking job of the inspection, no skimping. When Dewar had finished with the front rank, Ogilvie called to him.

'A word if you please, Mr Dewar. Can Mr MacInnes carry on?'

'Sir!' Formally, Dewar saluted, nodded briefly at MacInnes and came across. 'Well, James, what's next?'

'Flag of truce. A parley. The Colonel's going in with Black.'

Dewar snorted. 'Is he, by jove! Bloody parleys! How can you *parley* with natives? I'd go in and smash the place up, starting with the guns – '

'I rather thought you would, Hamish. That's what I wanted to talk to you about.' Ogilvie, though they had

56

moved some distance away from the ranks, kept his voice low. 'This is a different kind of soldiering, in a different sort of country from anything you've known before. For heaven's sake don't go on the rampage if we do enter the city. No more provocative parades, and above all, no thoughts of personal revenge. I think – I *know* – the whole battalion's feeling revengeful, but to a greater or lesser extent they've felt that ever since they first came out to India – and we've all learned to live with it and not let it show! Do you see?'

'Well,' Dewar said surlily, his heavy face dark and the lower lip jutting, 'I'll take your word for it if you insist.'

'I do. It's an order.' Ogilvie added, 'You've a hell of a lot to learn about India, Hamish.'

With a snap in his voice Dewar retorted, 'I'm beginning to be sorry I ever left the North Devons.' Turning on his heel, he marched away, exuding indignation. Anxiety gnawed wormlike at Ogilvie's mind: Hamish Dewar was going to be more than a handful once there was any contact with the tribes.

*   *   *

Before Lord Dornoch rode out, more orders were passed by Black: the battalion was to remain in its present position but was to stand-to in readiness to move the short distance to the city walls if need be, leaving its tents behind in the care of a quarterguard of half-company strength. If the Colonel should require them to march, his bugler would sound the Advance, and they would then go forward with the guns and await the next order. There was to be no firing except on the Colonel's own word of command: and if it so happened that the truce party were to be surrounded and taken, then the second-in-command, Major Hay, would act according to his own discretion.

'And what does that mean?' Dewar growled when the orders reached B Company. 'Pretend not to notice, and march back to the lines?'

'It means what it says.'

'For me, it's a little imprecise.'

'For God's sake,' Ogilvie said wearily, 'shut up and stop criticising the Colonel. He's got the weight, not you! Don't you ever use your head, Hamish?'

'How d'you mean?'

Ogilvie sighed. 'You'll learn – one day!'

Dewar snorted but argued no further. As Ogilvie sought out MacTrease he saw Andrew Black, with an attendant bugler, mounted and riding towards the Colonel's tent, carrying a flagpole to which was attached a white sheet that blew out on the breeze off the hills. As Lord Dornoch emerged and mounted his horse, a silence fell over the whole battalion. Black gave a smart salute, smartly returned by the Colonel; then the two officers rode out of the lines with the bugler in rear, to be joined by a mule-mounted escort of a bombardier and four gunners found by the mountain battery. The silence was maintained as though by mutual consent as the small group cantered away towards the walls of Kalundabad beneath a climbing sun shining down on the hills from a clear blue sky. There was a poignancy in that curiously-maintained silence, which, Ogilvie felt, was almost a premonitive one. In the vast terrain, with the snow-topped Pamirs far ahead beyond the foot-hills, the mounted group looked lost and forlorn. Through glasses Ogilvie watched the splash of colour, the Scots riders' trews bearing the tartan of the Royal Strathspey, the regimental flash standing out from the dun-coloured Wolseley helmets as they rode on across the rocky desolation of the track to Kalundabad and its mutinous citizenry.

SIX

As the would-be parleyers halted some two hundred yards from the close-shut gates of the city, Ogilvie was standing beside Major Hay, who was mounted and staring towards the Colonel's party.

'They've got there,' the Major said unnecessarily. His fingers held his horse's reins tightly, nervously: Hay, an elderly man for his rank, had no wish to assume the command as a result of his Colonel's capture or death. The two were old friends, and now Hay's set face showed the strain of waiting. In that face also, Ogilvie noted, was the promise of indecision should command be forced upon the Major. In John Hay there was no lack of guts for a fight; but he was what Hamish Dewar would undoubtedly call an old woman, and he would be mightily attentive to the as yet unknown wishes of Lieutenant-General Francis Fettleworth. 'There seems,' Hay went on, 'to be no reaction from the city.'

'I dare say they're making up their minds, Major. They'll have problems, as well as us!'

'Indeed, that's true, very true,' Hay gnawed at his moustache, frowning beneath heavy grey brows. 'As for me, I could wish time moved faster.' He looked around. 'Sar'nt-Major!'

'Sir!' Mr Cunningham bustled up.

'The men. They're in good heart?'

'Never more so, sir.'

'They'll need steady hands and tempers, if we're ordered to advance.'

'They'll have that, sir.'

'I hope so, I hope so indeed. This is a very difficult situation, Mr Cunningham. I – ' Hay broke off. 'Good heavens, now what's that?'

'A trumpet, I fancy, sir.' The R.S.M. stared towards the city, shading his eyes with a massive hand. 'But as yet no movement, sir.'

Hay nodded, gripped his reins tighter. The notes of the trumpet coming from the distant walls apparently, echoed off the hills, tinny but somehow threatening. After that there was resumed silence throughout the lines, silence broken only by the creak of equipment and the rattle of rifles as the men, fallen in by companies ready to advance, stood easy in the ranks, every head now turned towards Kalundabad. Within the minute another trumpet call came down on the breeze: and then there was the unmistakable sound of rifle fire, a sudden and prolonged burst that took everyone by surprise. There was a rising murmur from the ranks, and men broke out of line, craning their necks to see what was happening to the truce party. As Hay stood in his stirrups, the Regimental Sergeant-Major moved away at the rush, bellowing at the colour-sergeants, chasing the men back to the ranks with blood-curdling threats. Hay said, 'The Colonel's all right, at all events. He's standing fast by the look of it.' As he finished, more firing was heard, and smoke-puffs were seen rising above the city into the blue of the sky. Watching closely through his field-glasses, Ogilvie saw Lord Dornoch conferring, apparently, with Black. Then Ogilvie saw the Colonel's right arm go up, and a moment later the bugle sounded the Advance and as the stirring notes swept wind-borne down on the waiting battalion, Hay turned his horse, standing again in the stirrups, this time with his claymore drawn and pointing back towards the city.

'Battalion will advance by companies . . . Major Pilkington, you will assemble your guns the moment I halt the battalion. Company Commanders carry on!'

Ogilvie was already on the move for his company, where

Hamish Dewar had started giving the necessary orders: 'B Company, atten-*tion*! Slope . . . *arms*! B Company will advance in fours to the right . . . right-*turn*!' The men came round as one, kilts swinging around sun-browned knees, with a stamp of boots and a clatter of bayonets. As A Company was marched out, Dewar got his company on the move behind them. Arms swinging, rifles steady and faces eager, the 114th Highlanders moved forward behind Pipe-Major Ross with the pipes and drums beating out 'The Mist-Covered Mountains'. It was a stirring sound and a stirring sight, more than enough to make the blood run faster through Scots veins . . . Ogilvie, glancing at Hamish Dewar, saw the blood-lust naked and gloating. That man was going to need very careful watching, and very careful handling: it was never easy, and indeed not often desirable, to deflect a Scot from a fight, but there were fights and fights, and it could yet prove unnecessary to start one now. As the battalion advanced the firing was maintained sporadically inside Kalundabad; to Ogilvie, the situation had the ring of an internal conflict, of civil war or rebellion. In twenty-five minutes, the head of the advance bore down on the truce party, still patiently waiting beneath its white flag of peace. Major Hay detached, riding to the right, and halted the column. As the sound of the pipes died away, Hay rode up to the Colonel. There was a brief conference, then Dornoch came away from the group, and, sitting his horse, addressed the men directly. His words confirmed Ogilvie's theory. 'There seems to be discord in Kalundabad,' Dornoch said. 'All I can tell you is that the situation is confused, and we must await developments. With the battalion present, we may swing the balance in favour of Jahangir Khan's properly constituted authority. That, anyway, is my hope. Major Pilkington?'

'Sir?'

'When your guns are assembled, take position in the centre of the line. Major Hay, turn the companies into line, make room for the guns, then stand the men easy.'

The Colonel turned back towards the old city walls and the tight-closed gateway. By now, the firing from within had mostly died away, although from time to time the waiting men heard isolated shots.

* * *

'It's a confounded nuisance!' Fettleworth said angrily, mopping at his face with a handkerchief. Having been brought out from a ball given by the officers of the 1st Division, he was in full mess dress, and his starched shirt-front was soft and sticky with sweat. He glowered round at the assembled staff officers and brigade commanders. 'Where, precisely, is Dornoch's regiment – hey, Lakenham?'

Brigadier-General Lakenham, Chief of Staff, laid the point of a pencil on a map in front of Fettleworth. 'There, sir, in the Malakand – that is, at the time the runners were despatched – '

'And now?'

Lakenham shrugged. 'That must depend on many things, sir.'

Fettleworth thumped the table. 'Make an assessment, man, make an assessment!'

'Very well, sir. I imagine they should be across the Panjkora by now, and not so far from Kalundabad. It appears Kalundabad is Dornoch's target – '

'Yes, yes. Point is, what's he going to do when he gets there? Start a Frontier war, or what? Hey?'

'Dornoch's a tactful enough man, sir.'

'Really.' Fettleworth made a disparaging face, and pushed irritably at the map with a pudgy hand. 'Damned if I think *any* Scot's that – '

'You chose him yourself, sir, for this mission,' Lakenham reminded.

'But at that time I'd not heard about that patrol getting cut up! That alters the situation drastically, my dear fellow, don't you see? Dornoch's one of these clansmen – you know how they carry on – an eye for an eye! That can be – '

'Sir,' Lakenham broke in loudly, 'the same kind of situation could have arisen, and in fact *has* arisen many times, as

62

a result of *any* action in which men are killed. This is certainly not without precedent and I'm quite sure you can rely absolutely on Lord Dornoch's discretion. To my mind, there are other considerations that take priority now – '

'Which considerations, Lakenham?'

'The question of reinforcements, sir, of course.'

'No, not of course, Lakenham! Why of course? Dornoch has an entire battalion and a battery of mountain guns!' Again Bloody Francis thumped on the table-top. 'Damn it, haven't I said we don't want to bring this business to a war footing? If I send in more battalions of infantry, more guns, cavalry even – what's Whitehall going to say?'

Lakenham gave a cold smile. 'Let us look at the other side of the coin, General Fettleworth. What are they going to say if the 114th are cut up, and no reinforcements on the way to hold the tribes in check? What then?'

'That'll never happen,' Fettleworth said with confidence.

'Nonsense, sir – with respect, that's simply not true. We know the strength of the tribes in and around Kalundabad, and indeed we know Jahangir Khan asked for assistance. Had he not done so, Dornoch would not be in – '

'Yes, yes, yes!'

'I add one more thing, sir: Whitehall is not going to be pleased should you fail to support Jahangir Khan's position in Dir and Kalundabad – '

'I am aware of my duties and responsibilities, Brigadier-General Lakenham, thank you. I shall *fail* in nothing. I am anxious only not to exacerbate the situation – '

'Please allow me to finish, sir. I was going to say, in the first instance you wished for an exploratory probe in order to assess what that situation was. At this moment we still do not know the answer – except that your initial probe led to the cutting-up of a British patrol. Sir, in my view, that speaks of a badly deteriorating situation, and one that must be faced and met with force!' Lakenham's voice was hard, his face flushed with anger now. 'If, as seems most likely, Jahangir Khan's territories are in a state of rebellion, then one battalion is not going to be sufficient force to deal with it – '

'A battalion *and* a battery –'

'Bah!'

Fettleworth looked astonished. 'I beg your pardon? Did I hear –'

'You must reinforce, sir. You must reinforce! You must order out a brigade with full artillery support, to march once through the Malakand. You can do no less. If you do not . . .'

Fettleworth met his eye. 'If I do not?'

'Then I shall myself represent the matter to Army Head-quarters in Muree.'

'Sir, you are damned insubordinate –'

'Sir, I am not. I am only doing my duty.' Lakenham lifted an arm and waved it towards the north. 'There are lives at risk up there, General Fettleworth – lives, and the very basis of the Raj! I admit we don't *know* what the situation is, but we must plan on assumptions now, on past experience. And if my assumptions are the right ones, sir, then the defeat of a British battalion by a horde of tribesmen is going to do more than merely *exacerbate* – it promises to lead to mutiny!'

Fettleworth was still obstinately mulish. 'Stuff-and-non-sense. Exaggeration's no help. In any case, I've made my decision – I shall refer the matter myself to Sir Iain Ogilvie in Murree, and then act as ordered.'

*　　*　　*

'The men,' Cunningham said, 'do not like the inaction, Captain Ogilvie, sir.'

'Nor do I, but it can't be helped. The Colonel has no other choice for the moment.' Ogilvie looked towards the city, white beneath the moon – white and ghostly. During the day there had been more firing at intervals; and at the proper hours the waiting battalion had heard the call of the muezzin bidding the faithful kneel to Mohamet, an act that even rifle-fire could not disturb. Again there was indecision in the air: until there was some straw in the wind, the British force must wait: that was its ordained role. They had not come as conquerors. As Ogilvie had tried to explain to Hamish Dewar, Dornoch must not be seen to Division, to Calcutta, to Whitehall or to the world as the mere avenger of his lost patrol.

'So,' Dewar had asked sarcastically, 'we're waiting for a sign – is that it?'

'In a way, yes.'

'Like a bloody holy man!'

Later in the day, Dornoch had decided to transfer his encampment from its overnight position and settle down for what could prove a long wait closer to the city wall. The movement occupied the battalion for some while as they were marched back to strike camp, then marched back again with the tents and equipment. When the move was completed, the men were fallen out to wash and shave in the water of a stream running close to the lines: in this stream they stripped and splashed, cooling weary bodies, with their ready rifles close at hand. In spite of the pleasure of clean water there were many grumbles, many loudly-voiced complaints about officers who couldn't make up their minds – complaints that had led to Cunningham's words that night to Ogilvie as the two, unable to settle down to sleep, met at the head of B Company's lines.

'What do you think is happening inside the city, Sar'nt-Major?' Ogilvie asked.

'I've no idea and that's the truth, sir. There's a nasty smell about this place . . . enough to make the men see ghosties and bogles! There's been just nothing to say that the inhabitants have even noticed us! And I do not like it, Captain Ogilvie.' Cunningham took a long look all around the camp perimeter, at the alert, patrolling pickets, at the lines of tents and at the waiting guns; and then back at the high sheer walls enclosing the city, quiet now beneath the backdrop of the hills. 'I'm thinking,' he said in a low voice, 'that we could well do with more strength. We're very extended, Captain Ogilvie, a devil of a long way from base! If we had – ' He broke off. 'Now what's that – d'ye hear, sir?'

5   65

'Where?'

Cunningham pointed. 'Away there, by the wall. A sort of scraping it sounded like, then a thump . . . like a man dropping down – '

'An attack? We'd better sound – '

'No, sir, no.' Cunningham put a ham-like hand on Ogilvie's arm. 'No alarm, that's my advice, with respect. I've a feeling that if it is a man out there then he doesn't want his own side to know he's got out!'

Ogilvie's heart thumped. 'An emissary?'

'It's just a feeling, sir, but that's what I suspect. Come, Captain Ogilvie, keep with me and we'll go and find out.' Cunningham moved, fast but quiet, extraordinarily light on his feet for his great bulk, towards where he had pin-pointed the sounds. As he and Ogilvie reached the camp's perimeter, they saw, clear in the moonlight, a desperately running figure coming towards them, in flapping garments, making an obvious effort of will to keep going. The runner was within thirty yards of them when there was the crack of a rifle and a flash from the top of the wall; and after that a tearing cry, a scream of agony. The escaper fell in a heap. As Ogilvie and Cunningham ran forward, the battalion came to life behind them. Black, pulling on his trews, dashed from his tent, shouting. A moment later the bugles sounded the Alert, and as they did so Ogilvie reached the body on the ground. More bullets swept down from the walls, but Ogilvie, disregarding them, bent and felt beneath the tattered, filthy garments. There was a faint heart-beat: he became aware of bright eyes, wide open, staring into his own. He felt shock: the face was a woman's, and it was white. She seemed to wish to speak, but no words came. Ogilvie registered the fact that the face was a young one, and though now sick-looking, had been pretty: then, glancing up as he heard movement close by, he found Cunningham also bending over the woman, but not touching her, a strangely fearful look in his leathery face.

'By God, a woman . . . och, the poor wee lady!' Then his

voice hardened. 'Get up, Captain Ogilvie! *Get up, sir, I say, this minute!*'

'On the contrary, Sar'nt-Major, I suggest you get down, unless you want a bullet – '

'Sir!' Cunningham was shaking, his face almost haggard in the white light of the moon, haggard and suddenly aged. 'Bullets I can take. But that poor lady's face, the skin . . . you can see well enough in the moon, surely? God knows, I'm no doctor, but – '

'But what?' Ogilvie asked impatiently.

'I've seen the look too often. It's the cholera, Captain Ogilvie!'

SEVEN

'THE CHOLERA!' Black's voice, as the Surgeon Major reported, was horror-struck. 'My God, the cholera!'

'I'm afraid so.'

'You're sure, Doctor? There's no chance of a mistake in your – '

'None, Andrew. There are all the symptoms. Acute diarrhoea, vomiting, feeble circulation, coldness of the body surface together with a high intestinal temperature. The disease is far advanced – I think the poor woman will not live long. I'll arrange for her to be cared for – '

'You'll do no such thing!'

Surgeon Major Corton said coldly, 'Will I not?'

'No! You said she's going to die. Let her die without contaminating us, Doctor! You'll leave her where she is, and when she's dead, you'll leave the vultures to remove the body!'

'I'll do no such thing – to make use of your own words, Andrew – '

'I order – '

'Oh, no! You do not order me! Andrew, I am a medical man, and my duty is to save life, *all* life. Where I cannot save – as in this case I believe I cannot – then my duty is to alleviate.' Corton put a hand on Black's shoulder. 'Now listen, and don't panic. I'll look after the woman myself, with volunteer orderlies to assist. With the proper precautions, there should be little danger of the thing spreading – you may leave that to me. The point is, she can't be left to lie out there. When daybreak comes, she'll be killed by rifle fire from the walls – '

'A better death, surely?'

Corton nodded. 'Perhaps – perhaps. But we still cannot leave any person, let alone a white woman, deliberately, to die. Besides, Andrew, you should be remembering *your* duty, should you not?'

'My duty?'

'The woman lives. Isn't it highly likely she escaped with a message? Should you not get that message from her, before she dies?'

Black put his face in his hands: a low moan escaped him, a moaning prayer to any gods that might listen. Captain Andrew Black was most mortally frightened of disease.

*   *   *

Corton himself went out again to bring the woman in, with two volunteers called for personally by the Colonel, men who shivered naked in the night air so as to preserve their uniforms from contamination, their skins blackened with boot polish to make them harder to see from the walls. The operation was carried out at speed, the native rifles providing the spur. Bullets snicked into the ground around them, and one embedded in the sick woman's shoulder as she was borne away. She was carried around the camp's perimeter, towards a hollow in the ground five hundred yards clear of the lines, on the side farthest from the city. As the Scots passed behind their lines the firing from the walls died. It was a strange procession beneath the moon, with the whole battalion staring fearfully, and already feeling the uncleanliness of the filthy disease, endemic to all India and beyond, the dreaded disease that could weaken and kill within twelve hours from the onset, the disease that had wiped out so many British soldiers over the years of Empire. The woman vomited constantly as she was borne along: the bearers became wild-eyed, almost running in their desire to bring the job to a quick conclusion. Reaching the spot he had selected, Corton ordered the woman to be laid down; and the moment the burden was released, other men doused the bearers with water from the stream, water that had been heavily impregnated with a strong disinfectant. Corton, joined now by the Colonel, along with a trembling, ashen-faced Black, and the Regimental Sergeant-Major, bent over the suffering woman, whose gun-shot wounds he quickly cleaned and dressed with a bandage.

'Poor woman,' Dornoch said with compassion. 'Doctor, can you get her to talk?'

'I'll try.' Corton bent over the woman's head, smoothing the brow, giving her a few words of comfort. In the light from a storm lantern the watching men saw the haunted face, the eyes deeply shadowed and sunken, the rise of bile in the working throat, the terrible gush as the discharge came, and then the groans. Gently Corton wiped the suffering lips clean with a pad of gauze soaked in water, then spoke again, quietly but with persistence. There was no more vomiting, but after a while the lips opened again, a swollen tongue protruded, trying to lick away the terrible dryness: again Corton used his gauze pad, then put a water-bottle close to the lips and tilted it. After this, the woman seemed to be making an effort to speak: there was a murmur, no more. The doctor bent closer, putting his ear as close to the mouth as possible. Black stared down, his face working; Dornoch's face was set hard. Fighting was one thing, disease another; the doctor had guts! After a while Corton looked up for a moment, felt for the heart, then got to his feet.

He spoke to the Colonel. 'Missionary,' he said. 'There's more inside the city. Her husband and his sister, and another couple – man and wife. I think I got most of the message. Jahangir Khan's authority is in the balance – there's a strong revolt. Jahangir himself is in the city with a detachment of his native army, but though his own men remain loyal to him, as do many of the townspeople, the rebels hold the gate and the walls.'

'And the other missionaries?'

'Are in Jahangir's headquarters.'

'No more information?'

'None, Colonel.'

Dornoch's face was grim in the lantern's light. 'An English woman, Doctor?'

'Yes.'

'An Englishwoman, to come to this! Will she say more, d'you suppose?'

'Not now, Colonel. She's dead.'

There was a long sigh from Black: relief? At least any spread would now be checked more surely than if the woman had lingered on! Corton added, 'She did tell me one more thing, Colonel, one we could have deduced for ourselves: the city's full of the cholera. The first case occurred only yesterday, but the spread has been rapid.'

'Can you cope with an epidemic, Doctor?'

'I, Colonel?' Corton made a gesture with his arms, a gesture of impotence. 'With my current medicinal supplies and lack of trained orderlies – no, frankly, I cannot.'

'Then you must do your best, Doctor –'

'Of course. In any case I think I can promise no spread out here, Colonel. My precautions –'

'You misunderstand me.' Dornoch's voice was hard, harder than was normal as he buttressed himself for a cruel decision, one from which he could not shrink now. 'We are needed by Jahangir Khan, to say nothing of the known presence of English women in the city, and now I consider my orders to be perfectly clear.' He looked around the small circle of faces. 'Captain Black – Sar'nt-Major: first this poor woman is to be decently buried, then the battalion will prepare to assault the gates, assisted by an artillery bombardment in the first instance. Mr Cunningham, a runner to Major Pilkington and Mr Dewar – they're to report at once.'

* * *

There were no bugle calls: under cover of the loud digging of a grave the orders were passed by word of mouth, quietly. The battalion deployed as quietly also, though it was obvious they must be visible in the moonlight. Proof of some movement having been seen came in the form of renewed firing from the walls, but the dispositions continued under the quiet orders of the officers and N.C.Os. Two companies deployed right, two left; these would all give covering fire to the main advance, raking the walls as necessary when the remaining companies, including Ogilvie's, charged the gates after the artillery bombardment had softened-up the position. Once the gates had been taken, B Company would remain to hold the entry. Major Pilkington's mountain battery, its guns now assembled and ready for action, took up its firing position in the centre, opposite the great gateway into the city and immediately ahead of the main infantry attack column.

When all the reports had reached him, Dornoch spoke to the company commanders. 'I've not much to say at this stage,' he told them. 'Simply this: after we have fought through the gate, which shouldn't be difficult once the guns have been to work, our first aim will be to contact Jahangir Khan and ensure the safety of the missionaries. Until we've done that, I wish as few casualties as are consistent with a successful entry – you must watch very carefully indeed for blood-lust and you will permit no killing for the sake of revenge. Pass the word to every man via your N.C.O.s before moving out, that we are entering in support of Jahangir Khan and that until the situation becomes clearer we shall continue our action to such support for properly constituted authority. One more thing: you will avoid the sick. Is that clear? There will be women and children among the sick, but the time for compassion will come later.' Dornoch paused, looking closely at each officer's face. 'I wish you all good luck, gentlemen. Once inside, the fighting is bound to be confused – and we have no maps to lead us to Jahangir Khan! All we have is Mr Dewar's knowledge of the city. Mr Dewar will stay by me, and you will do your best to keep me in sight – and keep behind me. I can offer no plan beyond that.'

He nodded in dismissal. The company commanders

72

saluted and fell out, making their way back to their men, kilts swinging around knees chilled by the cold breeze of the night, tunics tight across hearts eager enough for the fighting to come but chilled by thoughts of the plague that they were about to enter. That night, there were many who thought the Colonel crazy: there were some, mainly amongst the rank-and-file, who said so, bitterly. Ogilvie, hearing some of the murmured discontent as he rejoined his company, felt sick at heart: undoubtedly the Colonel was asking a lot, and undoubtedly also a number of laggards were going to need chasing through the gates by threat of revolver or Court Martial.

Even Hamish Dewar was unhappy now. 'If the cholera gets into my stomach,' he said, 'I'll sick it up into the Colonel's face!'

'It's not the Colonel, Hamish.'

'Oh?' There was a jeer in Dewar's voice, an ugly look on his heavy face. 'Who is it, then?'

'No one person in particular. Just – well, the Frontier, that's all.'

'The Frontier, that's all,' Dewar repeated in the high voice of mimickry. 'God, you make me sick too! You seem to think the sun shines out of the Colonel's blasted backside, no matter what he does – or sometimes doesn't do!'

Ogilvie fought down his temper. 'Finished?' he asked. 'Because if you haven't – ' He broke off, what he had been about to say killed by the sudden, strident notes of the bugles. Dewar dashed away to join the Colonel. The call had scarcely started when Pilkington's guns crashed out in a fury of sound and flame, all six together, hurling their shells towards the gateway ahead. The din at close quarters was appalling: men stuffed fingers into ears as the bombardment went on and on, as it seemed. In fact it was contained to six rounds per gun, and it was enough. Thirty-six shells, all well and truly laid on the target, reduced the entry to a redly-burning shambles of crashed masonry and woodwork, a terrible picture of total destruction given voice in the crackling of the flames and the screams of dying men. As the

73

barrage ceased, the bugles sounded the Advance and the four attack companies, with bayonets fixed, charged for the gateway with the pipers standing bravely in the open ground to play them on. The rush of men, yelling out Highland warcries, thrusting with the cold steel as they poured like a torrent over the smashed doors and the fallen stonework, carried the gates with ease in spite of a hail of bullets from the top of the walls. As the support companies, deployed to right and left, returned this fire, natives fell screaming only to be replaced by more. Among these support companies, the casualties looked like becoming heavy. Dornoch, waving his claymore like a maddened dervish, his horse rearing over a press of natives running from the British bayonets, turned and looked back towards the gateway, now being occupied by Ogilvie's company which had followed in rear of the main assault. Looking along the inside of the great walls of the city, he saw the hordes of natives pouring fire down on his men still outside. Then, as Major Hay swept past him he called out:

'Major, the walls. Get them cleared – and quickly! Bring in the remaining companies, they've done their job now.'

'Very good, Colonel.' Turning his horse, the Major rode back along a shattered alley. Dornoch heard his voice bellowing the orders, and within the minute the British fire was being directed on to the platform running below the parapet of the walls – directed from within, and the Maxims now in stuttering, raking fury. The native defenders fell in swathes, dead from the bullets or dead from the impact as they crashed to the ground far below. As the Maxims ceased firing, the four remaining companies of the Royal Strathspeys charged the gateway, climbing over the rubble, yelling and cheering, with the pipes and drums exulting behind the leading company. A swarm of running natives poured past the Colonel's horse, and, looking about him, he saw that already Hamish Dewar had been separated from him.

Dornoch swore. Then, as a native who, by his dress, seemed of more importance than the rest of the mob, brushed past, Dornoch reached down and grabbed for the man's robe. Getting a good grip, he pulled the man backwards and up towards him. Dark eyes rolled fearfully. 'You'll take me to Jahangir Khan,' the Colonel said in a harsh voice, using Urdu. 'He wanted us, and we're here. Take me to him at once, or I'll slice your head off this instant!' He looked round, saw the Regimental Sergeant-Major picking his way towards him, avoiding a rude heap of bodies that had the look of the cholera death about them. 'Sar'nt-Major, this fellow will guide us to Jahangir Khan – providing we don't let go of him! Take him over, if you please.'

'Sir!' Cunningham moved towards the native, his face streaming sweat and almost demoniac in the red light of fires burning just inside the shattered gateway. Dornoch looked back.

'The fires, Mr Cunningham. I think we're sufficiently in control to spare men to fetch water from the stream. Kindly detail parties to douse the fires – I'll hold on to this man meanwhile.'

'Sir!' The R.S.M. swung about and moved away. He was back within a few minutes. 'Parties detailed, sir. Captain Black will take charge of fire-fighting. Major Hay's compliments, sir, and he is seeing to the posting of pickets all along the parapet. Sir!'

Dornoch nodded. 'Thank you, Sar'nt-Major. And now – to Jahangir Khan!'

The R.S.M. took the native in a big fist, heaving the garment tight as a binding rope. Also speaking in Urdu he said, 'Now, you'll take the Colonel Sahib and me to Jahangir Khan. No tricks – if you wish to live without pain! Now move.' Still holding the man with the one hand, he drew his revolver with the other, pressing the muzzle hard against the cringing backbone. Eyes rolling, the man moved ahead of the Colonel's horse, making for the mouth of a narrow alley between tall buildings, crumbling buildings with the very stench of death and decay about them. Added to this appalling smell was the sharp but clean smell of cordite hanging over all, plus the fumes and thick smoke from the fires behind. In rear of Dornoch came a half-company of Highlanders with fixed bayonets – men who had seen too many comrades die in the assault that night. The look of their faces was enough, apparently, for the civil inhabitants of Kalundabad, who pressed back and away fearfully, into doorways and cross-passages. Many of the doorways they passed contained the huddled, horrible bodies of the dead from the sickness, and behind them the hostile eyes of the yet living, women largely, in long dresses and veils, staring at the British soldiers. And those British soldiers, with all a strong man's detestation of sickness, were nervous with a desire to get away from Kalundabad as soon as the Colonel's business was completed. The colour-sergeants were going to need all their watchfulness that night to prevent any incidents arising from gun-happy fingers losing their self-control. This indeed was much on Cunningham's mind as he followed the directions of his captive. Won they had – so far! But an artillery-assisted assault, with some element of surprise at least, was a very different situation from that posed by penetrating such a spider's-web of alleys as this: every alley's mouth, every doorway could hold sudden death from knife or rifle; every filthy emanation from the hovels could bring the cholera to a man's guts.

None of this, however, showed in the R.S.M.'s face or bearing as he marched along. Duty was duty: as a Warrant Officer, he was charged by the Secretary of State for War, in the name of Her Majesty Queen Victoria, to do his duty and to uphold and obey his officers. And woe betide any N.C.O. or man who didn't do the same!

Coming out at last from the horrible confines of the alley, they found themselves in a kind of small square, with the roadway dividing to right and left around a large central building: not quite a palace, for though large it had a more functional aspect than the usual run of the palaces of the Frontier princelings. It was most probably, Dornoch thought, the seat of local government, of Jahangir Khan's representative in Kalundabad. And it appeared he was right: as the native-led soldiers approached, a body of men in the livery of a native army came out from a doorway at the head of a

76

broad flight of steps: twelve men who, under the orders of a richly-dressed and turbaned native, assumed some sort of line to bar the way to the inside of the building, while other men held lighted flares.

Lord Dornoch halted his half-company. Ahead of him, the Regimental Sergeant-Major, outlined by the red flickering light from the flares, hauled his captive to a halt also, but still retained his grip and the pressure of his revolver.

Dornoch surveyed the native soldiers, all of them armed with the old-fashioned long-barrelled rifles so familiar along the Frontier and inside Afghanistan. Then, again speaking Urdu, he said in a strong, carrying voice, 'I come by request of His Highness Jahangir Khan. My mission is peaceful, and is in support of the law. I come not as one who wishes to take possession of your city.'

There was no apparent reaction. The native guard remained silently in line, fingering their weapons. Ahead of the Colonel, Cunningham turned his head. 'Sir! I don't like the look of this.'

'No more do I, Sar'nt-Major, but we'll not do anything precipitate.' Dornoch raised his voice again. 'I wish to have words with your master, Jahangir Khan.'

This time there was an answer, from the man who was evidently their officer: 'Jahangir Khan is dead. The Colonel Sahib can have no words with those who die in the Prophet . . . until he also is dead. Have a care, Colonel Sahib. This city of Kalundabad is no longer loyal to its former rulers, who have been rejected by the will of the people. I say again, Jahangir Khan is dead. Go now in peace and you will be allowed to live. Stay, and you and your soldiers die in Kalundabad.' As he finished speaking, the native raised both arms above his head, looking skywards, and started a loud cry, a kind of keening it seemed: and as he did this, his twelve men brought up their rifles, aiming them at the British force.

Dornoch remained rock steady, sitting his horse imperiously. 'If Jahangir Khan is dead as you say, then I demand to see the evidence – I must see his body. And I would also

77

say this: if Jahangir Khan is dead, it makes no difference to my duty. Kalundabad remains within the province of the successor, the lawful successor, of His Highness Jahangir Khan.'

There was no response to this: but the rifles remained on their point of aim. After a moment the native officer turned away and vanished into the building behind him. Dornoch said, 'Sar'nt-Major, they may be speaking the truth. I believe he's gone for the body.'

'Aye, sir, it's possible. The cholera, sir?'

'Perhaps. Or the knife in the back.'

Cunningham looked around, at the close-set, stinking alley behind him, at the steady Highlanders with their rifles and bayonets, at the native soldiery in their commanding position at the head of the steps. Commanding they might be, but there was a half-company of Scots behind the Colonel . . . Cunningham, struck by a random thought, spoke again to Dornoch. 'Sir! They may try to hoodwink us. Do you know Jahangir Khan yourself, sir?'

Dornoch gave a hard laugh. 'No, by God, I don't, Sar'nt-Major, and I doubt if you do!'

'I do not, sir, but there is one who does. Captain Ogilvie, sir. Captain Ogilvie once met him, at a levée in Murree, sir, given by Sir Ian Ogilvie – he told me that, sir.'

'Did he, indeed! Thank you, Mr Cunningham.' Dornoch paused, looked back at the waiting men in rear, then towards the Regimental Sergeant Major. 'Four men and a corporal, if you please, Mr Cunningham, to detach and act as escort to Captain Ogilvie – at the double!'

'Sir!' The R.S.M. called the orders back past the Colonel's horse, and four privates detached and doubled to the rear under the orders of a corporal. They had just passed out of sight into the mouth of the alley when there was movement at the head of the steps. The native official came back, together with four more men bearing an inert burden. As Dornoch and Cunningham watched, these men swung their burden – which was now seen to be a naked body – back and forth to gain their momentum, then cast it strongly towards

78

the group of British soldiers. The grotesque brown corpse flew through the air, arms and legs spread limply and flopping, to drop with a smack immediately in front of the Colonel's horse, which reared up, snorting, on its hind legs, nostrils flaring at death's obscenity. There was a sharply indrawn breath from Cunningham as possible foul infection brushed his body in its flight: that was all. He remained as still as a rock, glaring, like Dornoch, towards the line of men on the steps.

Briefly Dornoch spoke: 'We wait, Sar'nt-Major. We wait for Captain Ogilvie.' He added beneath his breath, 'And I pray God he'll not be long in coming!'

EIGHT

MANY MILES TO the south in Murree, garrison life continued as usual, though today the social round was being interrupted by a ceremonial parade in honour of one of the high native rulers – the Maharajah of Kesh. The Maharajah – a young man educated at Eton and Christ Church, Oxford – stood on the dais with Lieutenant-General Sir Iain Ogilvie to take the salute as the might of the British Raj marched past in review order. It was a windless morning, heavy with heat. Sad-looking dusty trees drooped along the perimeter of the vast parade-ground, here and there among the packed natives watching from beyond silken ropes a thirst-mad pariah dog snuffled along with its tail between its legs, until it was chased away with sticks and stones. In the stands erected for the civilians and the ladies of the garrison, elegance and grace maintained at least an appearance of cool beneath sunshades and awnings.

Taking their traditional position at the right of the line, two batteries of Horse Artillery led the rich pageantry past the saluting platform, with a rattle of brightly-polished harness and a tang of horse sweat, the great wheels of the limbers making deep tracks in the sandy ground. After them came the cavalry of the Indian Army, one squadron each of the Bengal Lancers, Madras Lancers, and Skinner's Horse, colourful and splendid in their full dress uniforms topped by magnificent turbans.

'First-class fellows,' Sir Iain murmured as the squadrons moved past at a walk. 'Your country, sir, makes fine horse-men.'

80

'Yours too, General. I know – I've hunted with the Quorn.'

Sir Iain nodded. After the cavalry came the infantry, the Queen of Battles. Mostly regiments of the British, as opposed to the Indian, Army: Connaught Rangers, Duke of Wellington's, Dorsetshires, Manchesters, Hampshires, Middlesex, King's Own Scottish Borderers. The quick-step, short and sharp, of the Light Infantry and the rifle regiments – Rifle Brigade, King's Royal Rifle Corps, Duke of Cornwall's Light Infantry. Drums and fifes, the H.Q. brass leading . . . right arms swinging, left arms holding rigidly positioned rifles against shoulders, sun-browned, moustached faces dripping sweat, the rolling thunder of thousands of marching feet, a superb prospect of unending Empire to swell the heart of any General Officer Commanding. After the British regiments had passed, two battalions of Indian infantry followed in their wake, one of Mahrattas, one of Punjabis. And finally the support corps – the wagons and horses and mules of the Supply and Transport, bringing up clouds of dust.

As the rumble of the wagons and the rhythm of the marching feet passed on into the distance, the H.Q. brass band detached and wheeled to halt smartly under their bandmaster before the dais. As they crashed out 'God Save The Queen' Sir Iain's scarlet-clad arm lifted to the salute. It was a poignant moment; the notes of the National Anthem took on immediate meaning in that military setting, with the splendour of Her Majesty's regiments vanishing into the dust-clouds and, beyond them, a vision of the high, distant peaks of Himalaya and the Hindu Kush to remind the garrison of sterner things along the fringes of the Raj. Turning abruptly as the music stopped, Sir Iain caught the eye of his wife in the principal stand behind the dais. He interpreted her look accurately: she had felt a similar emotion, and her thoughts would be with their son, James, fighting along those northern hills.

'A splendid parade, General,' the young Maharajah said.

'Thank you, Your Highness.' Sir Iain ushered his guest towards the stand, towards his Chief of Staff, who was already on his feet and looking expectantly and with a touch of anxiety towards the G.O.C. Visits of Indian princes meant a good deal of preparation and a fine sense of timing was demanded on the part of all concerned. Next on the programme was a big reception, to be followed by luncheon in the Army Headquarters Mess. As Sir Iain held out an arm to assist Lady Ogilvie to her feet, the Chief of Staff approached.

'Sir – a word, if I may.'

Sir Iain noted the inflexion, the hint of urgency in the tone. 'Not about the luncheon, Leith?'

'No, sir. Er . . . a word in private?'

The General nodded. Turning to the Maharajah, he said, 'You'll not mind if I leave my wife to entertain you for a few moments? A matter seems to need my attention –'

'General, I shall be honoured. My dear Lady Ogilvie . . . ' With a gallant gesture, the young Indian lightly touched the hand of the General's lady. Sir Iain moved along the gangway with Brigadier-General Leith.

'Well, Leith?'

'A despatch from Peshawar, sir.'

'Fettleworth?'

'Yes, sir –'

'Damn and blast!' Sir Iain said disagreeably. 'What does he want?'

'This concerns Kalundabad, sir. You're aware already, sir, that –'

'That Fettleworth despatched the 114th to be held in readiness on the route to Kalundabad – yes. What's happened since?'

The Chief of Staff explained. 'The original patrol was cut up inside the city, it seems. That apart, all General Fettleworth knows is that it was Lord Dornoch's intention to advance on Kalundabad with his battalion. General Fettleworth doesn't know Lord Dornoch's further intention, sir – what he means to do when he arrives outside the city –'

'I don't suppose anyone but Dornoch *does* know that!' Sir

Iain moved impatiently. 'What does General Fettleworth want *me* to do about it, Leith?'

'He's asking whether or not a support force should be sent, sir. It seems he has in mind the possibility of a deterioration in the situation – in which case, the 114th may need assistance.'

'But he doesn't want to annoy the politicians?'

'The despatch doesn't say that, sir, but I believe that to be the case.'

'So do I!' Sir Iain laughed harshly, then frowned. 'To a point, Fettleworth's right. We have to maintain the status quo in Dir and Kalundabad, but we don't want to force matters unnecessarily. Myself, I'd trust Lord Dornoch to smooth things out short of war! I'll go into this again after luncheon, Leith – and in the meantime, tell Fettleworth he's to do nothing until he gets his orders.'

'Very good, sir.'

Sir Iain Ogilvie went back to join his wife and the Maharajah. But during the reception and the luncheon he was taciturn, morose: the mood had changed. Peaceful ceremonial and splendour was, in India, ever on the brink of giving way to blood and the rolling clouds of war. War, after all, was the whole reason for a soldier's existence; but though he had never consciously allowed the fact to sway his judgment, and indeed seldom allowed any hint of emotion to show, Sir Iain never forgot that he was a father as well as a soldier.

*　　*　　*

Lord Dornoch's face was grey with weariness and anxiety, with the result of feeling that he and the battalion were sitting neatly on a fused time-bomb. The night before, when Ogilvie had reached him, a quick examination of the flung corpse had yielded the information that the corpse was not that of Jahangir Khan. Making up his mind on the instant, Dornoch had given the order to his half-company to open fire on the natives holding the steps. The whole line had been mown down to a man, and the Scots, charging with yells and cries behind their bayonets, had taken the building after vicious hand-to-hand fighting along corridors of marble and in sumptuously furnished apartments. Barricaded into one of the rooms they had found the soberly-dressed missionaries – a Mr Ernest Wimpole and his wife Ada, and the Reverend Arthur Hopkins, husband of the young woman who had escaped earlier from the city; and his sister, Miss Mildred Hopkins. They were clearly terrified, but composed enough, though Miss Hopkins broke down at the sight of her brother's face when he was told the news of his wife. Lord Dornoch was given the story of earlier events by Mr Wimpole: the clergyman's wife had been taken by the mob, and raped, and they had already given her up for lost when she had been dragged away. Questioned, none of the missionaries had any knowledge of what might have happened to Jahangir Khan, though they asserted he must still be in the city, dead or alive. When full control had been gained inside the building the place was tooth-combed for Jahangir, and the natives who had survived the Highlanders' attack were closely and sometimes brutally questioned for some hours. The obvious fact of a successful insurrection, and the admission that the leader of this revolt had fallen to the British guns, were the only pieces of information to emerge: there were no clues to the whereabouts of Jahangir Khan. Even his loyal supporters, of whom the Scots found twenty-odd imprisoned in the building, were unable to help.

'His Highness has not been seen since your attack started, Sahib,' a big, heavily bearded havildar of the rulers' private army reported. 'I myself had not seen His Highness for some hours before that.'

'How much support has he in the city now?' Dornoch asked wearily.

'Sahib, there are few of us left. The rebels have been busy with their long knives. But such as are left will fight for the British Raj, and for His Highness Jahangir Khan.'

It was simply and honestly said, a soldier's words. Lord

Dornoch looked into the havildar's dark eyes. 'Do you believe His Highness lives?' he asked directly.

'Sahib, this I believe. I feel it here.' The havildar lifted a hand and placed it over his heart. 'His Highness lives, and is in need of help, Sahib.'

'That he will have,' Dornoch said. He looked around through tired eyes: the rich apartments were largely a blood-stained shambles now, but at least he had got himself a head-quarters. During the night another full company had fought through the streets to join him, and details had been hastily organised to begin a thorough and lengthy search of the city. The 114th's makeshift headquarters were strongly held, as were the gates. But the very air was vibrant with the screams and imprecations of the mob, while the insidious fly-borne cholera continued to make its horrible, obscene depredations – as, during the morning, Surgeon Major Corton reported to the Colonel. He said, 'There's no sickness yet among the men, but I can't control the spread so long as we're inside the city.'

'Can't is a somewhat comprehensive word, Doctor.'

'But a true one.' Corton spread his arms; his own face was tense, tired. 'The place is a festering cesspit, Colonel – literally! It's full of open drains, full of flies, full of corpses too, corpses that should be burned. To prevent the spread is impossible, and when it comes to us, it'll come fast. I've only one suggestion to make.'

Dornoch looked up. 'And that is?'

'Evacuate the city. Contain it from the outside.'

'And leave Jahangir Khan to die with the rest? He's not been found yet – and he's a British responsibility, Doctor! No, I can't evacuate the city. I'm sorry, but that's final – '

'Jahangir Khan may well be dead already – '

The Colonel smashed a fist into his palm. 'But I must make sure! Until I know what has happened to him we remain – all of us, Doctor, for I need the whole battalion. Without strength, we'll be massacred – you don't need to be a com-batant officer to see that, surely?'

85

'Colonel, is a native regime worth the sacrifice of a British battalion, for that is – '

'It hasn't been an easy decision, Doctor. I beg of you not to make it worse.' Dornoch's face twitched nervily and there was a shake in his hands as he rubbed at bloodshot eyes. 'But it's my decision and I take full responsibility. Now let us consider what we can do medically, Doctor. You speak of drains – we can do nothing about that, I think. But you also speak of corpses that should be burned. Very well then – we shall burn them!'

'But – '

'No buts, Doctor. The medical precautions are in your hands.' He waved an arm. 'This place is big enough – set up your medical centre in as many of the rooms as you need. See to disinfectants – do all you can. James?'

Ogilvie stepped forward. 'Colonel?'

'You'll take charge of the burning parties. You must set up an organisation in consultation with the Surgeon Major – you'll have any number of bodies to cope with. When anyone dies, they are to be burned at once. Select a burning area outside the city, commandeer all carts, provide as strong an armed escort as you consider necessary for the removal. Send men to forage for brushwood, to start the fires going. Mr McCrum has paraffin in his commissariat wagons – use it, James. Is all that clear?'

'Yes, Colonel.'

'Good – then carry on.' Dornoch glanced across at the Adjutant. 'Andrew, four men if you please – men who are good riders. Detailed, not volunteers. You will provide horses. I'll prepare a despatch for General Fettleworth, informing him fully of the position here. Four copies, one to each man, and the party to split into pairs after leaving the city. 'Understood?'

'Yes, Colonel.'

'Sar'nt-Major?'

'Sir!'

'The strictest discipline you've ever imposed. There is to

86

be no shooting except under attack. If any man disobeys, then he will himself be shot. The men are to provoke nothing, by word or deed. Remember we're very heavily outnumbered, and we can afford no casualties.'

'Sir!'

'And detail four of your best, most dependable colour-sergeants to assist the Surgeon Major and see to it that his orders in regard to disinfection and personal cleanliness are obeyed to the letter.'

'Sir!' Cunningham permitted himself one comment: 'I don't believe there'll be any lack of keenness to obey *that* order, sir!'

'I trust there'll be no lack of keenness to obey any other order, Sar'nt-Major. Now, when all this has been put in hand, I want you, Andrew, and you, Mr Cunningham, to report back here. We shall then see what can be done to increase the search details looking for Jahangir Khan – and consider how best, militarily, to withstand what promises to be a very unusual kind of siege!'

*   *   *

Everything felt unclean, as though the cholera lay in all that the hand or clothing was forced to touch. Flies were everywhere, buzzing and crawling in the enervating heat of the city, darting under flailing arms to the attack. The open drains with their sluggishly running contents sickened men's stomachs. It would, Ogilvie thought, be hard to distinguish such resultant vomiting from that brought about by the cholera. With a half-company of corpse burners, he gathered in such carts as he could find. While the living sullenly watched from windows, flinging down much muck and abuse and the occasional bullet or knife, fly-encrusted bodies were picked from doorways, from alleys, and flung into the carts to be trundled under armed escort to the gates and out to the piles of paraffin-soaked brushwood collected by the luckier details operating outside the walls. As soon as there were enough corpses to make a start, the fires were lit, and while some of the men stood by to keep them going, others went back with Ogilvie and the carts for more dead. There seemed to be an unending supply. Death had the city in its grip: even as Ogilvie watched, haggard sickly faces vanished from windows, collapsing into the last stages of the disease. To the smells of the open drains and the human effluents rotting in the oppressive heat was now added the peculiarly revolting smell of the burning dead.

Encouraging the men as best he could in a disencouraging situation, steadying them in their horrible task, Ogilvie heard the snatches of talk along the death-cart procession:

'When ye feel the terrible thirst an' get the squitters, then ye'll know ...'

'A bloody high temperature and a great muck-sweat they say ...'

'Pukin' up green bile –' Those who, on earlier service, had met the cholera before, had not been slow to air their knowledge and their fears.

'Yon Colonel's gone bloody mad, that's what! Why don't we cut an' run – get out while we're still fit?'

The processions continued towards the fires, smoking and flaming in red tongues into the sky, in the shadow of the hills. As each cart came up, it was tipped to discharge its cargo: flopping arms and legs, bony sightless faces, staring eyes and closed eyes, filthy stained garments, men, women, children. Offloaded, the cargoes were taken over by other men and lifted on poles serving as makeshift pitchforks, to be slung on to the fires. Probably never before in all their long history of service had the Queen's Own Royal Strathspeys been called upon to perform such a task. It was a task that continued right through the day and the following night before the current dead had been cleared. From now on, it would be simply a task of keeping pace with the fresh deaths; and after Ogilvie had reported, orders came from Black that the burning detail would be reduced to two sections under a sergeant, and that the remaining sections, after some rest and proper cleansing, would help to back up the parties combing the city for Jahangir Khan. Ogilvie fell out with immense relief and gladness, and reported to Surgeon Major Corton's disinfecting room.

*　　*　　*

The insidious germ did not long delay its attack on the Scots. The doctor, who had already made his dispositions in readiness, had the sick brought to the makeshift battalion H.Q. and isolated in the biggest of the state apartments, one that had evidently been the council chamber, the very seat of Jahangir's government, lofty, spacious, and comparatively cool in Kalundabad's stifling heat. All the missionaries volunteered their help: Corton was only too pleased to accept the nursing assistance of the ladies. Mrs Wimpole and Miss Hopkins were a gentle pair, both bespectacled, both with wispy brown hair, both with angelic expressions that Corton found profoundly moving. There was a curious serenity about them as they carried out their tasks among the suffering, vomiting soldiers, bringing comfort by their touch, even by the very sight of women's dresses. Mr Wimpole and the Reverend Arthur Hopkins also ministered to the men, using the precious water-bottles to wet their lips, fetching and carrying for the doctor, and helping to keep the sick quarters clean. There was no thought of self.

During that second day, the sick list to the Colonel showed eighteen men down with the cholera.

NINE

NEXT MORNING CAME up bright and fresh, with a strong
breeze blowing through the streets to carry away the stinks
and the dried dust of excreta. Ogilvie, with Hamish Dewar,
watched from a high tower as the sun came over the eastern
hills. The city, far below, seemed at that distance peaceful
and trouble-free and clean, its mud-coloured walls lightened
by the splash of the Royal Strathspey tartan around the knees
of the company providing the gate guard. Above that gateway there now floated the Queen's Colour, waving bravely
out before the alien walls.

Ogilvie turned as Dewar gave a sudden laugh. 'What's up,
Hamish?'

'Up? Nothing's up – I was just struck by a thought, that's
all. That flag down there. There's something about a flag...'

'I agree, there is.'

Dewar waved a hand towards the Queen's Colour. 'Look
at it ... waving over filth and corruption! James, what the
devil *are* we doing here, what *are* we defending when all's
said and done? Shall I tell you? We're just following a dream
... I don't refer to the Raj itself, of course. That's splendid.
But we're following a dream of the *old* India, an India of
rich and powerful princes – '

'They're still that.'

'I know! And why? I'll tell you, James: because we prop
them up, that's why! They're part of our dream, the *stupid*
part. Prince, Maharajah, Gaekwar – call 'em what you like,
they're all scheming bastards.' Dewar's voice was full of
contempt and hate. 'At this moment, we're breaking our-

selves against a bloody rock of – of native privilege. Good men are lying down there sick and probably dying, all to keep a bloody black princeling in his appointed station – '

'Shut up,' Ogilvie broke in impatiently. 'Good God, Hamish you just don't know a thing about it, do you! We prop them – as you call it – because we damn well need to! If we didn't, well, we'd have a damn sight bigger rock to break ourselves against – the mass of the people of India. Don't you see?'

Dewar laughed again. 'Do you mean the mass of the people don't love us then, James?'

'Of course I mean that. I'm not blind. And I don't think you are really.'

'No, I'm not. I agree with your view, and that's why I don't bloody well love them back! Frankly, James, I hate their guts. And I don't particularly want to die for them, especially by this filthy disease.'

'If I were you, I'd be careful where you say that.'

'I'd be thought to funk it?'

'Not funk a fight, no. I've said that before, and I meant it. But some people might wonder where your loyalties lie – '

'Then they'd be as stupid as the Colonel is to stay here and rot,' Dewar said in an over-loud voice. 'My loyalties are all right – they're to the country and the regiment, make no mistake! But I came out here to fight, not to go to bed with vomiting and diarrhoea like some old woman in the Union – '

'Put a sock in it,' Ogilvie said sharply, laying a hand on Dewar's arm. 'Someone coming up.' Dewar looked impatient but said no more. They listened to slow footsteps climbing the spiral stone stairs that led up to the tower. A moment later Surgeon Major Corton appeared, looking sick himself and deathly tired and strained. Seeming not to notice the two officers, he walked over to the farther battlements and stood looking down through one of the embrasures.

Ogilvie called to him. 'Good morning, Doctor. How is the sick list?'

Corton turned and stared almost blankly. 'I didn't see you,' he said. He tried to smile. 'Getting old, I suppose!'

Ogilvie repeated his question: 'The sick list, Doctor, how is it now?'

'Twenty-seven, and one of those down with it is poor old Cunningham.'

'No!'

'I'm sorry, but there it is. He's driven himself too hard, James – '

'What are his chances?'

Corton shrugged. 'I can't yet say. He's not a young man to fight it, but I have hopes, for he's tough. Meanwhile I've to report to the Colonel that I have four deaths.'

'Who are they?'

'Young Crichton of E Company. Corporal Bain. Two privates – Ross and McWhirter. There'll be more to follow during the day, and I expect the sick list to lengthen. It'll be a progressive thing, James, for some while. If it goes on long, I'll run out of medical supplies and disinfectant.'

'How does the course of it run, Doctor?'

Corton said, 'Well, as you probably know, it's spread by the flies, and God knows we have plenty of them! Incubation is normally about three days, but – '

'Then we've been hit early?'

'No, not unusually so, James. The period varies in fact from just a few hours up to five days, and cases can be anything from mild to severe. Death can occur at any time during the course of the sickness – '

'And the flies contaminate the food?'

'Yes, and the water too. They carry excreta and dried vomit on their legs and wings. In our present circumstances, it's devilish difficult to control the spread. We need much chlorination of water, we must cook all foodstuffs – nothing must be eaten fresh – we must obviously isolate all cases and suspected cases. The first we can do easily so far, the second less easily. We should also isolate all contacts now. We should, and in camp or cantonments we *would*, have a general tightening up of sanitary supervision – but here!' Corton rubbed at his red-rimmed eyes. Then, suddenly, he turned away and left the tower. Ogilvie and Dewar listened to his footsteps descending. There was a curious look in Dewar's eye.

* * *

'Ah, Captain Ogilvie.' Black fussed up as Ogilvie came down from the tower. 'I've been seeking you. There are orders . . . and there is no time for absence now, since we are short of an officer – Mr Crichton has died of the sickness – '

'I know. And I apologise for my absence. What are the orders, Captain Black?'

'You are the Officer responsible for . . . disposals. You will now attend to Mr Crichton and three others dead.'

'Attend to them . . . by what method? Surely not burning?'

'No, Captain Ogilvie, not by burning. We of the 114th Highlanders are not natives. You will see that all their clothing is burned, and then you will mount a decent burial, with a firing party. Kindly see to this as soon as possible.' Black hurried off, making for an apartment that the Colonel was using as the battalion office. Calling for an orderly, Ogilvie sent the man in search of Colour-Sergeant MacTrease: before mid-morning the bodies of the four dead men had been placed in funeral carts and were being wheeled under a heavy escort of Highlanders through the streets – streets that by now were almost deserted except for the sick huddled in corners and in side alleys waiting for death to take them. Faces, however, watched from windows: the concealed weapons were never far away, as Ogilvie knew. Until the cortège reached the gates, no overt marks of respect would be paid in case this should arouse hostility from the natives. But at the gates the shrouded dead were decently covered with the Union Flag and a lone piper stepped forward to take his place at the head of the procession. As the sad notes of a Highland lament wailed upon the still air the two missionary ladies who had nursed the dead in their last hours stood in silent farewell, with tears shining on their cheeks.

Shallow graves had been dug in some ground to the west of the gates, some five hundred yards from the city. Behind the thin and melancholy notes of the piper the carts headed for this, the likely cemetery area for heaven knew how many Royal Strathspeys to come. Reverently, silently, the corpses were lifted from the carts and placed in the graves. The Reverend Arthur Hopkins, relinquishing for the while his self-imposed sick-quarter duties, read the funeral service; after the lone piper, standing square and steady beneath the peaks and jags of the mountains, had played 'The Flowers of the Forest', the farewell rifles crashed out their saluting volleys. As the echoes of the firing resounded off the hillsides, Ogilvie turned to find Lord Dornoch sitting his horse in the rear, and bringing his hand down from the salute. At the same time the clergyman, frail-looking in his white surplice, also turned and met Dornoch's eye.

'A sad day, Colonel.'

'Indeed it is. I'm grateful for your presence, Mr Hopkins.'

Hopkins bowed his head. 'I am humbly thankful to be of some service. If there is ever any more I can do, please call upon me.'

There was something in his tone that made the Colonel ask curiously, 'What have you in mind, then, Mr Hopkins?'

'I believe my colleagues and I may yet have some influence upon the natives . . . I believe, or anyway I hope, that they have some respect for us still.'

'How can you, of all people, say that?' Lord Dornoch demanded briskly, then made a gesture of apology: his words had been a cruel and thoughtless wound, a reminder of the terrible treatment the clergyman's wife had received from the mob. 'You have done, and are doing, more than enough, Mr Hopkins. My Surgeon Major sings your praises loud!'

'It is little, really,' Hopkins said self-deprecatingly. 'But if you will excuse me, Colonel, I must return to the sick quarters now.' He went off: for a moment Dornoch watched him go, watched the flutter of the surplice round the tall, bony frame of a good man, a man whose goodness shone like a beacon in this savage land. Stumbling a little, clearly very tired and hungry and desperately missing his dead wife, the missionary went on towards the city gates and the Colonel turned to Ogilvie.

'This is only the beginning,' he said sombrely. 'God above, how will it end?'

There seemed to be no answer, and Ogilvie attempted none. Feeling awkward and clumsy, he waited. After a few moments the Colonel said more briskly, 'The doctor wishes me to evacuate the battalion, James. I cannot do this until we have found Jahangir Khan, but the moment we have done so, then I shall bring the men out into the clean air.'

'Colonel, suppose he's gone? Suppose he's left Kalundabad – '

'If he's left, it'll not have been other than in death.'

'Then suppose the body has been burned, Colonel?'

Slowly, heavily, Dornoch nodded. 'I know that's possible, but I cannot make the assumption yet.'

'The searches have produced nothing, Colonel.' Ogilvie hesitated. 'There is another point. When a search party closes in on Jahangir Khan, closes in on whoever is holding him prisoner, then isn't it likely he'll be killed when that happens, if he hasn't been killed already?'

'You imagine I have not considered this?'

Ogilvie flushed. 'I'm sorry, Colonel.'

'I think *you* have failed to consider the more pertinent point: if the rebels had killed Jahangir Khan, they wouldn't have needed to throw down the wrong body, James! This shows that for reasons of their own they do not in fact wish him killed. As for me, I am convinced he is in the city, and that he lives. In that case, he has to be found.' Lord Dornoch looked beyond Ogilvie towards the line of graves. 'See to the filling in, James, and bring your detail back as soon as may be. We have a need of every man.'

'Very good, Colonel.' Ogilvie saluted. Dornoch brought his horse round and cantered off for the gates. Ogilvie watched the filling-in of the graves and the building of low cairns of stones, and when this was complete the detail marched back with the empty carts and the pipes silent, back

95

into the filth of the city, back into the smells, the drains and the cholera-laden flies.

*   *   *

It was a nightmare of insufficient food, of disturbed sleep, of bodies sweat-pungent from lack of washing water, of guard-posting and of probes into filthy, infested hovels as the search for Jahangir Khan proceeded to the Colonel's orders. The only duty that found favour with the men was the daily foraging detail that scavenged the country-side beyond the gates for anything that would supplement the rations. Berries, wild fruit – whatever grew and could be eaten. The city's grain supply was commandeered and ground and baked by the field kitchens into rough bread. All the while the casualties continued, both from the cholera and from the native knives and rifles as small groups of men were attacked in the darkness of the criss-cross alleys, attacked by shadows who struck and fled before they could themselves be shot down or bayoneted. The mood of the rank and file grew morose and bitter, worsening as the days passed and the doctor's sick list grew into treble figures. Voices, loud voices, condemned the Colonel's action in remaining in the city.

And not only the voices of the rank and file: in the make-shift Officers' Mess there was much criticism voiced about obstinacy as the tension grew, the tension of the creeping disease. One by one the faces were vanishing into the isolation section: one by one the deaths continued. Another sub-altern, another thirteen men. The Major went down with the sickness, but only mildly. The Regimental Sergeant-Major was bad, and the doctor was gloomy as to the prognosis; and the doctor himself looked far from well. Hamish Dewar had lost his bounce but not his bitterness, his desire – a natural one – for a clean, open fight. And all the time the fruitless house-to-house search went on in the terrible sweating heat. James Ogilvie took his share of this duty, took it with fast diminishing hopes as men poked bayonets into recesses, into filthy bedding, into walls and ceilings that

96

might hide trapdoors, into mounds of obscene dirt in which a bound and gagged man might lie concealed until the search party had passed on its way. As each sector of the city was tooth-combed, men were left behind to cordon off the alley entrances – men who had at intervals to be relieved for food and rest. The battalion became over-stretched to its limit, but still there was no sign of the deposed ruler. And no sign that the Colonel would change his mind: Ogilvie himself was among those whose thoughts were soon infected by the bug of doubt. Lord Dornoch, he began to believe, was a tired man sticking too rigidly to his orders, even exceeding them. Neither Fettleworth nor Whitehall would expect a battalion to engage the enemy of cholera when they could make clean camp outside and lay siege to the city until the rebels surrendered Jahangir Khan.

*   *   *

Mild cases could, it seemed, turn into virulent ones: Major Hay became seriously ill. Black took over and assumed the joint duties of Second-in-Command and Adjutant. Mr Cunningham, who had been on the danger list, began to show signs of pulling through, to Ogilvie's immense relief. On the day following the Major's deterioration, the cholera struck Lord Dornoch, and Captain Black announced his second temporary appointment – this time to the command of the 114th Highlanders.

Black's first task was to assemble all fit officers and senior N.C.O.s not required for urgent duty and to address them pompously. 'There will be no change in the order as yet,' he said. 'I am in command, but intend to carry out the wishes of Lord Dornoch –'

'Then we're not withdrawing?' Ogilvie asked.

'We are not withdrawing, Captain Ogilvie. To the best of my knowledge, Jahangir Khan has not yet been found –'

'But every quarter of the city has been searched, Captain Black.'

'*Every* quarter? The last report –'

'Mr Dewar has just returned with a search party, having now been through the last sector.'

Black stared across the room. 'Mr Dewar?'

'That's correct, Captain Black.'

'I am now your Commanding Officer. You will kindly address me properly.'

'Yes – sir.' Dewar, meeting Ogilvie's eye, winked: did Black expect to be addressed as Colonel?

Ogilvie said, 'In my opinion, the time has come to evacuate the battalion and make camp outside.'

Black, obviously irresolute now, obviously wishful to agree, gnawed at the moustache that drooped over unshaven stubble. 'I don't dispute a certain desirability – indeed not! But this is a matter for the Colonel.'

'You've assumed the command, haven't you?'

'Yes, I have!' Black snapped, swinging his kilt. 'But such an order is still for Lord Dornoch – '

'Who is a sick man, and not to be bothered.' Ogilvie hesitated, choosing his words with a certain care. 'The cholera, as you know, Captain Black, leads to weakness. Decisions don't come easily, and a man's judgment isn't what it would be when fit and well.' He stopped; he had a feeling he had gone far enough.

Black frowned and licked at his lips. 'Doctor?'

'I've been pressing for withdrawal almost since we entered, Andrew, as you well know, I think it is vital that we do so now, without delay, and pray to God it's not too late to save the men who are still fit!'

'That's your considered opinion, Doctor, as a medical man?'

'It is,' Corton's tone was uncompromising. 'Andrew, you must give the order, and give it quickly.'

Black shook his head, rubbed at his jaw, obviously feeling the pressures of command, realising for the first time how difficult it could be to weigh one consideration against another. The sickness was terrible to bear, the battalion was clearly depleting daily, the deaths were appalling, Jahangir Khan did indeed appear not to be in the city; on the other hand, the situation had not changed in basis: the battalion was still under orders to assist Jahangir Khan, and the fact that he had not been found did not mean that he was positively not there. Calcutta, Whitehall, General Fettleworth at Division – they might all consider a virtual retreat without their orders having been carried out to the last to be in effect an act of disobedience, even of cowardice. Those were not the lines that led to permanent promotion or to honours and decorations: they could lead to premature retirement, to genteel rooms in Cheltenham and comments whispered behind a man's back in the clubs and drawing-rooms . . .

'Well?' Corton asked brusquely, his skin almost transparent with fatigue and under-nourishment.

'We should not be hasty. There are many things to be considered. One of these is the likelihood of reinforcements reaching us – '

'What difference does that make, Andrew? We don't need more battalions to fight the cholera – we need more medicines, more doctors, we need nurses, food, clean water – '

'Yes, yes – ' Black broke off as the hanging curtain of beads over the doorway was suddenly thrust aside by a red-faced, sweating colour-sergeant with his helmet awry.

'Sir – '

'What is it, man? Can you not see – '

'Captain Black, sir! There's a strong force approaching from – '

'A battalion – a brigade?' Black's eyes shone with hope.

'Sir, it's neither! It's a native army, coming from the direction of Dir.'

'Friendly – Jahangir Khan's men?'

'I don't know, sir. I don't know yet. But it's a big force, sir. I should say five thousand men.'

All eyes were on Black: Black's response was a natural enough one. He said, 'Well, gentlemen, no further decision until we know the purpose and loyalties of this approaching army. If it proves to be friendly – ' Once again, he broke off short. From the distance there had come a sound like rolling thunder, and the very ground beneath the waiting officers seemed to shake. Then a split-second later, the apartment shuddered to a series of appalling explosions as the shells of the native artillery took the city; and then came the crash and rumble of falling masonry. Alongside Black, a piece of pottery bounced into the air and fell from a wall bracket to the floor.

TEN

IN THE VARIOUS messes the officers of the Peshawar garrison were at breakfast behind the *Times of India*, preparing in leisurely fashion for another day of Frontier heat and dust while they listened with half an ear to the loud shouts, distant shouts, of the drill-sergeants already at work on the regimental parade grounds. As they drank coffee or chewed – after the kidneys and bacon – toast and marmalade, those officers were concerned with many varied things: Company orders for the day, defaulters, exercises, a visit to their Colonel for a reprimand or compliment, an appointment (with or without parental approval) with the pretty daughter of a Staff Major; or just in many cases the staving off of the boredom of another long Indian day until military tradition allowed, once the sun was low, an over-indulgence in alcohol. But today, into the quietude of breakfast-time, came a foot patrol of the York and Lancaster Regiment, a patrol whose duties had taken it on an extended beat to the northward, to a point not far south of the Malakand Pass into the plains of Swat. They had with them a solitary Highlander of the 114th, a man sore from an unaccustomedly long period in the saddle, a man weak from loss of blood, a man whose horse had been shot from under him shortly after leaving the Malakand. The officer in command of the patrol reported immediately to Brigade.

*   *   *

The report from Brigade reached the Divisional Commander as he was taking an after-breakfast stroll in the solitary privacy off his garden, sniffing the scents, admiring the riotously abandoned profusion of colour, relishing the heavy dark green foliage that had responded to a good deal of precious water lavished by his gardeners, hard-working venerable natives who performed their tasks under the General's soldier-servant corporal-in-change of innumerable bearers.

Fettleworth was approached by his Chief of Staff.

'A despatch, sir, from Lord Dornoch in Kalundabad – brought with great bravery and difficulty.'

Fettleworth stared. 'So Dornoch's actually in Kalundabad, is he?'

'Yes – '

'Let's see the despatch, Lakenham.'

Brigadier-General Lakenham handed it over. Bloody Francis ripped open the envelope, quickly scanned the contents. 'By God, Lakenham, they're in the midst of cholera! What the devil's taken hold of Dornoch, I'd like to know!' Fettleworth, eyes staring from the deep red of an angry face, waved the despatch. 'Feller's – '

'May I see his despatch, sir?'

Fettleworth thrust the sheet of paper towards the chief of Staff. Lakenham read it, looked up. 'He hasn't found Jahangir Khan, it seems. And he needs help.'

'That's what he says – '

'He must have it, sir. He must be sent medical supplies, and more doctors. Have you seen cholera, sir?'

'Yes!' Fettleworth snapped.

'Then you'll understand Dornoch's predicament – '

'One he might have avoided, had he held his damn battalion outside the city – '

'We can't judge yet, General Fettleworth. We don't know all the facts.' Lakenham paused. 'Sir, have I your permission to order out a brigade, with all possible medical – '

'You have my permission to do nothing!' Fettleworth said angrily, waving his arms in the air. 'It is my responsibility, not yours – and I shall do nothing whatever until I've referred the whole matter, once again, to Murree.'

102

'And waste more time, sir?'

'Time, what is *time* in India?' Fettleworth shook with fury. 'You know very well the orders must come from Murree!'

'Then, sir, for God's sake, get them speedily.'

*   *   *

Black, caught by surprise as he had been, and with all the responsibilities of sudden command, responded well. Sending Ogilvie to take charge at the city gates and the other company commanders to organise fire-fighting parties and to spread out their men in the best firing positions along the walls, he went himself, with Colour-Sergeant Anderson, detached from A Company temporarily to act as Regimental Sergeant-Major, to the tower. From here he had a commanding view of the advancing native levies, who had poured out of a pass in the hills to the north-west of the city – the pass that led from Dir.

'The estimate of five thousand seems right enough,' he said to Anderson. 'If they've come from Dir it would appear Jahangir Khan has lost his support in his own capital as well as here.'

'Aye, sir.'

Black stared through field glasses. There was cavalry as well as infantry, and something like a score of guns – heavy artillery, probably captured British pieces, with bullocks yoked to the limbers. That artillery looked cared for and effective. Puffs of smoke appeared along the battery line, and seconds later the city below shook to the explosions as the shells crashed home. More fires broke out, great spreading red flares with thick smoke, and the tower trembled. Black saw the flying standards of the foot levies, the colourful guidons fluttering from the lances of the cavalry. As the guns crashed out again, a shell landed close below and the tower shook more; stones flew, and a section of the battlements fell away to smash through the roof beneath. Black's face paled, and he seized the colour-sergeant's shoulder.

103

'We'll get down,' he said, 'before we follow faster than we'd like!'

The two men went down the twisting staircase, fast, almost falling over their own feet. At the bottom they found the doctor, his face smudged with sweat-damped dust. 'That lot just missed my sick quarters,' he said. He dabbed at his face with a dirty handkerchief. 'If the whole tower goes . . . Andrew, I'd like to evacuate the sick – '

'Where would you propose putting them, Doctor?'

Corton shrugged helplessly. 'I don't know. Can't you find me an alternative?'

'Only one that will be riddled with the cholera. You must make your own choice. More disease, or possible entombment in ruins.'

'Those who already have cholera can't be made worse, but I'll not risk the suspected cases – '

'Make your own arrangements, Doctor, as you think best – I have more pressing matters to attend to. Find other accommodation yourself, if you wish, then report to me later.' Brusquely, Black pushed past, making with the colour-sergeant towards the steps leading down to the square. He saw Hamish Dewar with a dozen privates, crouched behind a pile of broken masonry, firing into a mob of townspeople.

'What the devil are you doing, Mr Dewar?' he shouted.

Dewar looked round. 'Killing natives, Captain Black.'

'The Colonel's orders – '

'The Colonel's on the sick list and the situation's changed.' Lifting his revolver, Dewar calmly fired at a big, near-naked native jumping down from a window. In mid-flight, the man clawed at his stomach, and screamed. He hit the ground and lay writhing. Black and the colour-sergeant ran across the gap to join Dewar, bending low, amid scattered shots from the mob. Again Dewar looked round, grinning, his stubble-covered face wet with sweat and his uniform dishevelled. 'You see what I mean, Captain Black?'

'Yes, I do see. I think you're right, Mr Dewar, we have now to hit back and keep on hitting back.'

'It's what I transferred for, after all.'

"You are about to get your bellyful of action from now on, that's certain!'

'I don't mind. So long as we come out on top – which we will! I don't like this artillery barrage, though. Why can't we answer back with our own guns?'

Black clicked his tongue. 'How do you use guns, from within a walled city? Can you tell me that?'

'No, I can't,' Dewar said, grinning again. 'Unless you can drag 'em to the top of the walls . . . pity we haven't any howitzers, isn't it?'

'A great pity,' Black said sourly. 'Since we have not, we must manage with what we have.' He looked around: as he did so, the native heavy artillery opened again. There were more explosions: as they crouched behind their cover of rubble, a huge flash and a tremendous roar came from close by on their right. More rubble flew up into the air, spattered down around the cringing soldiers. There was an over-whelming smell of lyddite, sharp, bitter. As their surroundings steadied, Dewar and Black, both unhurt, looked up and around in wonder. The building to their right had gone, was no more than a pile of shell-shattered rubble lying beneath swirling clouds of dust. The mob, too, had gone – killed or fled. Bloody corpses lay all around. Many, too many, of the Scots had died as well: men were seen crushed beneath the rubble, in some cases only a foot or a hand visible. Colour-Sergeant Anderson and a private lay headless, out in the open. With the other survivors Dewar and Black scrabbled at the piles of broken masonry and woodwork, doing what they could to free men who might yet be alive. They managed to pull two of the soldiers clear: both were dead, with skulls smashed and chests caved in.

Black stood away, his own chest heaving as he drew breath. Beside him a sergeant, minus his helmet, wiped a hairy hand across a streaming forehead. Black said, 'God, but it's a mess!' He was shaking, white-faced. 'And this filthy dust!'

'Dust,' Hamish Dewar said lightly, 'will not hurt you, Andrew!'

'Oh, no? Man, man, it's cram full of the cholera! And other things too, maybe. Lice . . . and typhus, and – '

'Don't think about it,' Dewar broke in, clapping Black on his skinny shoulders. 'If you dwell on sickness, Andrew – '

'*Captain Black*, if you please! We are not in the Mess now, and I am in command of the battalion.' Black took a grip, drew himself up gauntly, and stared around. 'Sar'nt Machray, we must leave the dead for now. Have the wounded carried to the Surgeon Major. Those that are fit to walk and carry a rifle must wait their turn.'

'Sir!' The sergeant, his face pouring blood from a gash on the cheek, saluted smartly.

'Mr Dewar and I will make our way to the gates with the fit men. I think we shall have little difficulty in getting through!' Black swept an arm around. 'See – the natives have made themselves nicely scarce for us!'

He started forward, with Hamish Dewar at his side. The native inhabitants had undoubtedly gone to ground: faces peered from windows, faces in some cases frightened, in many others gloating – evidently a reaction to their individual interpretation of current events. Black, as they stumbled over the rubble, remarked on this.

'There is a look of triumph, I fancy,' he said with a touch of unease. 'Yet for all they know, those guns could be British – '

'Not, I think, from the north, Captain Black.'

Black coloured, glared furiously at Dewar. They went ahead, the gates coming into sight as they emerged from an alley. The gates themselves were in the same smashed condition as they had been left by the initial entry of the battalion earlier, but the space between what was left of the great pillars was being filled by the men of Ogilvie's company, working like beavers, dragging up the gun-shattered stones and rubble to construct what looked like a dryland dam. Black clicked his tongue and called out to Ogilvie, who was working with his men.

'The purpose, Captain Ogilvie – the purpose of all this work?'

106

'Isn't it obvious?'

'Not to me,' Black shouted back angrily. 'It's but a flea-bite, when the guns open on it –'

'It'll not go like the gates did, I assure you. It's solid. It'll provide some sort of obstacle at least, and to be able to pick off a trickle of men is better than trying to stem an avalanche –'

'Oh, have it your own way!' Black bared his teeth in a devilish grin: he had spoken hastily. He stared up at the walls, where the embrasures along the parapet were fully manned by soldiers with rifles and grenades, waiting for the native army to deploy outside. For the moment there was no firing: the range was as yet unpropitious for good results. 'Mr Dewar, come with me.' Followed by the subaltern, Black made his way to a steep flight of stone steps north of the gateway and climbed to the fire-step. He looked out through one of the embrasures; and as he did so, the tinny notes of a native bugle sounded out and the advancing natives came to a ragged halt, shouting and waving their rifles above their heads. Black waited. There seemed to be a conference going on in the centre of the native horde, where a small figure sat in an elephant-borne howdah. After an interval, a time of suspense that jagged at men's nerves and made fingers itch to squeeze triggers, more bugles sounded. There was no advance, but there was a good deal of commotion. The phalanx of natives ahead of the elephant and its howdah pressed away to either side, giving free passage. Slowly, ponderously, the elephant moved along the cleared human avenue, with files of horsemen coming in ahead and in rear, lean, savage-looking men with lances. A solitary rider in the van carried a white flag attached to his lance.

Black and Dewar looked at one another.

'A flag of truce,' Black murmured. 'A parley –'

'Damn their impudence,' Dewar said harshly. 'What have they to talk to us about?'

'We shall see, Mr Dewar, we shall see.'

'You're going to meet them, talk to them?'

'A flag of truce must be answered. And I must go myself.

The Colonel cannot – we know that! No, it's up to me.' In Black's tone was the hint that he would much have preferred it otherwise: with flags of truce, one could never be certain of the honourable intentions of the tribes, and a British officer could make a nice hostage.

'Do you wish me to come with you, Captain Black?'

Black hesitated: two was company, after all. 'You have a temper, Mr Dewar.'

'I shall control it. If it were my choice, I admit, I'd not parley – I'd open fire and be damned! But I'll be careful.'

'You had better be, Mr Dewar. I order you to be! I order you to say nothing, but to leave the parleying to me. You understand that, do you?'

Dewar nodded. 'Yes, of course, I –'

'Then you shall come. I agree . . . only because it will be excellent experience for you.'

Dewar grinned cheerfully. 'I only hope we're going to live to make use of the experience,' he observed. The acting Commanding Officer gave him a bleak look, and swung away towards the steps. Descending, he and Dewar made their way to the gates, looking back at a crowd of natives that had gathered at the mouth of one of the alleys. They appeared sullen but watchful, waiting their chance of a stab in the back. The two officers approached Ogilvie, who had climbed his roughly constructed barricade and was studying the advancing truce party and its lumbering transport. He turned as Black came up to the foot of the rubble pile.

'You're going out?'

'Yes.'

'Mounted?'

Black shook his head. 'A horse would find it difficult to climb your precious barricade, I fancy. I'll go on foot with Mr Dewar, but I'll want a strong escort, also a white flag. See to that, Captain Ogilvie, if you please.'

'Very good.' Ogilvie called up a corporal and passed the orders. Outside the walls, more bugle calls were heard, and a sergeant shouted down from the parapet that the truce party had halted some five hundred yards clear. An escort – a sergeant and ten file – doubled up with their rifles and were reported to Black.

'No firing, I need hardly say, from the walls, Captain Ogilvie, unless I should be seen to be under duress, or if I should break from the truce party and return at the double, in which case you will give covering fire. Are my orders clear?'

'Quite clear – '

Black turned to the sergeant of the escort. 'You will halt the escort on my orders, Sar'nt, and remain while Mr Dewar and I go forward alone and unarmed.'

'Sir!'

'Then if we're ready – '

Ogilvie broke in. 'One moment, Captain Black. The Colonel . . . have you discussed this parley with him?'

Black glared. 'Damn your impertinence, Captain Ogilvie, I have not! There has been no time, and he is a sick man. I – '

'The Colonel – '

'Will have the opportunity to approve or disapprove anything that is discussed before any guarantees are given.' There was a sneer on Black's face. 'Does this satisfy you, Captain Ogilvie?'

'I'm sorry,' Ogilvie said quietly. 'I didn't mean to – '

'Kindly leave me to my business. Mr Dewar, you're ready? Good. Sar'nt!'

'Sir!' The sergeant saluted, turned about with a crash of boots, and moved the escort towards the gate. They broke off to climb the barricade, slithering in clouds of dust that rose chokingly from the debris. Black, making heavy weather of the climb, went down the far side on his bottom and with a certain loss of dignity. The escort was fallen in again outside the walls and marched ahead, in the rear of Black and Dewar, the latter bearing the flag of truce. They marched over parched ground, withered and white in the strong sun, towards the massive backdrop of the northern hills, the beat of a solitary drummer marking their footsteps. Ahead of them the native party waited impassively, silent upon their horses, the lances steady. From the distance came a trumpeting of draught elephants. As the British officers came nearer to the small dark figure in the ornate howdah they saw the wizened face grinning down at them from a gold clasp set with rubies and emeralds. Black, turning, signalled the escort to halt: with a crash of boot-leather they did so, and the two officers advanced alone. Dewar, glancing sideways at Black, was aware of his senior's tension, of the fear that he was overcoming by an obvious effort of will. A muscle in his face was twitching, and he was bathed in sweat – not, Dewar fancied, from the heat alone. Great dark patches stained the khaki drill uniform, the once starched shirt collar beneath the tunic was a limp rag, dirty and wetly glistening. Dewar's lip curled: he had no time for fear, still less for its overt manifestations, giving no credit for the basic guts that were forcing Black on in spite of that fear. Fear was alien to Lieutenant the Honourable Hamish Dewar: intense anger and irritation were not, and his temper was rising fast. That grinning old native on the elephant's back was making a mockery of British officers, of the Raj, of the Queen-Empress herself. No doubt he could smell Black's fear as the latter approached! There was a scowl on Dewar's heavy, fleshy face as Black reached out, laid a hand on his tunic sleeve, and muttered to him to halt.

Dewar halted – slam bang, very smart, looking up sneeringly at the native in the howdah, the native with a king's ransom on his turban.

Black, his voice unsteady, spoke in Urdu: 'I come in response to your flag of truce, representing my Colonel, who commands the British garrison in Kalundabad.'

'I recognise no British garrison.' The voice was high and querulous, an old man's voice.

'It is nevertheless there. What do you want, and who are you?'

'I am Fazrullah Sahib, Ruler in Dir.'

'Jahangir Khan is Ruler in Dir, Fazrullah Sahib.'

'The British puppet?' There was a high, cackling laugh. 'No longer does Jahangir Khan rule, for he is dead – '

110

'Dead do you say?' Black glanced sideways at Dewar.

'He was killed in Kalundabad, and his body lowered from the city walls whilst your army was attacking the gates,' the high old voice said. 'He was brought to Dir – now I bring the body back again to be dragged through the streets of the city after I enter.'

'I see.' Black looked and sounded full of irresolution. 'Since clearly you have had contact with events in Kalundabad . . . you will surely have been told there is cholera in the city, Fazrullah Sahib?'

The turban nodded. 'This we know. You British fear cholera mightily, we do not.' The old man shrugged. 'It is part of our existence, and we accept it as the will of Mahomet. Men and women must die at some time, must they not? – be it by war or by sickness! You will not prevent us – if this is what you seek to do – from entering the city, Captain Sahib, by fear of cholera –'

'What is it you want?' Black broke in, wiping fresh sweat from his face and eyes.

'To enter in peace. We do not wish our countrymen to die from our own guns.' The ancient figure lifted a skinny arm, and pointed over the heads of the British Officers, towards the city walls. 'March out your soldiers, Captain Sahib, and we shall not harm you or them. You have seen what our guns can do. If you remain in Kalundabad, foolishly, you will be pounded to pieces –'

'Then you will kill your own –'

'At the last, yes, Captain Sahib, if it be necessary. In the beginning, it will be a siege only, to reduce you by sickness and starvation.'

'Yet you will still kill your own people!'

The man shrugged again. 'It is the will of Mahomet.'

'I think you speak with two tongues, Fazrullah Sahib. However, I shall convey your wishes to my Colonel, and then return. This is agreeable to you?'

The turban dipped in assent.

Black said, 'There is one thing, Fazrullah Sahib. I doubt if my Colonel will agree, in fact, to your terms . . . if he does not, you will have a long wait outside the walls. You should bear in mind that a relieving force will be marching to our assistance, and – '

'Captain Sahib, you speak glibly and perhaps only to bolster your own morale with hope. We have many people who pass information to us, and we know that there is no movement of British soldiers from Peshawar or Nowshera or Murree. If such a movement should be made known to us, as it will be if it takes place, then we shall call up our guns to blow you to fragments earlier than would otherwise have been the case, Captain Sahib.'

The old man gave a cackle of laughter; Black, his face stiff and drawn with anxiety, jerked his head at Dewar and turned away, looking as if he had difficulty in not breaking into a run towards the waiting escort. Dewar's face was like a thunder-cloud as they walked back. He asked harshly, 'What was all that about, then?'

'He wants us to evacuate.'

'The devil he does!'

'Or he'll lay siege to us, and then blow us to pieces with his guns!'

Dewar swore luridly. 'And the Colonel – he'll agree?'

'I would say he has no alternative, although I said to – '

'No alternative to surrender – is that what you're saying?'

Black wiped his face again: his hands shook, a fact not lost upon Dewar. 'I suppose so . . . yes.'

'A Scots regiment, surrender? Never! Never so long as I'm part of that regiment!'

'What would you propose to do to prevent it, may one ask?'

Dewar's bull-like face and thick neck suffused with blood: they had reached the escorting party by now, but he made no attempt to keep his voice down as he stormed at Black. 'Do? Why, the same as anyone else with any claim to guts, with any claim to be a soldier of the Queen, would do: *this*!' Before Black had realised what he was about, Hamish Dewar had snatched the rifle from the hands of the man closest to him, snatched it and aimed it at Black's stomach.

'Out of the way!' he screamed.

Black dodged aside, shouting at the sergeant, ordering Dewar's instant arrest. But Dewar moved away behind the rifle; and, before anyone had gathered wit enough to move, he had swung it towards the howdah and fired. Two shots in rapid succession: on the second, the old man toppled, the jewelled turban falling from his head to show blood pouring from a hole in the forehead. As the wizened figure hit the ground, Dewar let out a clansman's cry, and shouted orders at the escort: 'Back to the gates – at the double! *Get moving!*' Black, he saw, was already on his way, kilt flying, heels pounding the hard ground. Dewar, giving a loud and exultant laugh, turned to fire once more, this time towards the native cavalry, then he joined the belting rush for the gates.

ELEVEN

'OF COURSE THEY have to be relieved!' Sir Iain Ogilvie paced his room at Army Headquarters, thumbs jammed into his Sam Browne belt, face glowering. 'Fettleworth should have damn well acted before now – too much damn time's been wasted already, by God –'

'Calcutta, sir –'

'Balls to Calcutta, Leith. There's a regiment being cut to pieces by a damn creeping germ, to say nothing of the military situation, and you mouth Calcutta at me! I shall act first, *then* inform Calcutta, and if they want my head, they can have it!'

'I don't disagree, sir –'

'Then good for you,' the Army Commander said belligerently. 'Now – the orders: inform General Fettleworth he's to despatch a relieving force immediately, and I don't care how much it depletes the garrison at Peshawar or Nowshera – if necessary, the First Division'll be reinforced from here. He's to send out an infantry brigade with its attached artillery and an additional heavy battery. Also a couple of squadrons of cavalry. He's to organise a medical column to march with them – doctors, orderlies, all the medical supplies he can muster. Nurses – but as volunteers only. Have you got that, Leith?'

'Yes, sir.'

'Then see that Fettleworth gets the word at once, and warn all units here that they may be required for posting to the First Division as replacements.'

* * *

'The feller,' Bloody Francis said pettishly, 'is stripping me *naked*, Lakenham!' He thumped his desk. 'He knows very well I distrust the guns, too. Give me infantry – what?'

'Squares, sir?'

'Yes, precisely, squares – never failed yet. A hundred times better than the guns!'

'But the orders –'

'Yes, yes, I know the orders and I shall carry them out, of course.' Fettleworth hefted his stomach and got to his feet, going over to study a large wall map and a chart showing the disposition of his Division. 'Now, what brigades have we available, h'm?'

'Brigadier-General Fortescue's sir.'

'Ah! Composition?'

'2nd York and Lancasters, and Sherwood Foresters, 2nd Border Regiment.'

Fettleworth nodded. 'They'll do. I'll see their colonels at once, Lakenham. Guns?'

'A heavy battery of Madras Artillery, sir –'

'Right! Let's hope they can get through the Malakand, that's all. Heavy artillery indeed!' Fettleworth snorted, blew up his straggling white moustache. 'If they get stuck, the mountain batteries'll have to cope – I dare say they will. Horse?'

'I can detach two squadrons of the Guides from Mardan, sir, and one of Probyn's Horse.'

'Very well, do so. And Lakenham . . .'

'Sir?'

'A *chota peg*. All this confusion goes straight to my stomach, blast it.'

Sighing, Brigadier-General Lakenham moved across the room for the whisky decanter. This duty done, he passed the movement orders to the Brigade Commander and the affected batteries and squadrons. He emphasised the urgency: and quickly the word spread throughout the cantonments that a British regiment was in sad difficulty from sickness. The drawing-rooms in the quarters of the garrison hummed with rumour, with concern: there was no lack of volunteers from among the nursing sisters attached to the Medical Staff. The garrison became a hive of controlled rush as the various units were brought to immediate readiness for the long and dangerous march through the Malakand, and the succouring medical column prepared its wagons and its field hospitals. That day, miracles were performed: and by next morning the relief force was ready to march. Fettleworth, in response to the prevailing mood, made an occasion of it, taking the salute from a dais as the regiments and corps moved past a great cheering crowd of wives and daughters, and of men from the brigades remaining in garrison. And an occasion it was, as the infantry marched past behind the headquarters brass band, chests out, stomachs held flat, faces pugnacious, fixed bayonets glittering beneath the fierce sun, with the drill-sergeants busy with pace-sticks, shouting out the step to the drum-beats that accompanied the stirring grandeur of 'The British Grenadiers'. Past the saluting platform, the brass wheeled to detach, and the fifes and drums of the battalions took over. The long column moved out, its leaders already vanishing ahead with a rumble of limber wheels and the hoof-beats of the cavalry, the medical wagons carrying the nursing sisters bravely bringing up the rear before the support units of the Supply and Transport. Fortescue's brigade, the Brigadier-General himself riding a white charger at its head, moved finally out of earshot to the tune of 'The Girl I Left Behind Me'. There was a sparkle in the eye of Bloody Francis.

'A great company of men, Lakenham,' he said to his Chief of Staff in an aside. 'Splendid fellers, all of 'em! Worth any young woman's time . . . every one's an Alexander or a Hercules or a what-is-it, Lysander! Dammit,' he added, seeming to go off at a tangent, 'she's a fortunate woman, very.'

Lakenham lifted an eyebrow. 'Indeed, sir? Who?'

'The Queen, Lakenham, the Queen.'.

*   *   *

116

'Great God above us,' Dornoch said. His face was an almost transparent white; he tried to lift himself from his bed on one elbow, but the doctor gently pushed him back to lie flat. In the doorway of the Colonel's sick-room stood Black and Ogilvie: it had been necessary in Black's opinion to report to Lord Dornoch in person, sick and weak as he was; but the Surgeon Major would allow no man closer than the door, and was unhappy even about that proximity.

'A lunatic's action, sir,' Black said. He was as white as the Colonel: the shock, the fear, had been terrible. Black's stomach was still reacting to that dreadful dash for safety. Miraculously, under very heavy covering fire from the walls, the whole party had reached the gates without loss, though with several wounds, some serious, others not, sustained by the men of the escort. 'I have taken the precaution of placing Mr Dewar in arrest, Colonel.'

'In arrest?'

'Yes, Colonel. I –'

'Then take him out again at once, Andrew, d'you hear me?'

'But, Colonel –'

'At once! Do you not understand the situation, the absolute necessity for all fit officers and men to be available for duty? We cannot have men detailed for sentry –'

'*Open* arrest, Colonel. Not close arrest.'

'Oh – I see.' Dornoch lifted a hand to his face: the doctor reached out with a clean linen cloth, and bathed away the streaming sweat. 'I'm sorry, Andrew. Yes, you were right. He'll be dealt with as soon as we're in a position to attend to matters of that sort.' He shook his head wonderingly. 'To use a weapon . . . when under a flag of truce! It's utterly disgraceful and humiliating.' For a moment he closed his eyes: when he opened them he looked at Ogilvie. 'The fighting, James. How are the walls?'

'Intact, Colonel, and we've given the enemy plenty to think about with our rifle and Maxim fire – they've pulled back now, out of range. I can't say how long –'

'And their field guns?'

'Not in use, Colonel.'

'But if they do use them?'

Ogilvie hesitated. 'It'll go badly with us, I think.'

'I agree! Why, then, are they not using them?' The Colonel looked from one to the other. 'What are your ideas, gentlemen?'

Black said, 'Colonel, I think it's possible they fear the cholera more than Fazrullah Sahib admitted to me. If they attack with artillery, and breach the walls, then they would need to enter the city – or at least to engage men who could have the cholera on them. It's possible they prefer to leave us to the sickness . . . and then attack when it has passed.'

'Attack what's left of us?'

Black nodded. 'Yes, Colonel.'

'James?'

'I agree with Captain Black, Colonel. But there's one more thing: I believe they'll use their guns as soon as they get word that a relief force is on its way – if ever one does come, that is.'

Once again Dornoch closed his eyes: Ogilvie looked at him with concern. He had the look of a man who was not going to come through, and if he died, it would be an irreparable loss – not for himself alone, as fair and just an officer as had ever held the Queen's commission, but for the effect on morale. Lord Dornoch was much respected, much loved, by the men: that continued, notwithstanding the bitter comments about his bringing them into sickness. In their hearts they understood why, and knew he had had no real choice. If he – chief of his clan, father of the regiment, friend of all – should die in Kalundabad, a good deal of the stomach for resistance would go out of a large proportion of the men. Dornoch, so long a part of the Royal Strathspeys from subaltern to Colonel, acted almost in the combined role of a lynch-pin and a talisman . . .

Seeing that the Colonel had fallen into an almost comatose sleep, Surgeon Major Corton gestured to the two officers to leave.

*   *   *

During that morning, the native bugles were heard again. The opposing army began to deploy to right and left around the walls, totally encircling the city and positioning the guns before the gateway. The great grey-sided elephants were tethered to stakes driven into the ground in a makeshift compound behind. In another compound went the bullocks who would draw the heavy guns if required to move in action, taking over from the ever-excitable elephants, the mere draught beasts for hauling on the march. From now on, with Fazrullah's army encircling the walls, there would be no more foraging parties to add their garnerings to the slender food stocks held by the quartermaster, a fact that was given immediate and dreary point by the miserable meal served to the officers and men at noon: a thin soup, and hard biscuits more reminiscent of the victuals of a sailing man-of-war than of a regimental Officers' Mess. After the meal, which was accompanied by a continuous, thin dirgeful wail of native music from beyond the walls, Black mustered the officers and N.C.O.s and told them the water supplies must be guarded with the utmost care. All water-bottles were to be called in and their contents emptied into clean vessels under the supervision of Mr McCrum, who would thereafter, in the presence of the Orderly Officer, issue two mouthfuls per man per day, with – for the present anyway – unlimited supplies for the sick as required by the doctor. The city wells, of which there were two, contained a fair supply of water but all this had to be boiled before use and they had also to consider the needs of the native population, who could scarcely be allowed – despite loud protests by some of the N.C.O.s – to die of thirst. In the meantime, a round-the-clock guard was to be maintained on both wells.

Hamish Dewar, not noticeably abashed by his conduct that morning, agreed with the N.C.O.s in their comments. When the meeting dispersed he said savagely, 'It's all bloody wrong, James. *We* need that water. Those dirty natives shouldn't be allowed any – '

'It's their water,' Ogilvie pointed out. 'Their wells.'

'And our lives. We're not here from choice, we're here in

119

their interest, aren't we? And what are their stinking little existences worth anyway?'

Ogilvie shrugged and walked off: one could never argue with prejudice, with pre-conceived views strongly held. Dewar, he found – and had expected no less – had plenty of support from the rank and file. Men who, on Indian service, had become accustomed to being waited upon by natives in their barrack-rooms, to having *punkah-wallahs* literally to toe the line that kept the hot, close air stirring day and night, world without end – men who were accustomed to giving orders as well as taking them in cantonments – a novel experience for British private soldiers – these men were not going to relish any sharing of slender, vital resources with an inferior race; a race, moreover, currently very intent upon killing them when they could. (Black had spoken of this latter danger: he had underlined, somewhat unnecessarily, the need for constant vigilance against internal attack. Without saying so in so many words, he seemed to have let it be known that the Colonel's earlier dictum about no unnecessary killing could be considered to have succumbed to the changed circumstances; but had been vague enough to make any sensible man think more than twice about the risks involved should authority not go wholly along with Captain Black.)

That afternoon, Hamish Dewar was sent for by the Colonel. Ogilvie encountered him shortly after he had left the sick quarters.

'How was the Colonel?' he asked, noting Dewar's heavy scowl. He grinned. 'In good voice?'

'Oh, shut up!' Dewar snapped, turning on his heel. The sullen fury in his face alarmed Ogilvie, as did his too obvious self-conviction that he had been in the right all along no matter what the Colonel or anyone else might say or do. Hamish Dewar must surely know that he would face Court Martial proceedings on return to cantonments, but his lumpish, boorish manner went deeper than a mere brazening-out of disfavour: the man was still, in his own eyes, right. In all the circumstances, such convictions could prove a spark to ignite a powder-barrel. And later that same day the ignition started from outside the city, a slow-burning fuse; perhaps not entirely unexpectedly. Ogilvie had made his way to the tower, which was still standing firmly enough to take a man as look-out. The view from the top was wide and long, and any oncoming army, British or native, would be seen many miles away during daylight. Looking down at the besieging force, Ogilvie saw the erecting of a curious structure like a sheer-legs with a pivoting, pendulum-like bar heavily counterbalanced at one end.

'What the devil's that, Morrison?' he asked the look-out.

'It's likely a catapult, sir.'

'A catapult?' Ogilvie studied the contraption through his field-glasses. 'A substitute for the guns – a rock-chucker, d'you suppose?'

'Aye, sir, that could be well be, though I canna see the purpose, sir. I mean . . . why not use the guns?'

'I don't know,' Ogilvie said in a tone of puzzlement. He went on watching: there was a score of natives around the sheer-legs, semi-naked, turbaned, some of them haranguing others who were dragging up a chunk of rock. There was a good deal of gesticulating, and the rock was abandoned in favour of a smaller piece. Men gathered in a tight circle, bending. When they moved aside, Ogilvie could see the smaller stone with something tied to it. The unweighted end of the pivoting bar was hauled down, and the stone placed upon its flattened surface while the bar itself was held down by as many hands as could find room to get a grip, the end with the counter-balancing weight rising high in the air.

Ogilvie suddenly took in the meaning of all the activity.

'They're sending a message,' he said. 'A message tied to the stone.'

'They'll not be risking more flags of truce, sir?'

Ogilvie stared back; Morrison's gaze fell. 'That'll be enough of that,' Ogilvie said.

'I'm sorry, sir. But . . .'

'Well?'

'I'll say no more, sir.'

'I think you'll finish what you were going to say, Private Morrison.'

The man looked stubborn.

'A charge of dumb insolence on active service may well lead to the limber wheel, Morrison.'

'Sir! Begging your pardon, sir, but I mean no insolence. It's just that what Mr Dewar did is a subject of talk among us, sir.'

Ogilvie gave a harsh laugh. 'Well, I have to admit that's natural enough! Tell me – what's being said?'

'It's half and half, sir.'

'Half and half?'

'More or less, sir. Half think Mr Dewar's act was . . . dangerous for us all, and – and not the act of a gentleman, sir. The other half admit the danger, but think Mr Dewar did right to kill a treacherous native, sir.' As if relieved to be able to change the subject, Morrison pointed towards the catapult. 'Yon machine, sir – it's going into its fling.'

Ogilvie put up his glasses again. Evidently at a word of command, all the grasping hands had let go. The counter-balancing weight swung swiftly down, bringing up the other end sharply. The stone flew in an arc, rising towards the walls of the city, crossing them to drop inside. Still using his glasses, Ogilvie pin-pointed the fall: close by the gates. A Lance-corporal detached from the gate guard and ran across to the stone with its tied document. Ogilvie watched him pull away the thin rope and study the message, then make his way towards the officer in charge at the gate – Robin Stuart of E Company.

Ogilvie made his way down from the tower, fast, to find the doctor busily engaged in supervising the removal of his sick quarters with the assistance of a half-company under Colour-Sergeant MacTrease.

'Still worried about the tower collapsing?' Ogilvie asked.

'I am indeed, James – if they use the guns again, it'll not last long. I prefer the tents – for one thing, they're cleaner than any of these damn hovels!'

'Where are you setting up shop, then?'

'On the cleared space down by the gateway –'

'First in line, if there's a break through –'

'I know, James, I know. It's the best I can do, and Andrew's agreed. There isn't anywhere else in this damn rabbit-warren, anyway.'

Ogilvie nodded. If the break through should come, the sick would be no safer for being distant from the gates. He said, 'We'll just have to hope the tribesmen hold back long enough for a relief to catch them on the hop, I suppose. We may know more about their intentions any minute now.'

'How's that?'

'They've sent a message by catapult. How's the sick list, Doctor?'

'One hundred and seventy-eight, nine more dead. And they'll need to be burned, James, since we can no longer bury them outside.' Corton paused. 'I wonder . . . would the native army agree to allow burial parties, d'you suppose?'

Ogilvie laughed humourlessly. 'Another flag of truce – after what Hamish did today? I think not, Doctor!'

'Damn young fool! He's brought us trouble we can well do without, James – and may yet bring more.'

Ogilvie looked at Corton curiously. 'Why do you say that?'

'I say it, James, because I have just a wee suspicion what that message could be, that you've just spoken of. If *you* have not, then I suggest you use your imagination, for I'll say no more in case I'm wrong.' Corton turned as MacTrease approached and saluted. 'Yes, Colour?'

'It's the R.S.M., sir. He's asking for you. He wants to be returned to duty.'

Corton said with a twinkle in his eye, 'Does he indeed! He'll not be getting his wish for a good few days yet, but I'll tell him that myself. You'll excuse me, James.' Corton moved away with MacTrease by his side. Ogilvie was grateful to be able to deduce that Cunningham was on the mend: that, at least, was a ray of light in a darkening situation. Ogilvie made his way towards the gates, past the sentries posted at intervals to watch any movement of the native population, who had now by order of Andrew Black been herded into their hovels pending their concentration in a guarded pound. He met Robin Stuart coming through to Black with the catapulted message.

'What's it say, Robin – the message? I was watching from the tower.'

'They want their revenge,' Stuart said, swatting at flies. 'What do the Pathans call it? *Melmastia*.'

' 'What – '

'They want Hamish Dewar, James.'

Ogilvie caught his breath. He thought: *so that's what Corton meant*! He asked, 'As a hostage?'

'As a sacrifice more like! An eye for an eye, James. If they get Dewar, they'll talk about concessions and agreements. If they don't, so the message says, none of us'll come out of here alive.'

TWELVE

'IT'S A DEVELOPMENT that follows naturally enough when dealing with natives,' Black said, 'but God knows, for I certainly do not, what's to be done about it!'

'It'll not be your decision, Andrew. This must go to the Colonel, sick or not.'

'Yes, Captain Stuart, I agree. In the meantime, not a word to a soul.'

'As I've already instructed Lance-Corporal MacLean.'

Black stared. 'Lance-Corporal MacLean? How – '

'It was MacLean who picked the message up – and read it. He has Urdu. I don't think he'll talk – he has his stripe to lose.' Stuart glanced at Ogilvie, from whom he had as it were inherited MacLean. With some pleasure, Ogilvie had seen MacLean transferred from his own company due to re-organisation after casualties: MacLean had been one of those who had voiced criticisms of Hamish Dewar's action in getting clear himself of Kalundabad whilst losing his entire patrol. It was a moot point as to whether or not MacLean's regard for his stripe would outweigh his consideration for his safety in a life-and-death situation: should the Colonel make a decision in Dewar's favour – as Ogilvie knew he was bound to do – then Lance-Corporal MacLean's tongue might wag with disastrous results . . .

Black sought out the doctor, pressed the over-riding urgency of the matter and, before the Colonel was moved to his new sick quarters clear of the tower, was admitted at door's length. He was some time with the Colonel: when he returned his face was solemn. 'The Colonel will not hand

Mr Dewar over willy-nilly,' he said. 'This, I believe we expected. The contents of the message are not to go beyond those who already know them – that is, ourselves, and Lance-Corporal MacLean.'

'What about those who'll suspect?'

'They may suspect, but they'll not know. In the meantime, the Colonel intends to give Dewar the chance to make up his own mind. Frankly, I myself do not see Dewar as willing sacrificial material – but one can never tell, I suppose. He is to have the chance, I repeat, of delivering himself up to the enemy once the alternatives have been put to him. The three of us are to speak to him in private as soon as may be.'

'Does the Colonel think he'll agree?'

'I doubt it, Captain Ogilvie, though as a fair man he is not pre-judging Dewar even to me.' Turning, he called, 'Colour MacTrease?'

MacTrease doubled up and slammed to the salute, 'Sir!'

'A runner, with my compliments, to Mr Dewar. I wish to speak to him – at the top of the tower.'

'Sir!' Once again, MacTrease's right arm shot up, quivering, and he turned about, kilt swinging, and marched away. With Ogilvie and Stuart, Black went towards the steps leading up to the evacuating building, along the corridors to the spiral stone staircase, and up. Reaching the tower, he told the sentry to fall out and go down to ground level until he was recalled.

'That damn music,' Black said moodily. It came up to them clearly, sounding menacing now, somehow even more obtrusive than hitherto. Looking down on the besieging army far below, they waited for Hamish Dewar, not speaking, each of them seeming occupied with his own thoughts as to the cruel dilemma that the subaltern was about to be faced with. They turned as climbing footsteps sounded on the stone stairs, and Hamish Dewar appeared, looking surly and defiant. 'What's this?' he demanded loudly. 'A subaltern's Court Martial, to be conducted by captains who should know better than to behave like children?'

126

Black frowned. 'It seems you have a guilty conscience, Mr Dewar – '

'Does it? Well, I haven't – '

'That's enough, Mr Dewar. There is to be no subaltern's Court Martial – the matter goes beyond horse-play of that kind.' Black paused, scanning Dewar's beligerent face; Ogilvie, closely watching also, saw the beginnings of alarm flicker across that face. Black went on carefully, weightily, 'As you know, I have assumed the command of the battalion. Nevertheless, there are matters that must still be referred to the Colonel, and this has been one of them – '

'Why not come to the point?'

'I am doing so, Mr Dewar. The Colonel has asked us to speak to you privately – none of what I have to say will go beyond those of us here present, I assure you.' Again Black paused. 'The fact is, there has been a message from the enemy – '

'So I understand. Is that what all this is about?'

'Yes,' Black said, and added baldly, 'The enemy ask for you to be handed over to them. If that is done, they will talk. If it is not, they threaten to kill us all.'

Dewar stared, his mouth sagging open, eyes filled with horror. 'You're prepared even to consider doing such a thing?' he gasped out.

'I have not said that,' Black answered. 'The Colonel is not considering any such surrender of one of his battalion – that is to say, he will not give such an *order*. Do you understand, Mr Dewar?'

'I don't know that I do . . . '

'Then I will tell you. The Colonel wishes you to make a choice.'

Dewar seemed dazed. 'Me?'

'You, Mr Dewar. If you leave the city of your own free will – if you sacrifice yourself – you will save very many lives. It is a clear choice, and one for you alone.'

'My God!' Dewar's rump sagged against the tower's parapet and he put his head in his hands. 'I don't understand. I've done nothing against the regiment, nothing – '

127

'Except against its honour, Mr Dewar – but that is not the point. The regiment is not punishing you, the regiment is not asking for your body. The natives are, and you have sinned in their eyes by dishonouring a flag of truce and killing their leader – '

'A damn rebel – '

'Their leader in their eyes, Mr Dewar – '

'And d'you really believe they can carry out their threat, that they can take the city and kill the whole battalion? Do you believe that – all of you?'

Ogilvie and Stuart looked away as Dewar's eyes blazed at them in beseechment. Black answered evenly: 'We are British, Mr Dewar, and we always win our battles. But unless relief comes, we shall be hard pressed. The enemy has heavy guns – '

Then why not break out and attack, instead of waiting to be shot to pieces?'

'With so many sick, against five thousand well-armed men, with our own supplies running short?' Black shook his head. 'No, Mr Dewar, we have no choice but to await relief from Peshawar!'

'But we don't even know if the Colonel's message got through to Division.'

Black said, 'No, precisely. We do not! Hence the choice you're presented with, Mr Dewar. I repeat, you can save very many lives, including those of the mission ladies. Think about it.'

'Save lives,' Dewar said bitterly, 'at the cost of my own!'

Black shrugged. 'A soldier's choice, and one that has been made many times before now. You are not a coward – that we all know.' Black moved forward and laid a hand on the subaltern's arm, his voice softening. 'Now come, Hamish. We all realise what we are asking of you. Please think hard about it. There will be no compulsion, but I should, I think, add just one more thing, and it is this: you have dishonoured a flag of truce, and this must have its effect upon many British regiments after us, for the tribes have very long memories – and have an inbred passion for revenge. A flag of truce will not be trusted again. When we return to Peshawar, it will be the Colonel's duty, however unpleasant to him, to report the circumstances to Brigade for further action.'

'And then?'

Black said, 'I cannot say, Hamish. But I think you have enough imagination, have you not?'

'I have imagination for the alternatives as well. What I can't see is why you all have to kow-tow to the bloody natives like this!'

Black took a deep breath, sent it hissing out again through set teeth. 'I've done my best to put it to you . . . Hamish, I think you have little understanding of the Frontier and its ways, little knowledge of the problems – of course, this is not surprising, but – '

'And you, Captain Black?' Dewar's fists had clenched, and now he threw off, with a violent movement, Black's hand that still rested on his arm. 'You have this knowledge, I take it. So you know what would happen to me, don't you? Oh, I've heard about tortures, about slow death, about filthy humiliations, which I suppose is why I loathe and detest those stinking swine out there!' He waved an arm down towards the native army. 'Look at them – dirt and squalor and cruelty decorated with rubies and emeralds – it makes a man bloody sick, I tell you! The Colonel's got a softening of the brain to even consider this – and so have all of you. I think it's disgraceful – '

'Had you not committed a disgraceful act yourself – '

'You think the Colonel – and the natives – are right?'

Black said, 'In the circumstances, there is a certain inevitability. Well? I'm waiting for your answer, Mr Dewar.'

Dewar drew himself up, again defiant and stubborn. 'You shall have my answer,' he said flatly. 'I say no, and you can make the best you can of it! And good-day to you all, gentlemen.' Hamish Dewar turned about with an arrogant swirl of his kilt, and clattered down the steps. The three officers remained, staring at one another in silence; then Black gave a sudden laugh.

'It's strange to say it, perhaps,' he said, 'but there goes a brave young man! I'd not care to be in his shoes when we return to cantonments.'

* * *

Hamish Dewar withdrew into himself, avoiding company. The message from the besieging force was ignored; life continued in the midst of death and sickness. During that day the Colonel's condition worsened: there was much vomiting and he became very weak: the doctor was gloomy.

'I believe,' he told James Ogilvie, 'there's a weakening of the basic desire to fight the cholera. And it's due in part, I do believe, to your precious subaltern – the Honourable Hamish, whose courtesy title seems singularly inappropriate now! It had a sorry effect upon the Colonel, that any officer of his should use a weapon under a flag of truce. Dewar's been lucky. Many a colonel in the old days would have had him shot.'

Ogilvie nodded. 'A rum character – Hamish. No lack of guts.'

'Maybe not, but the man's a danger to any battalion in the field. He's too sure of himself, without any basis to be so. Over-confidence is always dangerous, when it runs hand-in-hand with total inexperience. I've seen it in my own profession too often not to be worried by it!'

'He'll not get another chance to be dangerous. Once bitten, twice shy –'

'I'll correct that, James: *twice* bitten already – don't forget, it was young Dewar who exacerbated the whole situation in the first place, even before our own arrival.'

'It does no good to remember too openly, Doctor.'

'Ah, well . . .' Corton sighed, and slowly filled his pipe, staring sadly at the almost empty pouch. 'Look at that! Soon there'll not be even the solace of a smoke.'

* * *

There was no immediate reaction to the ignoring of the message: still the enemy guns were not brought into action. When a man showed himself indiscreetly on the walls, there was rifle-fire: a few men were lost from time to time but that was all. The tribesmen seemed to realise that there was no reason to expend more ammunition when hunger and thirst and the deadly work of the cholera were all present to reduce the garrison and bring it, in the inevitable end, to its knees. Day succeeded day in enervating sameness: at night the tribes lit their camp fires to flicker all around the walls and bring for a while a halt to the day-long sounds of reedy pipes and flutes and chattering drums that seemed designed to bring down the garrison by insanity. The overall gloom, the anxiety, the depression and sense of claustrophobia were indicated in the morose, sullen faces of the N.C.O.s and men as they went about their tasks of guard and relief, of ration and water issue, of burning their dead and of containing the native population, moved three days after Hamish Dewar's débâcle to a heavily guarded encampment in a shell-wrecked central area of the city. Here, with their bundled paraphernalia, they lay or squatted in their own filth, a breeding ground for flies and disease but one that had to be tolerated. With the consequent need for continual use of disinfectant by the soldiers guarding the perimeter of this make-shift camp, the Surgeon Major became more and more gloomy as to his medical supplies.

'Everything'll be used up soon,' he told Black, who, unable to do anything about it, pulled angrily at his moustache. 'No disinfectant, no chlorine, no mixtures for the diarrhoea, no bandages for the wounds . . .'

'We shall simply have to manage, Doctor.'

'We simply can't,' Corton retorted edgily. 'We should face up to it, Andrew.'

'For what purpose? I can't produce medicines from the empty air!'

Corton shook his head in near despair. 'When the devil is Fettleworth going to send us a relief?'

'God knows! We must just pray to Him, Doctor – pray

131

hard that help will come – that's all.'

'I think we're all doing that. He seems deaf to us – perhaps because of the voices rising beyond the walls to Mahomet, with an opposite message!'

'Yes.' Black, sitting down suddenly in the shade of the rubble-filled gateway, spoke seriously. 'Is Mahomet God, do you suppose?'

Corton lifted an eyebrow, quizzically, giving Black a hard scrutiny. 'You have seldom spoken of God, Andrew – '

'I'm doing so now. Are all gods the same god? Theirs and ours?

'I would say . . . yes, they are, though our missionaries might not agree! In basis, all human hopes and prayers must be directed to the same target. There can be only one Creator, surely? We differ only in what we call Him. God, Mahomet, Buddha and the rest.' Corton laughed, a grim sound rather than humorous. 'If that's so, He must have an awful lot of conflicting requests to listen to!'

'Indeed yes. If only He would send a sign! I have a thought . . . ' Black's voice trailed away, and a boot began scuffing the sun-baked earth.

'What thought is that, Andrew?'

'Oh, a thought to do with something Dewar said the other day. That we might go out to the attack, in the open where we can use our guns – '

'Dewar's ideas have not so far been of any assistance, as you well know – '

'True, true. I'll not deny that,' Black sighed.

'And this one sounds as crazy as any. Of course, I'm not a combatant officer, but I'm not young in the Service either. To go out now would be, in a sense, to abandon the sick – '

'No, no – '

'But *yes*, Andrew!' The doctor leaned forward, tapping Black's knee. 'Think! At this moment the sick are safe within the walls – safe, until Fettleworth's relieving army reaches us. Once there is a breach from inside or out, that safety vanishes like a puff of smoke!'

Black raised clenched fists and pressed them against his

burning cheeks, lifted them again to flail viciously at the buzzing, crowding flies, his eyes red-rimmed and staring. 'You speak of a relieving army –'

'Yes, indeed I do. Our best course is to wait as patiently as we can. Relief is bound to come –'

'No. The message may never have got through.'

'They're not all fools at Brigade or Division.' Corton said harshly, speaking as much to convince himself as to reassure Black. 'Our destination was known. You may depend upon it – if no word comes through from us, no report – they'll send out a probe, and a strong one too.'

Black stared hopelessly across the dust and rubble, shaking his head from side to side, face twitching as he listened to the wretched music from the tribes. As he stared, a man appeared – the missionary, the Reverend Arthur Hopkins in his parsonic black frock coat, his clerical collar a limp damp band around a long neck. Looking incongruous, Hopkins was approaching across the shattered space between the gateway and the maze of filthy hovels, picking his way, approaching with diffidence but clearly with something to say, his eyes bright and eager and his adam's apple working in the scrawny throat.

'Captain Black . . .'

'Yes, Mr Hopkins, what is it?'

'Captain Black, you are in the room of the Colonel now, and there is a matter of some import . . . it is to you I must talk.' The clergyman cleared his throat nervously, a hand pulling at his thin, eyes blinking.

'Go on.' Black moved his shoulders impatiently.

'Thank you. Captain Black, I believe we – my party of missionaries that is – can be of some help. You see, we know these people, the natives. We know those who have rebelled, and we believe that by and large they will trust us –'

'Even after what they did, Mr Hopkins?'

The clergyman's face worked with pain, but he said, 'Yes. For our part we must forgive –'

'Forgive? *Even that?*'

'Yes. It is not easy. But our mission is to work the will of

133

God on earth, Captain Black, to teach by Christian example. We must not be seen to fail at such a time as this. We have an opportunity both of service to your garrison and of offering proof to the natives that God lives.' The parson's eyes beseeched. 'Do you not see?'

Black laughed, harshly. 'By God, sir, I do not!'

'I mean this,' Hopkins said, licking at bone-dry lips. 'My party, all of us – my sister and I, Wimpole and his wife – ask permission to be allowed out of the gates so that we may talk with the leaders of the army from Dir. We have been in Dir and we know these men. Now that Fazrullah Sahib is dead, his son will be the new leader – his name is Gaftar Sahib. He is no friend of the Raj, but I believe he will listen to us.'

'What would you have to say?'

Hopkins shrugged his thin shoulders. 'I would talk of peace, of an end to death.'

'And of what else?'

'Of hostages – ourselves. We would ask Graftar Sahib to hold us as hostages – '

'For what purpose, Mr Hopkins?'

'We would ask him to hold his army in check, and to let your garrison march out for Peshawar – '

'By God – '

' – and we would say that in Peshawar you would advise your General to seek negotiations with both Gaftar Sahib and the constitutional successor to Jahangir Khan, so that a solution could be arrived at peacefully, without more bloodshed, and so that the city of Kalundabad would see no more suffering.' The missionary paused. 'To us, who try to walk in God's way, that seems by far the better thing, Captain Black, than war.'

Black was almost gasping. 'You have put this to the Colonel?'

'No. He is too sick a man for that. Can you give me an answer, please?'

Black blew out his cheeks, glanced at Corton, who was shaking his head in amazement. Black opened his mouth, shut it again, shook his own head, and then said, 'What you suggest is . . . brave. Very brave and gallant, and I'm obliged. But my answer is no, Mr Hopkins – '

'But surely you will – '

'That refusal is final.' Black rose to his feet, tall and straight. 'I shall not countenance your ladies risking their lives – or you either. And this is no time for parley or abject withdrawal, since we expect relief daily – relief by an army that will with our assistance *hammer* those scum into the very soil of their land! Good-day to you, Mr Hopkins.'

He strode away.

*   *   *

They marched, a fit and healthy body of men, into the treacherous Malakand Pass, men from many parts of England stepping to the beat of the drums and the thin music of the fifes, popular tunes or regimental marches that brought the voices roaring out to echo off the hillsides.

' 'Tis my delight of a Friday night
  In the season of the year . . . '

The Lincolnshires were not marching with them, but 'The Lincolnshire Poacher' was a catching tune: so was 'John Peel', and the Border Regiment was there to give it spirit. In spite of cholera ahead, all the men were eager: there was something very special about this advance, and revenge was not the least of the troops' emotions. They had women with them too, and this gave men's backs a straighter bracing, their shoulders a decided swagger. They were the flower of England, and the very spirit of England marched with them to the relief of a beleaguered regiment of the line. And ahead of them, ahead of the drums and fifes, ahead of the cavalry and the guns and the marching feet of the infantry, the word ran fast along the crests of the Malakand from one concealed, hawk-faced tribesman to another, the word that the British were coming.

*   *   *

'Captain Ogilvie, sir!'

Ogilvie halted and turned to a familiar and welcome voice. 'Mr Cunningham! You're back to duty?'

'I am, sir. The doctor didn't like it much, but here I am –'

'I'm delighted.' Ogilvie reached out a hand, warmly shook that of the Regimental Sergeant-Major. 'Don't overdo it, for heaven's sake, or we'll have you on the sick list again. You don't look over fit to me.'

'I'll be right as rain, sir, don't fret. One good meal . . . but there, why talk of that! It's not yet to be, and that's all about it.' Cunningham paused. 'The Colonel's bad, sir. Recent worries'll not have helped him.'

'You're up to date with events, Sar'nt-Major?'

'Aye, I am that, Captain Ogilvie. Including what Mr Dewar was up to out there.' Cunningham nodded towards the northern wall. 'It's not for me to pass comment, but I'll be very surprised if the tribes let that pass.'

'Have they an option?'

'Come now, Captain Ogilvie, sir, you know the Frontier better than that!' Again Cunningham paused, looking Ogilvie in the eye. 'I hear there was a message, sir.'

Ogilvie nodded. 'That's right, there was. It's been dealt with, Sar'nt-Major.'

'I see. Yes. Well, now, I'm an old Frontier hand, sir, as you know. As I said, it's not for me to pass comment . . . but I'd be surprised if they didn't demand the body sooner or later.'

'The body, Mr Cunningham?'

'I think you know what I mean, sir.'

'Perhaps. Meanwhile I'm not in a position to discuss this any further –'

'I'm sorry, Captain Ogilvie –'

'Don't apologise.' Ogilvie laid a friendly hand on the R.S.M.'s shoulder, and smiled. 'We're all glad to have you back with us, and as for me, I'll be more than ever grateful for your support.'

'Sir! That, you'll have in full.' Cunningham gave his usual swinging salute. 'Now if you'll excuse me, sir, I have many things needing my attention. Lord, but the battalion's grown slack while I've been sick!' He turned about smartly and marched away, his pace and his arm-swing as regimental as ever it had been, his helmet precisely square on his head, his back straight. Ogilvie chuckled at the old warrior's parting remark: there had been truth in it, though it had been said humorously. The slackness would vanish now, if Cunningham's loudly raised voice was indicative of his intentions! Ogilvie saw men straighten to attention, and straighten helmets, as discipline bore down upon them, barking. The R.S.M. was a tonic: against Bosom Cunningham, the cholera had manifestly failed. He was the loud-voiced, very living proof that the Royal Strathspeys could and would pull through. Ogilvie turned away and walked on towards the gate to take over the guard. He would have wished to confide in the R.S.M. over the native demand for Hamish Dewar, but in fact there had been no need. Cunningham had guessed; and in guessing had issued an unspoken warning: other men, the older men with Frontier experience equal to Ogilvie's if not to Cunningham's, could also guess. Therein might lie the spark of trouble.

* * *

Yet another conference of officers, presided over by Andrew Black in the continuing sickness of the Colonel and Major Hay. This took place in the cool of the evening as the enemy camp fires were lit beyond the walls and the interminable tinny music came clearly across to ears that were driven close to madness by the never-ending irritation.

All the news seemed desperate.

'The doctor,' Black said heavily, his face twitching, 'reports a sick list of three hundred and four men, and seven officers. Forty-one men have been returned to duty in the last twenty-four hours – that is good, of course, but . . . ' Black's voice trailed away; he raised a hand to his eyes, and seemed for a moment to stagger, but recovered. 'In the native compound they all seem to be sick, but since they were rounded up and isolated they have not contributed to the spread – '

'Except insofar as the flies settle on their filthy droppings,' Dewar said contemptuously, 'and then on our bodies and our food, or what there is of it – '

'Mr Dewar – '

'They'd be better shot and their bodies burned,' Dewar interrupted, looking round with bitter, haunted eyes. 'If I had my way – '

'Which you have not, Mr Dewar. Kindly be silent or I shall ask you to leave. Now. Mr McCrum?'

The Lieutenant and Quartermaster got to his feet.

'Oh, sit down, Mr McCrum, we're all too weary for formality now.'

'Thank you.' Mr McCrum gave a preliminary cough. 'The commissariat position. It has not changed except that we have a day's less supply than yesterday, Captain Black.'

'Yes, yes. How many days have we left?'

'I told you yesterday – ' McCrum broke off with a sigh. 'Very good, Captain Black. We can exist for seven more days, maybe a day or two beyond that if the ration is shortened even further. We have flour, a fair amount of water, some rice and potatoes, and biscuits.' He threw up his hands. 'It'll sustain life, which is all we can ask until relief comes!'

'We shall have to shorten the ration, Mr McCrum. Go into it with the Surgeon Major. Work out your maximum number of days on the smallest amount that will keep us going, and reduce the issue accordingly. Mr Cunningham, what is the state of the ammunition?'

'Plenty in hand, sir, very little having been expended.'

'And your shells and charges, Captain Bingham?'

Bingham, commanding the mountain battery in the absence on the sick list of Major Pilkington, indicated, somewhat caustically, that since no firing had been possible no shells at all had been expended. 'If we had food,' he snapped, 'we'd be as operational as when we entered the city. Soon, with no food at all, we may as well make a bonfire of the

138

guns and blow the place to Kingdom Come –'

'You're impertinent, Captain –'

'All right, I'm impertinent, and if you like I'll be bloody rude!' Bingham said hotly, getting to his feet. 'I've told you before, we should get out there and fight while we can still put one foot before the other, and I'll tell you this: you're the one that's stopping us, Black. My fellows have had just about enough of your –'

'Captain Bingham, I –'

'I've not finished yet –'

'Yes, you have. Sit down. That's an order.'

'I'm not having you –'

'Somebody . . . *Captain Ogilvie!*'

Ogilvie was already on his feet, making towards the gunner captain. Reaching him, he said, 'Take it easy, old man, none of us are having much of a time.'

Bingham, a tall, dark-faced man not unlike Black himself, sneered in Ogilvie's face. 'You're as bad as the rest of your bunch,' he said flatly, 'and I'm not –'

'Do as you're told and shut up, will you?'

'No, I won't!' Bingham's mouth slitted. Balling a fist, he punched Ogilvie full in the face before the Scot could dodge aside. Ogilvie gave his head a shake, felt blood run, and struck out himself. The gunner went down in the dust, spitting blood from a split lip. His fists clenched, Ogilvie stood over him.

'Get up and –'

'James, James.' Ogilvie heard Stuart's lowered voice, felt a hand on his shoulder. 'Leave it. It's doing no good, and Black's in a bad way by the look of it. It's all getting too much for him.'

Ogilvie relaxed and turned round. Black appeared to have virtually collapsed on to a camp stool. His hands were covering his eyes, his shoulders were heaving, and there was a sound of sobbing. Everyone present was looking extremely embarrassed. Ogilvie moved towards Black: there was a sound of deep and terrible retching. In a gush of sour-looking bile-filled vomit, Black was sick.

139

Ogilvie stopped in his tracks. 'The doctor!' he said. 'Some-one bring the doctor, quickly.'

* * *

'Black's down with the cholera,' Ogilvie said later, coming back from sick quarters. 'Bingham – that little fracas . . . no hard feelings now, I hope?'

Bingham smiled somewhat sheepishly. 'None, Ogilvie. You have my apology – the strain's been telling, I'm afraid – '

'That's all right. What's your seniority?'

Bingham said, 'December '96.'

'In that case I'm a little ahead of you.' Ogilvie looked around the group. 'During Captain Black's illness, gentle-men, I'm assuming command of the battalion and the city, and that includes the guns. I shall – '

'*Use* the guns – to attack, Ogilvie?' Bingham interrupted.

Ogilvie took a deep breath. 'No. I'm sorry, because I know how you feel, but in my opinion Captain Black was right not to attempt a sortie with a sickness-weakened force against the numbers we know the natives have out there. We must wait for relief – it's all we can do. I'm certain relief will come. If, on the other hand, it does not . . . '

'What then, Ogilvie?'

'When all the food's gone, then we'll mount a sortie. It'll be no more than a gesture, a calculated sacrifice – but it'll be a better way than starving.'

THIRTEEN

As THOUGH THE fight between two officers had acted as a flash in a powder-barrel, trouble came to several heads among the men next day.

The R.S.M. sought out Ogilvie and made a report. 'They're at each other's throats, sir. I've handled much of it myself and no more need be said about that, but an example's got to be made in a couple of cases, sir.'

'Defaulters, Sar'nt-Major?'

'Aye, sir.'

'I don't like sounding Defaulters in this situation, Sar'nt-Major.'

'Sir! I think you'll like the alternative less. With respect, sir, two men must be seen to be disciplined. Lance-Corporal MacLean and Private Monk.'

Ogilvie sighed, feeling the blistering impact of a high sun, a sun whose scorching heat was enough to make any man step out of line, let alone men starving and thirsty and unknowing when the cholera would hit. 'The charge?' he asked.

'Lance-Corporal MacLean is charged with mutinous talk, sir, with seditious talk. I myself heard him haranguing the men of his section to the effect that the rank and file should take up arms against the officers, sir, and open the gates to the enemy. Sir! If that is not dangerous, then I'm a bloody fairy – sir!'

'All right, Sar'nt-Major, I take your point and he'll be charged. Monk?'

'Making water, sir –'

'*Making water!*' Ogilvie gave a laugh. 'We're not a group of young women –'

'Begging your pardon, sir. Making water on rice destined for the officers' rations. Sir!'

*   *   *

A bugler sounded Defaulters, notes that had not been heard since the battalion had left cantonments in Peshawar. James Ogilvie, as the call died away over the sun-hot walls and the hard earth, over the Queen's Colour at the gates, over the watchful waiting levies outside, took his appointed place behind an ornate table in his headquarters. To his right stood the Regimental Sergeant-Major bearing a file of papers to strike an incongruous officious note in the besieged city. Also present were the accused soldiers' company commanders – Stuart in the case of Lance-Corporal MacLean, Hamish Dewar in Private Monk's case, Dewar having taken over Ogilvie's company for the time being. Monk, being on the lesser charge in a military sense, was the first man to be doubled in. Ogilvie listened to the ritual, which began outside and finished in front of him:

'Prisoner an' escort . . . double march, left-right-left – left . . . *wheel*! Halt! Salute!'

Private Monk, crashing to a halt, saluted, looking mighty scared. The Regimental Sergeant-Major, flicking away flies, went into his spiel. 'Number 047765, Private Monk, Angus James. Sir! On the fourth day of June at nine-thirty-five hours a.m. was observed to urinate on a container of rice the said container and its contents being part of the officers' luncheon ration. Sir! This action being witnessed by Number 14563, Colour Sar'nt MacTrease, Alan. Sir!'

Ogilvie nodded. 'Thank you, Sar'nt-Major. Colour Mac-Trease?'

MacTrease sprang forward, halted, saluted. 'Sir!'

'State what you saw, Colour MacTrease.'

'Sir! At nine-thirty-five hours a.m. on the fourth of June, sir, I was proceeding about my duty which was to post

142

sentries for guard changing on the native camp within the city. Sir!' MacTrease, rigidly at attention, eyes staring at a point a little above Ogilvie's head, was sweating like a pig. 'As I passed the point where the rations for the Officers' Mess were in preparation, I saw Private Monk, detailed to assist the ration fatigue, standing in suspicious circumstances close by a pan of rice – '

'Suspicious circumstances, Colour-Sar'nt?'

'He was withdrawing a part of his person, sir.'

'I see. Go on, please.'

MacTrease did so: in some detail, as per Queen's Regulations, the evidence was given and the story emerged. When the Colour-Sergeant had finished, Ogilvie spoke to Private Monk.

'Well now, Monk, you've heard the evidence. What have you to say?'

There was no reply: just a black look.

'Come now, you must have an answer. Do you deny the charge?'

Monk scowled; though he was clearly frightened of the consequences of his act, something was making him obstinate and surly. 'I don't deny the charge,' he said.

'Sir!' This was Cunningham.

'Sir,' Monk said after a pause.

'Then, as stated in evidence, you did in fact urinate on the officer's rice, Monk?'

'Och, I pee'd on it, yes.'

'*Sir!*'

'Sir.'

'Why did you do that, Monk?'

'I was fed up. Sir.'

'That's no excuse and you know it very well, I think.' Ogilvie spoke coldly. 'Every man in this city is fed up, but they don't do as you did. I'm not going to stress the disgusting nature of your act, Monk – you obviously realise this for yourself. But this I am going to say.' He paused, looking closely at the soldier, who stared back in defiance. He asked, 'Tell me first, Monk: did you understand what the results

143

might have been, had you not been seen?'

'The results – sir?'

'The results, yes – the results of persons eating . . . what could well have contained the germs of the cholera? Are you in such a way mentally, Monk, that you deliberately attempted to infect so-far healthy officers with cholera?'

'No! No, I didna do that.' Monk's face had changed. 'Gosh, no, sir, I didn't think that way at all, at all!'

'You're sure?'

'Certain sure, sir, as God's ma judge!'

'Then you must be half a lunatic not to have realised what you were doing!' A thought struck Ogilvie, a thought brought about by the curious mixture of fear and bravado in the man's manner. 'Were you put up to this, Monk? Is someone behind you?'

'No! No one's behind me . . . sir.'

Ogilvie leaned forward, his face threatening. 'Again I ask – *are you sure, Monk?*'

'Yes, sir.' Monk licked at his lips, face twitching. 'There is no one else, sir. I'm sorry for what I did, sir. It'll no' happen again.'

'Not for a while anyway,' Ogilvie said shortly, and passed sentence. 'Seven days cell punishment –'

'Cells!' Monk's face was a study. 'We have no bloody cells – '

'Hold your tongue, or you'll be in them for fourteen days. The Sar'nt-Major will provide you with an equivalent to cell accommodation, Monk. Right, Sar'nt-Major.'

Mr Cunningham came back, as it were, on stage. 'Salute! Prisoner an' escort, about *turn*! Double *march*! Left-right-left and take that insubordinate look off your bloody *face*, Monk, or you'll double *back* again! Left *wheel*!' As the party vanished, the R.S.M. spoke to Ogilvie. 'You put your finger on it, sir. When you said he was put up to it.'

'You think so?'

'Aye, sir, I do. Mind, I'm saying no more yet – but I hope you'll deal severely with yon MacLean. Sir!'

144

'We'll see what he has to say first. Wheel him in, if you please, Sar'nt-Major.'

'Sir!' The ritual was repeated: Lance-Corporal MacLean came to a halt in front of Ogilvie and saluted. The charge was read: listening to it, Ogilvie saw on MacLean's face a surly look similar to that on Private Monk's earlier.

'Well, Lance-Corporal MacLean,' he said formally when the reading was finished. 'What have you to say?'

'Sir, I wish first to state a complaint –'

Cunningham roared: 'Hold your tongue –'

'All right, Sar'nt-Major, let him go on.' Ogilvie paused. 'Well, MacLean? What's this complaint?'

'The witness to what I'm said to have done, sir, is the Sar'-Major. And it's the Sar'-Major that's prosecuting. That's not fair, Captain Ogilvie –'

'Not fair?'

'Not in accordance with the Queen's Regulations, Captain Ogilvie.'

'You're a barrack-room lawyer, are you, MacLean?'

'When it's ma future at stake, I am, yes.'

Ogilvie was in fact unsure of his ground, but knew that it would in all the circumstances be unwise to let any such uncertainty show in his voice, manner or actions. Any injustice could be righted later: the over-riding consideration for now was to stop incipient trouble in its tracks. He said, 'I take note of your complaint, Lance-Corporal MacLean, but for now I am disregarding it. You will answer the charge as read by Mr Cunningham –'

'I'll not do any such –'

'Lance-Corporal MacLean! You will do as you are told, or you will incur the punishment for mutiny. As acting Commanding Officer, in this situation representing Her Majesty the Queen Empress, and the British Government, I shall feel entitled and obliged to act exactly as I see fit. Consider your position well, MacLean – that is my advice to you! Now – you will speak out, and answer the charge made against you. Did you, or did you not, utter sedition and mutiny?'

'I did not,' MacLean answered flatly.

'Sir!'

'Ah, bugger the sir.'

Cunningham virtually exploded: Ogilvie signalled to him not to interrupt. Turning to MacLean again he said evenly, 'I'd like some explanation of that last remark. To me it smacks of mutiny – of substantiation, in fact, of the charge. Well?'

MacLean said, 'I'm sorry.'

'That's no answer.'

'It was not meant mutinously, Captain Ogilvie, not in the sense you're meaning. I have spoken no sedition, only common sense – '

'Do you, then, admit the words used, as heard by the R.S.M.?'

MacLean nodded, his eyes blazing. 'Aye, I do. The words, not the intent. Maybe I let off a little steam, Captain Ogilvie, but I'm a loyal soldier both to the regiment and to the Queen. All I said was not meant to be taken truly, though some of it was and I'll not deny that – '

'What part, MacClean? What part did you mean?'

'When I said the officers were not leading us as they should. When I said they'd made a balls, Captain Ogilvie, and would go on making a balls so long as we sat down under their bloody incompetence! Aye, that was true, and I'm saying it again, d'ye hear, Captain Ogilvie?' MacLean lifted a fist, and waved it in the air until he was seized by the escort and held still. 'You bletherin' lot of – '

'Silence!' Cunningham roared. 'Captain Ogilvie, sir, let me have him removed and put in irons – '

'Ye'll do no such thing, you old – '

'*Colour-Sar'nt!*'

'Aye, sir.' The colour-sergeant in rear of the escort took the struggling MacLean from behind, and clamped a vast hand over his mouth. Ogilvie watched, sweating: all three of them – he, Cunningham, the colour-sergeant – had all realised the one thing: MacLean must not be allowed to say more, and never mind Queen's Regulations. To contain the situation, not to allow the spread of a dangerous poison and to stop that spark reaching the powder-barrel – these were the vital things. They almost got away with it, but not quite: with a violent movement MacLean threw off one of the escort and at the same moment bit deep into the colour-sergeant's hand. The N.C.O. withdrew the hand with an oath, and MacLean pointed his accusing finger at Hamish Dewar – and spoke the words that none present wanted to hear.

'Yon's the wee birkie that's got us where we are, Captain Ogilvie – not you, nor most of the others. Mr bloody Dewar's the one and if you kicked him oot the gates the regiment would be all right! Och, he's a dirty big coward, a bloody yellow-guts, and we all of us know *that*!'

Too late, MacLean was secured again and held quiet, this time with the colour-sergeant's sash hauled tight about his mouth like a tourniquet. When he was frog-marched out, he left a stunned silence behind him. Everyone avoided looking at Hamish Dewar when he broke the silence by saying bitterly, 'Well, now I suppose you all want me to die.'

No one answered him, and he walked away from the defaulters' table defiantly.

* * *

'MacLean'll be kept in close arrest pending Court Martial.' Ogilvie said to the gunner captain, 'but what do we do about Hamish Dewar?'

Bingham shrugged. 'Your problem, not mine.'

'We're all in this together,' Ogilvie said.

'A trite enough observation –'

'But true!'

'Yes, I know. But I'm not one for interfering in regimental concerns. I mind my own guns . . . and I wish to God I could *use* 'em, Ogilvie!'

'Yes, I know you do, but let me concentrate on Dewar. I'm asking your help, so forget your principles, will you, and tell me this: what would *you* do, if he were one of yours?'

Bingham pondered for a moment. 'I'm damned if I know,'

he said, frowning. 'It *is* a poser I'll not deny! I'd hate to order a man out to certain death, but if he doesn't go, it begins to look like the death of a regiment. Can't he be shamed into going voluntarily?'

'That's been tried. Dewar's not the sort to feel shame, he's too bloody thick-headed –'

'Or thick-skinned?'

'That too.'

'Why not,' Bingham said after some more thought, 'give him a job? Detail him to do something outside the gates . . . I don't know what, but if we think hard we may come up with something!'

'Something that doesn't need anyone else but him! I won't risk men on a caper of that sort.'

'Well, I don't know . . . ' Bingham shook his head. 'I wish to God you'd –'

'Let you use your guns – I know!'

'I wasn't going to say that. Make a sortie – a *real* one, with Dewar in it. We can't last much longer, you know! There'll have to be action soon. Don't you realize that? It may just as well be now, Ogilvie.'

'I'm getting closer to the idea,' Ogilvie said, 'but – not yet. Not quite yet. I have to think of the sick . . . and I have to face the fact that we won't have a dog's chance. It's still our role to wait for Fettleworth. It may be ignominious, but it's –'

He broke off: there were rapid footsteps behind, steps that broke into a run towards the rubble-filled gateway where the two officers were talking. Ogilvie swung round. The Regimental Sergeant-Major, purple in the face, was coming hell-for-leather, shouting out something about trouble.

'What trouble, Sar'nt-Major?'

'Sir, the . . . the battalion . . . ' Puffing like a goods train, Cunningham eased to a walk. Looking over his shoulder, Ogilvie suddenly stiffened. Behind the R.S.M., still some distance off beyond the sick quarters, a group of the men had assembled and were moving towards the gate. Armed men, men who had an intent and determined look, men led by a private soldier, a hulking fellow from Ogilvie's company – Private Meldrum of the long tongue that, during the march from Peshawar, had been in need of the R.S.M.'s silencing via Lance-Corporal MacLean.

Ogilvie looked at Cunningham, his heart thumping hard. 'Mutiny?' he asked.

'It hasn't quite the whole feel of that, Captain Ogilvie, but be very careful now. And just look behind you.'

Ogilvie did so. The men of the gate guard had turned inward. There seemed to be a potential threat in the way they were handling their rifles.

FOURTEEN

OGILVIE FELT DEATHLY cold in spite of the heat of the day. As the group of men advanced with their rifles held loosely across their bodies he felt tremendously glad of the Regimental Sergeant-Major's rock-like presence at his side. He himself had no experience of a possibly mutinous situation: Cunningham would know instinctively how to interpret the mood of the men. Ogilvie's own instinct was to react violently, for his whole upbringing revolted against the idea of mutiny, of any kind of disobedience of orders. It was alien to the British way of life, to the British concept of an army – it had to be. Yet violent reactions, he knew only too well, would not be likely to help matters now.

He glanced sideways at Cunningham, at the massive jaw and the moustache that was still, by some miracle, wonderfully waxed. Cunningham was standing very steady and very straight, with his pace-stick rigid beneath his left arm. He was staring at the oncoming men. Suddenly he opened his mouth and roared out: *'Halt!'*

The men halted: some with a fair grace, others with bad, but they all halted. Ogilvie let out a long breath of relief. Cunningham called, 'Now what's all this about? Come on, speak out. You have a purpose. Name it!'

There was no answer: the men eyed each other, looking uneasy now.

'Private Meldrum!' The R.S.M. snapped.

'Sir!'

'Six paces forward – march!'

Meldrum got on the move.

'*Halt*! Meldrum, you appear to be in the lead. What are the men about?'

'Sir! We wish to speak to Captain Ogilvie.' Meldrum, black-haired, dark-faced, stared over Cunningham's head. 'We insist on speaking to Captain Ogilvie – '

'Oho, you insist, Private Meldrum! We shall see about that – '

'All right, Mr Cunningham,' Ogilvie said. 'I'll talk to Meldrum.'

'Sir! A word in private first, sir, if you please.'

'Very well.' Ogilvie turned away from the watching men, walking to one side with the R.S.M. Cunningham said in a low voice, 'A word of warning, Captain Ogilvie, with respect. *Don't talk of mutiny*. I do not believe this is mutiny except in a strictly by-the-book sense, but to use the word, in their present mood you understand, might precipitate the fact. For the same reason, sir, I would not give orders that might be disobeyed – '

'But – '

'*No sir*! This is not a time for buts. We are not in a position to ensure obedience, so we must not provoke. At the same time, sir, we shall not be seen to lose control – if we are careful as to what orders we give! Do you follow me, Captain Ogilvie?'

'I suppose so,' Ogilvie answered grudgingly. 'I don't like it – '

'No more do I, sir. It's still the only way.'

Ogilvie nodded. 'Oh, very well, Sar'nt-Major. But if it's not mutiny, what d'you suppose it is?'

'That we'll be finding out, sir, but I think it's what Meldrum says – they wish to talk to you.'

'And if I don't, or can't, say what they want to hear?'

'That's when the trouble will come, sir – '

'Actual mutiny?'

'Very likely, sir. In the meantime, we must still not provoke it. I repeat what I said earlier, sir: be very careful now.' Cunningham paused. 'Shall we go back to the men, Captain Ogilvie?'

Ogilvie met his eye and give a tight smile. 'I'm ready, Sar'nt-Major. Thank you for your advice.' He turned away and walked across towards Meldrum, with Cunningham at his side. He stared at the private, looking the man up and down, noting the sullen, determined look, the look of a desperate courage screwed to the sticking-place. He saw the shake in the fingers as Meldrum stood rigidly at attention, the slight tremor of a muscle in the face, the tongue that protruded to lick at dry lips – lips dry from a current nervous reaction as well as from sun and lack of water. Ogilvie went on staring, trying to assess the man, assess his potential for stubbornness, the point – if there was one, and surely there must be – at which he would crack. After a moment he heard Cunningham's cough by his side, and made an accurate interpretation: Cunningham was urging him to get on with it and not exacerbate any nerves.

'You wish to speak to me, Meldrum?' he asked, his voice sharp with tension.

'Sir!' Meldrum was taking pains to be correct: he gave a smart salute, which Ogilvie returned. 'If I may make so bold, sir.'

'Say what you have to say.'

'Sir! We're afraid for our lives, sir, if things go on as they are.'

'Oh, nonsense! Relief'll be here shortly. You don't imagine Division's taking no action, do you?'

'We have seen no action, sir, and relief is no' here yet, sir. When it comes it may be too late. Meanwhile we have a way of saving ourselves, sir.'

'By making a sortie out of the gates? That's the – '

'No, sir. No' that, sir.'

'Then what?' As he spoke, Ogilvie saw the answer for himself: the answer that he had sub-consciously feared all along, the thing he had pushed to the back of his mind because its consequences were too horrible to contemplate. 'What else have you in mind, Meldrum?'

'That, sir!' Meldrum spoke hoarsely, in a voice that seemed filled with hate and contempt. He raised his left arm, and pointed up at the walls to Ogilvie's left: looking up, Ogilvie saw Hamish Dewar standing there with his back towards what was going on just within the gateway. Dewar was staring down at the encamped army just outside, through field-glasses, and seemed unaware of any trouble inside the city. Meldrum went on, almost shouting now, 'That bloody coward, sir, that lost a whole patrol in this very city and then used a rifle under a flag of truce and so –'

'Stop it, Meldrum –'

'I'll no' stop, sir, as long as yon Dewar's allowed to flaunt himsel' around the regiment! Send him tae the enemy, Captain Ogilvie, send him where he's wanted – and save all our lives!'

Ogilvie's head felt feather-light: he was aware of Cunningham's steadying hand on his arm . . . then realised that Dewar, still on the walls, had turned to stare down at the gathering of men, that by now he had heard Meldrum's shouting tones. Amazingly, he heard a laugh from Dewar, and his call: 'Hold on, James, I'm coming down.'

Dewar walked towards the steps, and ran lightly down. He went across to Meldrum, gave him a cool stare, then turned his back and approached Ogilvie and Cunningham. 'I heard my name mentioned,' he said. 'I'm not sure that I got the context. What it's about?'

'Hamish,' Ogilvie said in a low voice, 'don't make this more difficult. We've reached a turning point. You heard, I think, what Meldrum said – didn't you?'

Dewar nodded, his face hard now, the easy manner suddenly gone. 'Yes,' he said, 'I heard. And I'll personally horse-whip the bastard for –'

'No, you won't. You'll do nothing. Leave this to me. I'm just asking you one thing: will you do as the man asks, as it seems *all* the men are asking, Hamish?'

Dewar stared at him. 'Why should I?'

'For the sake of the battalion, for the sake of the sick . . . and to prove Meldrum's lie about your cowardice.'

'I don't think I need to prove that, James.'

'Not to me. To Meldrum. To his – accomplices.'

153

'His accomplices in mutiny?'

There was a hiss of breath from the Regimental Sergeant-Major. 'Mr Dewar, sir, *please*! No talk of that!'

'Why not? It is mutiny, isn't it?'

Ogilvie said, 'Not quite – not yet. It's a request – a request involving insubordination and insolence towards an officer, but still only a request.'

'Made unconstitutionally and in disregard of Queen's Regulations.'

'But condoned by me, and made with my permission. The men are in the clear, Hamish. And now the whole thing's up to you.'

'You'd sacrifice me, would you, James?'

Ogilvie sweated. 'Not willingly, no, of course not. But it's one life against many now. If this situation gets out of hand, we're done for – don't you see? If I don't give Meldrum the answer he wants, then the knife-edge tips towards mutiny.'

'I see. In other words, you *would* sacrifice me. Well, I can't say I blame you, James. Perhaps I'd do the same in your shoes. Now it's my turn to make a request.'

'Go ahead.'

Dewar smiled slightly and said, 'I want to talk to the men myself. Oh, I promise I'll be discreet! I won't upset any of their precious little susceptibilities and tip that damn knife-edge of yours.'

Ogilvie glanced at Cunningham. 'What d'you think, Sar'nt-Major?'

'I'd say yes, sir. But please, Mr Dewar, sir, be very careful. I can't stress that enough, sir.'

Dewar smiled again. 'Touch and go, is it?'

'Indeed it is, sir, and I'd have thought you could see that for yourself.'

Dewar said lightly, 'Hoity-toity, Sar'nt-Major, you're feeling the strain and letting it show, I think! Well, James, I have your permission, then?'

'Yes.'

Dewar swung round and moved slowly towards Meldrum. He looked the man over coldly, then moved on behind him towards the rest of the men, still standing silently holding their rifles. He ran his gaze, somewhat superciliously, over them all. Some stared back, others looked away. Dewar gave a loud laugh, then again turned his back and, walking round Meldrum, stopped in front of Ogilvie.

'I thought,' Ogilvie said, 'you wanted to speak to them.'

'In my own time.' Dewar answered. 'First, another request. Meldrum's the biggest and strongest. I want to fight him.'

'Fight him?'

'That's what I said. *Fight him*. Man to man, without gloves, and without the Marquess of Queensberry. You heard what he called me. I have the right, you know! We'll forget we're officer and man. All right, James?'

Ogilvie hesitated, very much in two minds. Such a fight would be an unheard-of breach of good order and discipline, but the North-West Frontier often enough made its own rules and the city of Kalundabad under siege was a far cry from the white-gloved, top-hatted gentlemen of the Commander-in-Chief's office at the Horse Guards. Whoever won, the air might be a little clearer afterwards and attitudes might change – which was probably Dewar's own hope. At the least, time would have been gained, time for screwed-up resolves to loosen a turn or two, enough, perhaps, for military discipline to re-assert itself in the minds of private soldiers . . . coming to a decision, one that had to be taken quickly, Ogilvie nodded his approval. 'If Meldrum agrees, I'll give permission.' He raised his voice. 'Meldrum!'

'Sir!'

'Mr Dewar wishes to fight you, without the rules. Do you agree?'

A big smile, a smile of astonishment as well as pleasure, crossed the big Scot's face. 'Aye, sir, I agree! That is, just so long as I'll not be accused afterwards of striking an officer!'

Ogilvie said, 'You have my assurance, with Mr Cunningham as a witness, and Captain Bingham too, that there will be no reprisals of any kind, whoever wins. Does that satisfy you?'

'Aye, sir, it does. When's the fight to be, sir?'

'Now.' Ogilvie glanced up at the sun; it had passed over the great gateway, and there was a pool of shade a little to his right. This, he indicated with a wave of his hand. 'Get ready at once, both of you. Strip to your kilts, and remove any rings. All men to remain well clear, and no interference with the contestants. Mr Cunningham, send for the Surgeon Major, if you please –'

'Sir!'

' – he'll be the judge of when the fight should stop, if there's no knock-out. His decision will be obeyed without question. Carry on.'

Dewar and Meldrum saluted smartly. Cunningham had already sent a man from the gate guard detail for the doctor: that man had obeyed instantly and smartly. Already there was a different feeling in the air, most noticeably. Ogilvie felt a strong sense of relief, of a terrible tension leaving him. Dewar and Meldrum stripped off tunics and shirts and sporrans, then stood with bare chests heaving as they took deep breaths. Both were thin; though both had fine muscles in arms and backs and thighs, there was a haggardness in both their faces that spoke eloquently of the siege conditions: this would not be a long fight, Ogilvie knew. They waited for the doctor's arrival from sick quarters; there was a buzz of anticipatory talk from the men behind Meldrum and from the stand-by files at the gateway. Word had spread around the city by some form of bush telegraph, and more men were crowding in from the alleys while others took quick glances down from their watchful stations along the wall. Looking somewhat testy, Surgeon Major Corton came up.

'Is this necessary, James?' he asked. 'I've any God's amount to do in –'

'It's very necessary, Doctor,' Ogilvie interrupted. He gave Corton a few words of explanation. 'I'd be obliged if you'd let them carry on till they're both fairly exhausted, then put a stop to it. I've a feeling it'll do a lot of good.'

'I can only say I hope you'll be proved right! I don't know what the Colonel would say.'

'I believe he'd agree. How is he, Doctor?'

156

A shadow crossed Corton's face. 'Holding his own still. He's very weak, though. Now get on with this caper of yours, James, and then I can get back to sick quarters, where I'm much needed.'

Ogilvie nodded. 'Mr Dewar, are you ready?'

'All ready.'

'Meldrum?'

'Aye, ready, sir.' Meldrum lifted his hands and spat into the palms, rubbing them together: his expression was keenly anticipatory. Both he and Dewar lashed the air around them, trying to disperse the flies that clustered and buzzed around bare, sweating skin. Ogilvie was about to give the word for the two to shake hands, but he never did so for the fight started with a sudden rush from Dewar, who bounded across the debris-scattered ground towards Private Meldrum. Ogilvie, realising that it was too late for his interference, shrugged: perhaps, after all, to have given the order to shake hands would have been a mistake. Hamish Dewar, in his present mood, might well have refused. Ogilvie concentrated on the fight: Meldrum had dodged that first rush nimbly enough, and Dewar had blundered past him. A laugh came from the men, and Dewar looked angry, but he seemed to have learned a lesson, for instead of rushing at Meldrum again he lowered his head and raised his fists and approached with caution, slowly. This time, it was Meldrum who made the rush, Dewar who dodged. But Meldrum, in passing the officer, turned suddenly and lashed out at his head. Taken by surprise, Dewar failed to dodge the blow entirely, and Meldrum's fist drew blood from his forehead. Dewar's mouth tightened, and he swung heavily at Meldrum, landing a fist plumb on the man's nose. There was a good deal of blood, and the nose appeared broken.

Beside Ogilvie, the Surgeon Major clicked his teeth. 'More work,' he said. 'Work I haven't time to do in the middle of a cholera outbreak!'

Ogilvie watched the men, the spectators. They, for their part, watched every move of the fight, largely in a tense silence broken now and again to cheer Meldrum on, or to laugh at the officer's antics – in all truth, there was little science about Hamish Dewar, Ogilvie saw. He was strong and tough and very eager for the fight, but he was lumpish and awkward where Meldrum was swift and nimble. More officers had come up now, to watch: McCrum, Robin Stuart, Neil Fergusson of C Company with one of his subalterns. Ogilvie felt a sense of unease as the officers applauded a good move from Dewar, who had landed a telling blow to Meldrum's chest, a very heavy blow that made Meldrum gasp and stagger. Was this, after all, to turn into an Officers v. Other Ranks vendetta, thus making matters worse? If that was the case, feelings would run higher than ever on the men's part afterwards, whoever was the winner. Having landed that good blow, Dewar was quick enough to follow it up with another, this time to the jaw. Again Meldrum staggered, shaking his head as though to clear it; and recovering, rushed blindly at Dewar with his fists flailing before him. One of them, more by chance than design, took Dewar on the side of the head: tripping over a stone, he went headlong on the ground. The soldiers cheered and laughed. Ogilvie, waiting for the end now, for both men were streaming with sweat, almost purple in their faces, and clearly both in vicious tempers, was surprised when Meldrum held back. The man stood with his chest heaving and fists slack by his sides, looking down at Dewar, waiting for him to scramble to his feet.

Dewar got up quickly: only his dignity was hurt. The look in his eyes was not propitious: the laughter that had swept the ranks had clearly infuriated him but had in some curious way given him the control he had so far lacked over his movements, as though it had thoroughly concentrated his mind towards winning. Gone now was the wild swing, the stupid bull-like rush: on his feet again, he stood and waited for Meldrum to come in to the attack, waited behind a barrier of weaving fists, his eyes narrowed, his whole expression dangerous. It began to look like a fight to the death. Ogilvie glanced at Corton: the doctor was watching closely, but seemed as yet disinclined to interfere.

As Meldrum closed, boxing well but, in his siege-weakened condition, obviously tiring already, Dewar's right fist darted out, attempting to cut through Meldrum's guard. But Meldrum deflected the blow easily, came in himself beneath it, and landed a blow of his own that looked like blackening Dewar's right eye and sent blood streaming down his face from a cut below the socket.

Again Ogilvie looked at Corton. 'Doctor?'

'No, I think not. Not yet.'

'But the eye – '

'I doubt if it's serious, James. To let the fight be undecided might be more serious. Somehow I feel we need to have a winner. Don't you sense the mood, James?'

'Not really, but you may be right.'

'I'm sure I am, but don't worry, I'll put a stop to it before there's real damage done. That is, if they take any notice of me!'

The sun, moving on its way into afternoon, had shifted the patch of shade. The two contestants, who were covering a wide area in any case, fought mainly in the full glare now, their blood-stained torsos gleaming with sweat, and blood dripping off them to dapple the stones and earth. Dewar had landed another fist on Meldrum's chest, but not, it seemed, such a heavy one as before; and Meldrum was fighting back hard, pressing the officer who, after a while longer, seemed to be on the retreat, moving back and away from Meldrum's fists. The whole atmosphere, the arena, had become tense, almost vibrant with feeling as the fight went on: still the doctor made no sign that he would stop it. The tempo, the movement, had slowed considerably: energy on both sides was draining fast, though the blows, when they landed as aimed, looked just as heavy and punishing. And suddenly, as with many a fight, the fortunes shifted. Meldrum, appearing to tire more rapidly than his adversary, let two blows through his guard in rapid succession: one to the nose again, the other slamming against his forehead with such force that the crunch could almost be heard. After that, it was Meldrum who began to move backwards; and Dewar, taking his advantage as it were with both hands, pressed cruelly. Blow after blow crashed through Meldrum's guard; he reeled, staggered about, but kept on his feet, fighting as best he could. Corton was about to call out the order to break off when Meldrum's covering arms fell away and Dewar simply walked straight in and gave the man a smashing blow to the point of the jaw that sent him down and out.

Dewar stood back. There was no cheering; only a sullen, resentful silence. Dewar had gained no friends. A coldness settled around Ogilvie's heart: this whole thing had very likely been a mistake. But Dewar had not finished yet. As the doctor ran across to Meldrum and bent, and felt for pulse and heart-beat, Dewar looked along the silent, sullen ranks, then at Ogilvie and the other officers.

'Now I'm going to talk to the men, as you said I could, James.' He turned towards the soldiers, glancing down at Meldrum, who had now lifted his head. 'Well, you've seen the fight. A fair fight, Private Meldrum?'

Meldrum looked up at him from the ground. 'Aye, a fair fight, Mr Dewar. You won on your own merits – '

'As a coward?'

'You have guts for a fight, I'll no' deny that,' Meldrum said.

'Thank you.' Dewar turned back to the watching men, men with unbuttoned tunics, with helmets on the backs of their heads, sweat-stained, hungry and smelling to heaven, dirty, unshaven. 'This . . . *demonstration* led by Private Meldrum has been a disgrace to the regiment. There's not one of you who looks like a soldier any more, and if you'd been soldiers you'd not have tried to hound one of your officers, or indeed any man, out into the enemy's lines to be tortured, dishonoured and killed. It's you who are the cowards. I shall not even address you as men. Worms would be more appropriate – or rats. You're not worth saving. Nevertheless . . . '

Dewar was shouting now, shouting over a rising murmur of sound, of a protest that now in Ogilvie's ears was fast approaching open mutiny. He caught Cunningham's eye, and Bingham's: with them he moved across towards Dewar.

Dewar's voice came out loud and strong above the sounds of anger. 'Nevertheless, I shall save you! I am going out towards the enemy of my own free will. There is, however, a condition: you will all disperse about your duties, or I shall not go. I want the area cleared within two minutes, and no more seditious talk that will certainly take you to the gallows when we reach Peshawar. You have been dirty, mutinous dogs! Now prove you are men, and soldiers of the Queen. Sar'nt-Major?'

'Sir?'

'Clear the area at once. Any man who refuses to obey will be placed in close arrest and taken in irons to Peshawar, where he will be charged with mutiny. Now – do as I say!'

'Sir!' For once in his life, Cunningham appeared to be taken utterly aback. He dithered, fumed: an order was an order, and it happened to be one he itched to carry out. But it could be suicide, and Dewar had not the right to give it in the presence of the acting Commanding Officer. Looking helpless, the Regimental Sergeant-Major turned towards Ogilvie. 'Sir! Do you confirm Mr Dewar's order?'

'I – ' Ogilvie broke off, staring. All attention shifted towards where he was looking: a thin, white-faced figure had appeared in the flap of the tent that housed the officers' sick quarters, a figure bare to the waist, wearing only a white towel around the loins – a travesty with staring, red-rimmed eyes and a thin white hand clutching for support the shoulder of a scared medical orderly. *'Colonel!'*

At the run, the Surgeon Major went across to the sick man. The Colonel's voice came out thinly, but was heard clearly in the sudden appalled hush: 'Make away with this disgrace immediately. Mr Dewar is right. Sar'nt-Major . . . '

'Sir!'

Lord Dornoch's mouth opened, but he was not heard to say more. Gently the doctor took his arm and, together with the orderly, half carried him back into the tent. The Regimental Sergeant-Major caught Ogilvie's eye. 'Sir! With your permission.' Without waiting for any answer, he marched to the gates, straight-backed and square and eagle-eyed as ever, left hand clasping his pace-stick at precisely the right angle. He halted in front of the men and lifted his voice high.

'You heard the Colonel! You heard Mr Dewar! Get away from here *at the double* . . . and if I catch up with any stragglers they'll hang in the civil gaol in Peshawar after being stripped of their regimental badges! *Move!*'

FIFTEEN

'THE COLONEL – how is he?'

Corton had just come from sick quarters. 'No worse, James, thank God, in spite of his foolishness, but still a very sick man. So's Andrew. You're still in the saddle.'

Ogilvie stared around. Cunningham, his orders obeyed with a good deal of haste, was marching back to join the others at the gateway, and all around men were back to normal, watching, guarding, patrolling the walls against the enemy. 'Well, Sar'nt-Major?'

'All over, sir. I don't expect more trouble, not for now anyway. It was the sight of the Colonel that did the trick, I believe, sir. Almost as though God had decided to act, sir.'

'God?'

'To send out the Colonel, sir. The men have great affection and respect for him, sir.'

'Yes, I know, Sar'nt-Major, but we shall have to manage without him a while longer yet. Have you anything further to report?'

There was an almost devilish look in the Regimental Sergeant-Major's eye. 'I had a word with Private Meldrum, sir.'

'And?'

'I think the men are now without a leader, sir. Private Meldrum, sir, sees the error of his ways and has a regard for his perishing neck, sir. I shall – ' Cunningham broke off, swinging round and staring. From beyond the walls there had come a burst of rifle-fire followed by savage shouting. With Ogilvie and Dewar the R.S.M. ran for the south para-

pet, taking the steps two at a time. They looked down: a
cloud of dust was rising, some distance off. In their field-
glasses they saw clearly four figures in a group, bunched
together inside a ring of the native rifles: a long, scraggy
man in clerical black, another in a dark frock-coat, and two
women in long dresses that trailed the ground. One of the
latter carried a white flag. All of them were being prodded
by the bayonets on the rifles.

It was Cunningham who broke the startled silence. 'What
is the meaning of this, sir?'

'They've been wanting to parley,' Ogilvie said. 'Captain
Black told me . . . it never occurred to anyone they'd take
matters into their own hands! There's courage for you,
Sar'nt-Major!'

'Aye, and foolishness too, sir.' Cunningham's voice held
hard anger. 'They should have been stopped, but we've all
been blind to everything this last hour – '

'How could they have got out – how could they have got
past the gates?'

'They'd not have done that, sir. You know as well as I do,
Captain Ogilvie, there are scaling-ladders laid along the
parapet ready for use – and they've used them!' He stared
through his field-glasses. 'Have they gone out to talk peace,
or what, sir?'

'Peace,' Ogilvie said, 'and to give themselves up as hostages, to ensure us safe passage out.' He looked bleakly down.

Cunningham muttered something under his breath. Then
he said, 'A hard decision for you, Captain Ogilvie, sir.'

'My decision's made, Sar'nt-Major.'

Cunningham glanced quickly at his set face. 'No rescue,
sir?'

'No rescue, Sar'nt-Major. We wouldn't have a hope, and
there's the sick as always. We have to think of them first, and
none of those missionaries would have it otherwise for one
moment. We have to remain intact until relief comes, Mr
Cunningham.'

There was a pause, then Cunningham said heavily, 'Aye,
sir, you're right, of course.' He glanced at Dewar. The sub-

altern was looking white around the gills, and his hands were shaking. Sardonically, Cunningham thought of Dewar's recent promise to the men: most probably he was now seeing himself, like the missionaries, in the tribesmen's hands. There was no more shouting now, but there was a sudden movement of the natives: more dust rose up as they closed in, there was a scuffle, and the white flag went down, to lie with its pole, pathetically, under the natives' trampling feet. Ogilvie shook his head in utter disbelief that anyone could have been so foolish as ever again to risk a flag of truce outside Kalundabad. *If it had not been for Hamish Dewar . . .* but it was pointless now to have such thoughts! Ogilvie looked along the walls: more men had come up to watch, to watch in a stunned silence, all of them knowing inside that something horrible was about to happen, none of them knowing what would be the form. Overhead vultures circled, dipping, swooping, floating up again, black and beaky beneath a harsh sky of burnished steel, filthy birds whose ravening appetites had not been slaked even by the meals so amply provided by the cholera in the interval between death and disposal. Then, as the Scots soldiers watched, the missionaries were thrown to the ground and secured with rope to heavy stakes driven in by the tribesmen. After this a horseman galloped across from the group towards the gun-batteries opposite the gateway, carrying another man on his pillion. Rider and passenger vanished behind the batteries: a few minutes later the horseman rode back alone across the hard, sun-baked ground. Behind him, his former passenger was seen seated behind the flapping ears of a great elephant that came lumbering like a moving mountain out from the compound in rear of the guns.

Beside Ogilvie, Cunningham swore roundly. 'By God, sir, can we not do something? We must bring down the elephant, Captain Ogilvie!'

His face almost bloodless as imagination drew terrible pictures, Ogilvie looked along the line of watching men. 'Stand to!' he called. 'Aim for the elephant and its mahout. Fire independently as soon as you've taken aim.'

The firing started on the instant, the Scots rifles crashing out from the gates and along the south parapet. The great gun-elephant lifted its trunk, and loudly trumpeted: its mahout shook a fist towards the city. The only effect the rifle fire had was to speed the elephant on its way. Trunk lifted still, ears flapping like sails, the huge animal gathered way and hurtled with earth-shaking feet towards the group of captives, helpless between the stakes, flat upon the ground. Ogilvie, staring in horror, felt Cunningham's hand on his arm.

'Turn your back, Captain Ogilvie, sir. Do not watch, sir, I beg you!' The R.S.M. had himself turned his back and was staring blindly across the city. Ogilvie followed the old soldier's advice, and Cunningham went on in a low, hard voice, 'It's what the tribes do to their criminals. It's to be a criminal's death . . . like Jesus, Captain Ogilvie, like Jesus. Those poor souls followed Jesus, and now may He have mercy upon them, and upon us.'

*　　*　　*

When it was over, a fast return to current problems became an unspoken necessity as if by common consent. Horror and revulsion sat heavily and would go on doing so, but all a sensible man could do was to hope to forget in time. As they went back down the steps Ogilvie, sounding strained and unnatural, forced their attention back to those current problems. 'You reported, I think, Sar'nt-Major, that you expected no more trouble from the men?'

Cunningham made an obvious effort. 'Sir! Yes, that is correct, now that Meldrum's been dealt with especially. Even so, there is a proviso, Captain Ogilvie.'

'And that is?'

Cunningham turned his gaze on Hamish Dewar, where the shock of the recent carnage showed plainly in a quivering face. There was something formidable, something threatening in the Regimental Sergeant-Major's look: it was not normally a look he turned upon officers. He said, speaking to Ogilvie, 'It is now entirely up to Mr Dewar, sir. The men are watching and waiting.'

'For what?' Ogilvie was still dazed.

'For Mr Dewar's action, sir!'

'Yes, Sar'nt-Major, I understand. Mr Dewar will, of course, do as he told the men he would do.'

'Just a moment,' Dewar said loudly.

The R.S.M. bristled at him. '*Just a moment, Mr Dewar?* Sir! A statement was made, and –'

'What statement?' Dewar's lower lip thrust forward belligerently. Already personal considerations, personal perils, were set to blur the outlines of the appalling scene beyond the walls. 'Tell me, Sar'nt-Major, exactly what I said, if you please?'

'Sir! You said this: "Nevertheless I shall save you" . . . referring to the men as I took it, Mr Dewar. You went on to say, "I am going out towards the enemy of my own free will." Sir!'

Dewar nodded. 'Quite correct. But there was a condition –'

'Which has been met, Mr Dewar.'

'Yes. That's true. But now I'm making another –'

'Mr Dewar, sir!' Cunningham's tone showed pure shock and utter disbelief that he could have heard correctly. 'Do you leave bravery to missionaries alone, then?'

'Do me the courtesy of listening!' Dewar snapped back. 'What, exactly, were my words again? Did I not say, by your own admission when you quoted me, that I intended *going out towards the enemy* of my own free will? Was not *that* what I said, Mr Cunningham?'

'It was, sir.'

'Thank you!' Dewar gave a cold smile. 'I intend doing precisely that. I am going out towards the enemy – not now, but after dark. *Towards* the enemy, gentlemen! If you think I mean to give myself up to the damn natives as a human sacrifice, especially after what we've just seen them do to those poor bloody missionaries, then we have failed to understand one another. Now, James, a word in your ear if you please.'

'I think some explanation would be in order first,' Ogilvie said. 'It seems to me you're making a play on words and meanings, and – '

'Come now, James, I mean to do this in my own way, and no one else's.' Dewar waved a hand around the walls and the ruined, rubble-filled gateway, around the tented sick quarters and the fallen masonry of the nearer alleys. 'Do you wish all this to be over-run, and ourselves slaughtered, blown to pieces by the guns outside? Do you?'

Ogilvie snapped, 'Of course not!'

'Then come, James, come with me to the walls. Mr Cunningham too, if he wishes.' Dewar paused. 'I'll not waste your time, I promise you!'

'All right,' Ogilvie said, shrugging. 'Sar'nt-Major?'

'I'll come, sir.'

Dewar led the way to the steps, the other two climbing behind him to the parapet. They looked out over a brooding silence, towards the nearer foothills and beyond to the great rearing crests of the Panirs in the far distance – snow-capped, remote, mysterious. They looked down at the encamped army of Fazrullah Sahib, its leader dead at Hamish Dewar's hands, down at the heavy gun-battery still drawn up to face the gates into Kalundabad.

'Well, Hamish?'

Dewar looked at Ogilvie, shaking his head and frowning.

'Do you notice nothing?' he asked curiously. 'Nothing at all different?'

'There's a coolish breeze,' Ogilvie said, lifting his head to it as it came down from the north.

'Nothing else?'

Ogilvie hesitated. 'Perhaps. I don't know. A silence?'

'That's it!' Dewar said eagerly. 'There's usually been movement in their camp, hasn't there? And that *bloody* music, or what they call music. Tin discord, I call it. Now there's nothing. They were quiet earlier too – before that horrible business with the missonaries. Isn't that a little odd?'

168

'Odd in what way, Mr Dewar?' Cunningham asked.

'Well, I don't know! I'm not used to the Frontier, am I?' Dewar was heavily sarcastic now. 'To me it suggests the calm before the storm. I could be wrong, of course.'

'You mean they're going to attack, Hamish?'

Dewar nodded. 'That's my impression, yes. There's another thing. When I was up here earlier . . . before that wretched Meldrum began his shouting . . . I was watching the guns.'

'Well?'

'They were being inspected, checked. I swear they were! A native wearing one of those decorated jackets, and red pantaloons or whatever they call them. An important native, in other words.'

'So?'

Dewar said, 'Well, I suppose it's just an impression really, but I think they're working up to something. If they are, you realise what that means – or might mean, anyway?'

Ogilvie and Cunningham exchanged looks: each was aware of a mounting excitement. It was Cunningham who spoke first: 'A relief, sir?'

'It's possible,' Dewar said in a dispassionate tone. 'The words reached them, and they're getting ready for action – '

'You may be right indeed.' Ogilvie turned interrogatively to Cunningham. 'What d'you think, Sar'nt-Major?'

'It follows, Captain Ogilvie, sir.'

'Well, if they do attack, we're as ready as we can be to meet them, but I've no great hopes of victory!'

'We shall give a good account of ourselves, sir, nevertheless,' Cunningham said, lifting a hand to twist the end of his moustache. 'My first anxiety is for the sick.'

'Mine too, Sar'nt-Major.' Ogilvie swung round on Dewar. 'What's the connection, Hamish?'

'Connection?'

'With your proposal to . . . what was it? Go out towards the enemy. You brought us up here to – '

'Yes. Oh, it's just that I shall take the appropriate action to deal with the situation, that's all.' Dewar sounded quite

casual, almost off-hand about it. 'As I said, if you can bear
the repetition, I shall go out towards the enemy, towards his
bloody guns, James, after dark tonight, and blow them up.
That's all. It should be easy enough. Of course I'll need your
permission, but I don't suppose you'll have any objections,
will you? It's a way out, isn't it? A way of killing two birds
with one stone, you might say.'

* * *

It would be a deliberate sacrifice, so much was clear: Hamish
Dewar would have little hope of survival in his lone attack
upon the batteries – and lone it would be, for he refused any
assistance. 'My show entirely, James,' he said later when the
two were alone. He said it with finality. 'It seems I got the
battalion into a mess, now it's up to me to get them out so
far as I can. I *want* to do it this way.'

'How do you mean to do it?'

'Oh, I'll bunk out over your pile of rubble and trust to
speed and darkness. And silence, of course. You'll have your
dispositions to make inside the city, with the sick in mind –
in case anything goes wrong.' Dewar grinned. 'Make them
quietly, James! If you use old Bosom Cunningham to spread
the orders, for God's sake tell him to use his bedroom voice,
not his parade-ground one. Or do you think he even yells at
his poor bloody wife?'

'You're making it sound easy, aren't you? What about the
actual blowing up?'

'Hand grenades, old man! Hand-grenades rammed down
each of the gun-barrels, behind a powder charge that I'll get
from Bingham. When that lot is tamped down hard and fast,
and blown, it'll split the bloody breech blocks to Kingdom
Come, won't it?'

There were also the gun sentries to be dealt with: Dewar
saw no difficulties there either. He was full of confidence,
confidence which Ogilvie felt was no act. Hamish Dewar had
dreamed up a plan, Hamish Dewar had decided upon it,
ergo, it must be possible and what was possible would be

done. There were dangers insofar as the priming of the gun-barrels would take time: time in which the enemy would move to protect his artillery. Dewar might not have enough time to complete the job; and again there was the certainty he would in any case be killed or captured.

'Not captured, James. I'll take good care of that! I'll keep the last bullet in my revolver for myself.'

'You'd do that?'

'Rather than be taken by the natives, yes. It's my way, old man. Damn it all, I've seen the mood of the regiment – I'm not that insensitive! Today, they'd have taken charge and handed me over without giving a fig. I had to have an alternative, hadn't I? This one strikes me as being as good as any.' He added somewhat self-consciously. 'I don't mind dying all that much. We all have to go sometime. That's trite, isn't it? But it's true too. At times like this, it helps, to remind oneself of it. I take it – if I might be melodramatic for a moment – the past'll be forgiven and forgotten?'

'Of course it will.'

'I'd like that, for my father's sake chiefly. He's a military-minded old boy, you know, and I can't let down the clan. The Bruce, Prince Charles Edward and all that. It means a lot to the Earls of Taymouth not to have their escutcheon blotted! I've been thinking. It was rather a poor business – that flag of truce.'

'That's over and done with now.'

Dewar laughed. 'You mean it *will* be – once I've buzzed off out of those bloody gates tonight! Oh well, let's hope there won't be a moon, that's all.'

* * *

Dewar, his cut face patched now by the doctor, went into a huddle with Captain Bingham of the artillery, discussing the theory of grenades and gunpowder charges.

'It could work,' Bingham said, though he looked dubious. 'If they'd been the old muzzle-loaders – you know, the ones the British Army reverted to for a while in the seventies, God knows why – then it'd have been easy enough. Just a straight-forward job of spiking, closing up the vent in the breech, literally, with an iron spike. The breech-block's a tougher proposition altogether. Remember, the thing is *built* to withstand the explosion of a charge in the barrel –'

'But plenty of tamping down the muzzles, Bingham –'

Bingham shook his head. 'I'd not rely on it. The best thing you can do is to place your hand-grenade and charge in the open breech, I think, pack 'em hard with clay, and hope you'll blow off the closing mechanism. If you can, well, that'll be one hundred per cent effective in stopping them being used again.'

'What, really, are the chances?'

'Fifty-fifty,' Bingham said, shrugging. 'Worth a try – since you've the guts to suggest it, Dewar! More than I'd care to do . . . but you can count me in if you want –'

'No. This is going to be my own show.'

'But you –'

'No! I mean that. I'm going it alone. All I want from you is advice, thank you.'

'Oh – very well then,' Bingham said with a touch of coolness at Dewar's angry tone. 'You shall have that, of course. Ready for the details?'

'Yes.'

Bingham put a hand on his shoulder. 'Come along to my armoury, if you can call it that, and have a word with my battery Sar'nt-Major. I'd suggest fuses – you'll never have the time to release the handles individually and count the seconds – but a fuse-trail leading to the charges . . . '

They moved away. Whilst they conferred, Ogilvie was organising, or re-organising, the city's defences. As unobtrusively as possible, the blocking of the gateway was extended with more of the rubble that littered the maze of alleys. Once their guns had been destroyed, the tribesmen would get in only by an infantry assault, and the walls were strong. An attack would meet with a fairly withering fire

172

from the defence: and Ogilvie, speaking to the assembled officers and N.C.O.s, instructed them that, in the event of the gateway being forced by the superior numbers outside, then the companies were to withdraw from the walls and form up between the gates and the sick quarters, holding off the assault for as long as was humanly possible in the hope that at least the sick could be preserved until relief marched in.

'Do we form square?' Robin Stuart asked, only half seriously.

'That's the idea,' Ogilvie answered, beating at the swarming flies that rose from the dung-heaps and other refuse that had not yet been burned. 'In this situation, the good old British square really is the best defence, so we'll use it – '

General Fettleworth,' Stuart interrupted with a chuckle, 'would be proud of you!'

Ogilvie grinned back. 'By the same token, he'd probably say the guns weren't worth the effort of destroying them!' Bloody Francis Fettleworth had always taken a distinctly hostile view of artillery: it was noisy and smelly and in his opinion ineffective, always landing its shells in inappropriate places, making much ado about nothing. The effect of shells, Fettleworth always maintained, was out of all proportion to their thunder: just a few square yards of earth shifted and that was all. Artillery detracted from the glory of the infantry, the everlasting Queen of Battles; and he revelled in the British square, self-replacing of casualties, ever firing, ever sure. Ogilvie continued with his orders to cover all foreseeable contingencies after the departure of Hamish Dewar, which would take place at eleven p.m. and would be covered by a diversionary move to the east where E Company would commence rifle-fire and appear to be sending men over the wall on the scaling ladders to mount an attack. Disregarding the probable advice of General Fettleworth were he there to give it, Ogilvie ordered Bingham to bring his mountain battery towards the gate area and have his guns assembled and positioned on the flanks of the infantry's squares, to blast away at any sizeable inpouring of tribesmen.

173

All-in-all, there was fair confidence in the air as the officers and N.C.O.s dispersed.

* * *

At ten-thirty that night, the whole battalion was counting the minutes. There was a moon; but by the grace of God there was also broken cloud stretching as it seemed back to those high peaks of Himalaya. Dewar would have to take advantage of that helpful cloud and make his moves beneath its spasmodic umbrella.

At the gates, Dewar himself, his face blackened with charcoal, waited with Ogilvie and the Regimental Sergeant-Major. Their nerves twitched badly as the seconds ticked away on Ogilvie's watch. At one minute to eleven o'clock, Ogilvie nodded at Cunningham, who lifted a lighted storm-lantern high above his head. A moment later, at the head of the tall tower, another lantern was seen. As its light disappeared again, a volley of rifle-fire crashed out from the eastern wall. Sweat glistened on the faces of the waiting men by the gate – glistened as the clouds failed them, and admitted moonlight to the earth. Ogilvie clenched his fists, and swore. Dewar was morose and tense now, his earlier confidence seeming to have deserted him when he most needed it. To the east the firing continued: from the wall to the south of the gate, a runner came to report commotion among the tribesmen, of men streaming towards the east. A similar report came from the north wall: the moment, but for the moon, was propitious.

'Damn it all, I'll go now and chance it,' Dewar said.

'No!' Ogilvie reached out a hand. 'The diversion'll last a while yet. Wait for more darkness, Hamish.'

'But – '

'That's an order. We're not going off at half cock now. Anyway – look!' Ogilvie pointed up at the sky: cloud was sailing close to the moon again, a long and wide patch of dark moving with majesty across the heavens. 'Just one more minute, Hamish!'

174

One more minute: it seemed an age, but the moon compliantly vanished: the dark came down, black as ink, an excellent cloak.

'Now,' Ogilvie said, and held out a hand. Dewar took it in a strong grasp. 'Good luck, Hamish.'

'Thanks. Remember what you said. There won't be enough left of me for a military funeral, I suppose, but you'll see to the rest, James?'

'With my last breath.'

There was a light laugh, and Dewar was gone, climbing swiftly up the rubble with his bags of hand-grenades and charges and packing material hanging from hooks on his Sam Browne Belt, fuses and matches in his pockets, the stars of his rank removed from his shoulders along with his tunic buttons, so that any returning moonlight should not strike fire from polished brass. At the top of the pile of rubble he gave a last wave and then slid down the other side. The watching officers heard the slither of stones, then there was silence.

SIXTEEN

'CHOTA-PEG. AND ONE for the Brigadier-General Sahib.'

'Yes, General Sahib.' The bearer, a venerable, white-bearded old man wearing a turban and a long coat, backed away, salaaming, from Bloody Francis. The Divisional Commander appeared to be worried: and when the Divisional Commander was worried, the lives of Indians were not worth the living. The General Sahib had the look of a man with an itching boot, and had he succumbed to that itch and planted the boot firmly in his elderly bearer's backside, it would not have been for the first time. The bearer left the cool verandah, moving into the bungalow behind where the punkahs, stirred continually by the string attached to the big toe of the patient punkah-wallah outside, kept the air relatively pleasant. *Chota-pegs* at the command of the General Sahib, and may a thousand million devils castigate the porcine stomach of the General Sahib upon his eventual retirement to his bed . . .

'Damned if I like it,' Fettleworth said petulantly to the Chief of Staff. 'Damned if I do! Not a damn word from any-one.' He gnawed at his moustache, fretfully, his blue eyes even more protuberant than usual.

'No, sir.'

'Like as not, all Dornoch's regiment is dead of the damn cholera!'

'A pessimistic view, sir –'

'Well, why not? We have to face the possibilities, Laken-ham, not bury our heads in the sand! And where's Fortescue, I'd like to know!'

176

'The brigade should be well through the Malakand by now.'

'*Should* be – oh, yes!' Fettleworth mopped at his sweating face and neck. 'Damn this bloody heat. Should be is all very well. The point is – *is* he?'

The question being seemingly rhetorical, Brigadier-General Lakenham left it unanswered. In all truth, he too was worried: not a word, as Fettleworth had said, not for the first time these last few days, from anyone at all – except Calcutta, where the Civilians were sharpening their knives, albeit paper ones, to the discomfiture of the military. Sharp words, Calcutta-instigated, had been issuing from Army H.Q. in Murree, where Sir Iain Ogilvie was bearing the main brunt. Nobody seemed to know, least of all Division, what the situation might currently be in Dir, for one thing – the most important thing in the minds of Calcutta's office-wallahs. Dir, and Jahangir Khan's propped-up authority, were in the office-wallahs' eyes the whole reason for the despatch of troops when all was said and done. That very morning, when Bloody Francis had been assailed by what he called 'one of the bloody clerks from Calcutta' in person, Lakenham had been witness to an undignified squabble. The Civilian, a Mr Peters-Henderson, had been undeniably indiscreet when he had suggested that soldiers were, however unfortunate the fact might be, expendable; but that a native ruler was unique.

'Unique my bottom!' Fettleworth had said loudly. 'What's *unique* about Jahangir Khan, may one ask, Mr Peters-Henderson?'

'Ah.' Peters-Henderson removed his spectacles and rubbed thoughtfully at the reddened flesh on the bridge of his rather long nose. 'Unique in the sense that there is only one Jahangir Khan, and that his continued rule is necessary to the Raj – to the balance of power as it were. Should he be deposed through any fault of the military, Whitehall would – '

'Yes, yes, yes!' Fettleworth snapped. 'I take your point I suppose, but unique's a damn silly word to use. So far as that goes, my soldiers are unique too – every blasted one of 'em!

If only to their own mothers! And they are *not* expendable, Mr Peters-Henderson. They are not mere cannon-fodder for the support of a damn bloated princeling with more wives than table manners.'

A gleam had appeared behind the Civilian's replaced spectacles. 'This is how you regard His Highness, Jahangir Khan, General Fettleworth?'

'Of course it is, and so do you if you're honest. Trouble is, you're not! None of you are. You don't face realities in the way we soldiers do. By God –'

'The realities, General,' Peters-Henderson broke in huffily, 'are the power and the money. Soldiers come two a penny – '

'You – '

'Lose even a fragment of our power and influence, and you diminish the Raj out of all proportion to the actual loss. You must agree, General, that the death of a soldier is, shall we say, bearable? Even the loss of a regiment – provided we don't lose the power and the influence.'

'Rubbish!' Fettleworth hooted, waving his arms in the air. 'I shall not put up with such talk – '

'And Calcutta will not, as you will find, put up with such a paucity of results as you have produced, General Fettleworth. Bear that in mind.' Peters-Henderson, while Bloody Francis fumed and muttered, dropped a sheaf of papers into a Gladstone bag, which he then closed with an ominous snapping sound. After a frigid farewell, the Civilian had left in a carriage for the railway station, taking with him an all too evident distaste for the Commander of Her Majesty's First Division – hence, that evening in the cool of the veran- dah, Bloody Francis's worried brow.

'What the devil do they expect me to do?' he asked in an aggrieved tone. 'They never say anything precise, do they? Damn it, Lakenham, I've sent a regiment, and I've sent a brigade in support! Dornoch's walked into cholera, and Fortescue's got lost. It's not my fault! What does Calcutta want me to do? Send the whole damn division – *go myself*?' His eyes swivelled as his bearer came back with a silver tray on which stood whisky-and-soda. After Lakenham, the guest,

178

had taken his glass with a word of thanks, Fettleworth reached out, grabbed, and gulped. There was a frenzied look in his eye, and the bearer gave silent thanks to his own gods that the white sahibs, in their wisdom, had decreed that Indians should leave their presence backwards. Once again, Lakenham treated the last question as rhetorical: any answer would be difficult. But he too sent a brief prayer heavenward: a prayer that God should not put too strongly into the Divisional Commander's head the idea that he might go himself. That way would lie considerable frenzy and disorder ... Lakenham gave an involuntary sigh. Poor Bloody Francis was one of the last officers to have taken his commission by purchase, in the days before the establishment of the Royal Military College at Sandhurst. In the fullness of time, the quality of General Officers would doubtless improve.

*   *   *

In the grim grey tracks of the Malakand Pass the attack on General Fortescue's brigade had come in volleys of sustained rifle-fire from massed tribesmen along the peaks, wild men who had ambushed and killed the advanced scouts and brought down the pickets as they made their rushing descent to re-join the column. Fortescue, dispersing his brigade into such cover as they could find, had fought back hard; but the action had been a long one, and when finally the attack had been beaten off, the casualty count to the British was high in men, horses, mules and wagons – wagons, carrying ammunition in many cases, that had been set on fire or fallen from the high, rocky track down into the splintery fingers of the rough ground below. But the column, mauled and bloody, moved on again after the dead had been decently buried and the wounded tended and bandaged by the medical orderlies and nurses, moved out to the music of fife and drum. With red-stained khaki-drill tunics, with dark patches of sweat beneath the arms, with the Wolseley helmets, bearing the regimental flashes, keeping the cruel sun from men's heads, the relief brigade force-marched out of the pass, the halts for rest and food kept to the strictest minimum. Here and there a man fell out exhausted, to be picked up by the tail of the column and laid for a spell in what remained of the wagons, then turned out on his feet to march again.

In the footsteps of the Royal Strathspey, they came out of the Malakand in due course, emerging into the plain of Swat for the Panjkora. General Fortescue, tall and gaunt, riding his horse ahead of his depleted brigade, could only pray that he would yet arrive in time.

* * *

Hamish Dewar's slither down the rubble filling the city gate had carried him right to its foot, and carried him in merciful darkness. For a couple of minutes he lay where he was, still and silent, listening and looking. From behind him came the sound of Ogilvie's continuing diversionary move, the firing from the farther wall. Ahead of him lay the target of the enemy guns, guns that were currently unmanned, with the draught elephants still in the compound some distance behind. Though unmanned, the guns were not unguarded: Dewar could not in fact see his quarry in the total dark, but his reconnaissance had been adequate to the task: he knew precisely where to head, and he knew the sentries' beats.

Carefully, making no sound, he got to his feet, felt for his revolver, for his hand-grenades and charges.

Very slowly he advanced, keeping an eye on the antics of the clouds above as well as on the ground ahead. He cursed: silver was approaching the fringe of the covering cloud. He dropped flat, just in time, as the moon emerged to sail like a brilliant lantern of danger across the night. The whole area was lit: behind him the city walls stood sharply out, and in front, the gun-batteries, vast and threatening with the great barrels pointing, as it seemed, straight at him. From his recumbent position he watched the slow walk of the sentries, two men, armed with jezails and wearing turbans and rough animal-skin garments to keep out the chill of the night.

Dewar's lips framed a silent, urgent prayer: *Oh God, send*

180

the bloody moon back behind the clouds! But God appeared to be in no hurry: the moonlight stayed, silver-bright – beautiful but lethal. Dewar shifted his cramped limbs, pondering on what his action should be. Should he risk a movement, a slide forward on his stomach, to bring him closer for the strike when the moon should go? If he could get close enough and still remain unseen, perhaps he could shoot down the sentries and carry out his task before the tribesmen in the main encampment around the walls could gather their wits to stop him: perhaps!

To wait would be the wiser course, but Hamish Dewar was not cut out for waiting.

He began to move.

*   *   *

'Sir!' The Regimental Sergeant-Major was keeping his voice as well as his body low as he watched from an embrasure on the wall close by the gateway. 'Mr Dewar's moving, sir!'

Ogilvie joined him. 'God, the bloody fool!'

'I don't know so much, sir. Time must be taken into account. We'll not get away with our diversion much longer, sir.'

'But that moon!'

'Aye, it's going to be tricky, sir, but he's not been seen yet.' Cunningham watched closely through his field-glasses, as did Ogilvie. As usual, the city was ringed with the camp fires, and there seemed tonight to be some restive movement among the elephants in the compound. Along the walls the Scots kept watch over the surrounding tribesmen, ready to report any movement towards the gun batteries. To the east the diversionary firing was being maintained while the rest of the battalion, and the mountain batteries whose guns were now ready for immediate action, waited between the gates and the sick lines, waited for the possible inrush of the native hordes. They would not easily give ground. Ogilvie, looking down on them from the walls, hardly dared think about the dawn. When that dawn came over the mountain peaks, the

Royal Strathspeys might well have ceased to exist. Looking through his glasses, he saw that Dewar had stopped again. Still he appeared to be unseen except from the wall's height. Still the sentries paced in front of the guns, their attention clearly on the firing in the east. There had been more movement of tribesmen towards the diversion: not much, in fact, but enough to withdraw some strength, and enough to help clear the ground for Hamish Dewar, put more space between his target and the nearer enemy infantry concentration.

Ogilvie looked up: there was shadow again, spreading out from the hills – more cloud! Again the moon's light was dimmed to extinction. Now he could no longer see Dewar. It would be a question of waiting, a time of nail-biting and hoping and praying, until the explosions sent back, thunderously, their undoubted signal of success. Within a minute of the descent of the friendly dark, Ogilvie heard a sound: what seemed to be a cry, strangled almost before it had come. Soon after, another – similar but louder, and followed by the beginning of a scream.

Ogilvie felt the tension in Cunningham as the R.S.M. spoke. 'That'll be Mr Dewar, sir, dealing with the sentries. He'll be placing his charges any moment now.' Cunningham wiped his sweat-streaked face. 'I've a feeling it's going to go all right, sir!'

*　　*　　*

Dewar looked down contemptuously on the twisted bodies of the native guards, one strangled, the other with his throat bayonet-slitted and with blood still soaking into his filthy garments. After that one look of hate, Dewar wasted no time. Running for the first of the guns, still unseen, he swung open the breech and placed his hand-grenade and powder charge, packed them down with clay, fixed his fuse-line to the charge and for the moment left it dangling. On then to the next gun in the battery line, then the next . . . it all took time, and in spite of the night cold, Dewar was sweat-soaked and panting by the time all his grenades and charges were in place. It was nerve-tingling work too: throughout, an eye and a half had to be kept on the perimeter of the battery. In the event he had not been disturbed by anything other than the menacing sounds from the elephants, who seemed to know something was amiss. In the occasional light of the fitful moon he had seen them, moving restlessly, jerking at the ropes that held them tethered, jerking so that once or twice Dewar had seen the stakes move a little in the ground. There had been a thump of monstrous feet, a sail-like flap of outlandish ears, and now and again the moon had lit upon small, red-glowing eyes that had appeared concentrated solely upon Hamish Dewar, concentrated and filled with malevolent hate . . .

The charges set, Dewar ran back to each of the breach-blocks, gathering up the fuse-lines and bringing them together to a point where the igniting of them would give him good time to run for safety before the fizzing sparks took the charges. The last of the job was done: squatting on his haunches, Dewar felt for his matches. Striking flame, cupping it in his hands, he lit the fuses, watching until all the snaking trails had caught.

Then he ran for his life.

*   *   *

The watching men on the walls saw the thin sparkle moving along the ground, a worm of reddish fire, followed by another, and another in quick succession as the tiny trails ran on their set courses for the native guns. *Too slow – too visible?* Ogilvie felt a shake in his hands as he waited. Then it came, seeming to rock the very hills, to burst the world asunder: a series of shattering explosions, the first two singly, the remainder erupting simultaneously as the great guns blew up, the breech-blocks smashing under the impact of the grenades and powder charges, wedged firmly into place in accordance with Bingham's advice. The scene stood out in vivid light as the explosions threw chunks of broken, jagged metal in all directions, some of them coming over the walls to clatter into the city's rubble. In three instances the exploding charges failed to dislodge the closing mechanism of the breeches, but in three only: and in one of these instances the hand-grenade leapt from the breech, spun through the air and dropped. There was a further gigantic explosion as the grenade blew up in the stowage box containing action-ready charges handy by the guns. There was a roar and a dense cloud of smoke fringing a white-hot blast of flame. As more fragments flew out and up, Ogilvie and the others along the wall ducked down below the parapet: and then through the embrasures saw, in the wicked light from the fires, the running figure of Hamish Dewar, pelting for the gates while a body of tribesmen rushed towards their broken batteries. Then there came a fresh sound, over-riding the now dying explosions: a terrible trumpeting, a maddened animal-sound of rage and fear.

Stuart grasped Ogilvie's arm. 'The elephants!' he shouted. 'They're on the move – broken out from the compound! Look at them!'

Ogilvie stared. Clear of the smoke and flame still surrounding the smashed guns huge forms were on the move, trunks raised high, screaming their fury and their terror – great grey hides like mobile buildings rushing like the very wind towards Hamish Dewar and the city gates.

SEVENTEEN

OGILVIE'S VOICE CARRIED through the night, trying to compete with that furious trumpeting: 'Covering fire, Sar'nt-Major! Every man on the walls . . . shoot to deflect the elephants!'

The bullets sped down, spattering uselessly off the thick hides. One, a purely lucky shot that took one of the beasts between the eyes, brought its great victim down screaming, sinking heavily to its knees like a torpedoed battleship, not so far behind Dewar. Then Dewar himself went down flat on his face, and lay still. Ogilvie, turning on Robin Stuart, shouted: 'He's got to be brought back. I'll not send any of the men. Are you game, Robin?'

'You and me?'

'Yes!'

'All right, I'm with you.'

'Good man!' Ogilvie raced for the steps, flung himself down followed closely by Stuart. Stumbling over stones and rubble, the two officers went fast for the gateway and began climbing up the debris that blocked it. Their chests heaving, they made the top. They were about to start down the other side when a sergeant at the top of the pile called to Ogilvie.

'Where are you going, sir?'

'To get Mr Dewar in –'

'It's too late, sir. The –'

'What d'you mean, man, too late?' Ogilvie stared from a dust-streaked face. 'Those elephants'll –'

'No, sir! The bloody natives, sir – they've got Mr Dewar. Two horsemen rode across behind the stampede –' The sergeant broke off, staring outwards. '*Look out, sir* – get back down for your life!'

Ogilvie caught just a glimpse of a huge body charging for the pile of rubble, then the sergeant had given him a push that sent him slithering down the slope to comparative safety. Behind him came Stuart, head first, in clouds of dust, and the sergeant. As they scrambled to their feet, an earthquake seemed to hit the rubble. Rocks flew off the pile and crashed to the ground, just missing the running men. The whole mass shook and trembled, small pieces of the rubble dislodging in a cascade, then there came a fresh onslaught as another of the charging, frenzied elephants slammed into it.

Ogilvie ran for the mountain battery. 'Come on, Bingham!' he shouted. 'You've got your chance – aim through the gates, and be quick about it!'

Bingham's voice was exultant now: 'We're all ready, Ogilvie, and we'll not keep you waiting!' He gave a signal to his sergeant, and the line of guns opened on the instant in shattering sound and a vomit of smoke and flame. There was a wave of sharp, acrid smell and the rubble flew in all directions, pounded by the exploding shells. For a moment the great trunk, the vast ears and tiny eyes of an elephant were seen beyond, the animal stock-still and the trunk lifted in a scream, and then the picture vanished as a shell took the brute smack in the face, exploding and fragmenting the animal into strips of bloody flesh. There was more screaming and a thunder of heavy pounding feet as the guns ceased fire on Bingham's order. The watchers from inside the gates, as once more the moon sailed out high and bright, saw the other animals turn aside to right and left and pound into the enemy lines, scattering the natives, bringing confusion and terror as they ran amok seeking victims.

'What now?' Bingham asked, grinning like a devil as the moonbeams struck silver fire from his badges of rank. 'Go after 'em and give 'em bloody hell, I say!'

Ogilvie's response was short: 'They've got Dewar.'

'*Have* they, by jove! What are you going to do?'

'Get him out, of course.'

186

'Get him out? But he's done what he himself wanted – '

'He's blown up the guns, Bingham. He's given us a fighting chance. He meant to put a bullet in himself if he looked like being captured . . . I'm not leaving him in the hands of Fazrullah Sahib's successor!'

Slowly, Bingham nodded, standing in the flooding moonlight with his hands on his hips. 'Well, I don't blame you. I'll bet that successor's no sahib when it comes to one of us! What d'you want of my guns, Ogilvie?'

'Just cover the gate, that's all. Open fire without further orders if any sizeable body of natives tries to enter. Small detachments can be left to my chaps to pick off with rifle-fire.' Ogilvie turned as someone came up fast. 'Ah – Sar'nt-Major – '

'I've just been told about Mr Dewar, sir. The men want to cut him out, sir – '

'The men?'

Cunningham wiped streaming sweat from his face. 'Aye, Captain Ogilvie, sir, the men. Things have changed now. They're all good lads at heart, sir – '

'I never doubted that! Well, they'll have their wish, Sar'nt-Major. I'm going out myself. I'll take B Company, and Captain Stuart will remain in charge inside the city.'

'I'll come with you, sir – '

'No.' Ogilvie met Cunningham's eyes. 'I'm sorry, Sar'nt-Major, but that's final. I want you here as a stiffener for the defence – we mustn't forget the sick. Have B Company formed up to advance, if you please, Sar'nt-Major, at once.'

'Sir!' The Regimental Sergeant-Major gave a crashing salute: turning about, he strode away. Ogilvie followed on towards the gateway, under the long shadow of the wall. Outside, the elephants could still be heard, loudly angry, and there was a good deal of firing. Ogilvie caught Cunningham up, found him giving Colour-Sergeant Mac-Trease the orders for B Company's foray.

Seeing Ogilvie, MacTrease saluted. 'We're all ready, sir.'

'Then we'll not delay.' Ogilvie turned to his company. 'We're going out to get Mr Dewar. We can assume he's being

187

taken to the enemy command post, and our job is to reach him before he gets there. Keep together unless I pass the word to scatter. You all know what happens to anyone who's captured. That being so, I'm not detailing anyone. I want volunteers. Any man who prefers not to go may fall out now and there'll be no recriminations.'

No one moved. Ogilvie allowed a few more precious seconds, then said, 'Thank you – all of you. I'm hoping the elephants will have proved a fairly effective preliminary bombardment in their own right!' He glanced at MacTrease. 'Carry on, Colour-Sar'nt – a quiet advance, no highland yells – but fast as we can go!'

Within half a minute, B Company was scrambling across the remaining rubble. In the lead, Ogilvie brought out his watch: four minutes only since the sergeant at the gateway had reported Dewar seized by the horsemen, but possibly four minutes too long. Doubling round the outside of the walls, looking for leads, Ogilvie felt the irony of the situation: so short a while ago, the whole battalion had wanted nothing so much as Hamish Dewar's departure enemy-wards; now, they were raring to cut him out again. Such was the change wrought by an obvious display of guts. Guts or not, however, Ogilvie found himself wishing devoutly that Dewar had never made his exchange into the Royal Strathspeys: the man was a confounded embarrassment who had now led him into doing what he had adamantly refused all along to do: make a sortie, and thus, perhaps, expose the sick to slaughter. What the Colonel would say, Ogilvie knew not; but felt, deep inside, that in fact there had been no choice.

B Company plunged on, finding no opposition yet. The elephants had indeed cleared the way very nicely, all the natives in the vicinity of the gate having beat it ahead of the thundering feet. Fire-crackers were being let off and there was a lot of rifle-fire that had an undisciplined, ragged sound about it, to the south of the city walls, and a few moments later Ogilvie was able to assess what was happening: it was an attempt at deflection, clearly, for ahead in the moonlight he caught sight of the stampeding herd, sheering off to the right and turning, and continuing to turn until the fresh target of the advancing Scots caught their attention, and they steadied, and charged down towards the soldiers.

'Keep together!' Ogilvie called. 'Fire independently, Colour-Sar'nt.'

MacTrease gave a brief nod and fired himself towards the charging elephants. There was a fusillade of shots, and some of the men threw hand-grenades to burst in the faces of the monstrous animals. As the fire was maintained at a high rate, the elephants divided to right and left of the explosions and pin-points of light, thundering down close beside the terrified men. There was a scream from one of the privates who had failed to dodge in time – a long-drawn sound of agony. With MacTrease, Ogilvie ran on behind his company, sprinting ahead through the ranks to take the lead, keeping his eyes skinned for any horseman with a human burden in tow, finding nothing, well aware that once Hamish Dewar reached the enemy field headquarters it was going to take more than one company of infantry to cut him out . . .

'Sir! Captain Ogilvie, sir!'

MacTrease was shouting, yelling.

'Yes, Colour-Sar'nt?'

'To the rear, sir –'

Ogilvie swung round fast. Once again the elephants had turned, their furious trumpeting heralding a renewed attack. Outlined by the silver light of the moon, they looked like something from pre-history, gigantic, roaring, threatening, moving like the wind. For a moment Ogilvie stood and watched as though petrified; then, taking in the direction of the charge, he called to his company.

'No firing! Down on the ground and move back towards the walls. Colour-Sar'nt!'

'Sir!'

'See that the men obey. It'll take guts to lie down, but they've to do it – quietly and fast!'

'Sir!' MacTrease doubled away, pushing men to the ground, not making too much of his voice now, sensing the officer's tactics. Crawling on their stomachs out of the line of the elephants' advance, the men lay still as the great feet smashed their way past them. Some of the Scots were still so close, Ogilvie saw, that they must have felt the wind as the hurtling bodies went past them, but none was hurt. As soon as the last animal had gone, Ogilvie shouted them back on their feet.

'We'll use the elephants as our cavalry spearhead,' he called, 'and double in behind. You'll see where they're heading.' He pointed with his revolver. 'The big tent with the pennons – the enemy's H.Q.' He ran ahead, waving the men on, and they followed, cheering now and yelling, charging on behind their fixed bayonets, the steel shining like living fire in the moonlight. The heathen had got one of their own, a brave officer: he would not be held long provided a well-armed if hungry bunch of Highlanders could, with the welcome help of a battery of maddened elephants, change the situation! One thing was undeniably certain: those elephants, well ahead of the military advance now, were going to change the physical contours of the enemy headquarters – were indeed already doing so. As the men pounded on, they saw the pennons go down in a tangle of rope and rich silk and smashed tent poles. There were screams of terror from the native levies, and in places, as the elephants tore rampaging on, showers of sparks flew up from scattering camp fires, sparks that ignited clothing and parched, tindery grass tufts. The situation appeared to be improving; but still they had not found Hamish Dewar.

Reaching the site of the headquarters tent, Ogilvie called a halt. Here there was sumptuous furnishing: tables decorated in sadeli work, tapestries, soft cushions, carpets – all now in total disarray and spattered with blood. Dead lay around, those who had not got away in time: a fat turbaned native in rich clothing like that of Fazrullah Sahib, with his loins trampled flat. Two other men, of lower estate this time, with heads and chests stove in. Three women, concubines probably, two dead and one cowering, sobbing, half concealed beneath a pile of silken hangings. Setting the men to the business of looking in the wreckage for any sign of Dewar,

190

Ogilvie yanked the woman to her feet. She was young, perhaps no more than eighteen years of age, semi-naked, with tight sharply-nippled breasts, and a peach-like skin, and a precious stone set in her navel to glint and sparkle in the moonlight streaming down. Long, dark hair fell around her breasts as she stared fearfully at Ogilvie.

He spoke to her in Urdu: there was no reply. He tried other tongues with an equal lack of success, then found MacTrease at his side.

'No luck, sir?'

'None.'

'You'll be wishing to know the whereabouts of Mr Dewar, sir. You'll need to persuade the woman, sir.'

'Force?'

'If needs be, sir, yes.' MacTrease met his eye. 'Time is short, sir, and it's a fair way back to the city gates. Leave the woman to me, sir.'

'But she simply doesn't speak any of the dialects!'

'Sir! With respect, you've been long enough on the Frontier . . . Captain Ogilvie, this is no time for chivalry or for protecting the women.' MacTrease paused. 'Leave her to me, sir, please.'

'All right, then.' Ogilvie said shortly. He walked away, turning his back on what he had no wish to see, and joined the men in their poking and probing of the silken ruination of the tent. There were cries, and the harsh voice of MacTrease came; then a long, terrible scream and sobbing that seemed to come from the heart itself. The sobbing continued, but more quietly, as within a couple of minutes MacTrease approached Ogilvie, wiping the blade of a bayonet on a piece of crimson silk.

'Sir! The woman talked, for what it's worth. Mr Dewar is alive yet, but is awaiting death, and under heavy guard. She knows no more than that.' Suddenly, MacTrease's expression altered. 'Sir, look behind you! I think we have delayed too long!'

Turning, Ogilvie saw the silver glitter of long knives shining in the moonlight, knives held by silent-moving, near-naked men with skins agleam with oil. Catching his breath, he ran a glance around the perimeter of the ruined tent and its immediate area. They were totally surrounded, a fact that the men were only just realising. MacTrease said in a low voice, 'We'll not stand for this, sir, will we? We still have our arms.'

Ogilvie nodded. 'And we'll use them!'

MacTrease took a deep breath then yelled the order: 'Stand to, lads, and fire, and keep on bloody firing!'

EIGHTEEN

AT THE FIRST volley of rifle fire from the Scots, the men with the knives vanished, dropping to the ground. Some had died, others had been wounded, but there were too many more to back them up. A trumpet call came from close by, and, swinging round, Ogilvie saw native cavalry charging towards him with lowered lances. The horsemen were upon the Scots before they had had time to react: the squadrons parted to right and left as they thundered up, then pulled up their mounts in a cloud of dust and sat with long points of the lances aimed into the bunched highlanders. From the darkness behind them, an order came in English:

'Throw down your arms, infidel pigs.'

There was a snarl from Colour-Sergeant MacTrease. 'Sons of pigs yersel's, and of bitches too!' He turned to Ogilvie. 'Do we fire, sir?'

'We do not,' Ogilvie answered shortly. 'What good d'you suppose that would do, Colour-Sar'nt?' He raised his voice. 'Lay down your arms, all of you. We have no choice now.'

There was a long clatter as one by one, grudgingly, the rifles were thrown to the ground. No one spoke. Sick at heart, Ogilvie waited for the next move, feeling the men's resentment at an abject surrender, their fear as to what was going to happen to them now. There was not long to wait: as the last rifle was thrown down, the ranks of the cavalry parted and a hook-nosed man, splendidly dressed, rode into the gap flanked by an armed escort. The moon showed strong

193

features: a firm mouth and chin, clean-shaven, and steady eyes. It also showed cruelty, hauteur, an emperor's imperiousness.

Speaking in English this man said, 'Your officer, which is he?'

Ogilvie stepped forward. 'I am in command. Who are you?'

'I also am in command,' the horseman said, showing very white teeth in a smile. 'In command, I think, of many more men than you, Captain Sahib! I am Gaftar Sahib . . . son of Fazrullah Sahib, and now succeeded to my father, and thus, Captain Sahib, now ruler in Dir – '

'That is a matter for dispute, as you well know, Gaftar Sahib – '

'On the part of your people only. I have the full support of mine, and this is all that matters to me, and I think, Captain Sahib, you would be unwise to dispute it – '

'For now perhaps, but a time will come.'

'Then that time shall wait, Captain Sahib – '

'But not long,' Ogilvie said with assurance.

'How so?'

'When a relief comes from Peshawar, then your numbers will not worry us any more. You would do well to have a care, Gaftar Sahib, for the British Raj has a long arm – and as for you, I think you now have few guns capable of firing, thanks to – '

'Thanks to your Dewar Sahib, that part is correct, but your relief force will arrive too late. Already, you see, I have word of its coming, of successful attacks upon it in the Malakand which have reduced its strength. In spite of this reduction, however, I have made plans to withdraw to the north, and fall back upon Dir, where I shall be reinforced by the greatest army yet seen along the North-West Frontier of your piratical Raj, Captain Sahib!' There was every confidence in the leader's voice, every self-assurance of victory. 'We march soon after the dawn, Captain Sahib, but first there are other things to be done.'

'What things?'

'The destruction of your regiment inside the city.'

'You would risk the cholera, Gaftar Sahib, you would expose your men to this?'

'It is a risk of war, and one to which, as my father told you, we are not strangers.'

'And when the British force arrives?'

Gaftar shrugged. 'I have told you, we shall be gone.'

'And the city? Will they not retake the city, Gaftar Sahib?'

'Yes, they will do this, and then they will be struck down by the cholera, which will march on with them.'

'But with you also! Surely it is a stupid thing to do, to enter a fated city, simply to destroy a sick garrison?' Ogilvie paused, staring into the man's arrogant face. 'You are taking a military risk, simply as an act of revenge? Is this the mark of a leader, Gaftar Sahib?'

'*Melmastia* demands that I avenge my father's death at the hands of a so-called sahib who betrayed a flag of truce – '

'Such as you yourself betrayed a flag of truce, when you killed the English missionaries, men and women who wanted only to help. How do you justify such treachery on your own part, Gaftar Sahib?'

'An eye for an eye,' Gaftar said dismissingly. 'The English sahib, your officer, was not delivered up to me. Instead, he came out and destroyed my guns.'

'Where is he now?'

'He is awaiting death, Captain Sahib. I said there were other things to be done, and I have told you only one of them. The second is the death of Dewar Sahib, which will in fact be the signal for our attack upon the city – but you shall see for yourself,' Gaftar added, 'since you shall be witness to the betrayer's death – which shall be a woman's death.' He made a sudden gesture to his waiting cavalrymen, who at once closed in. 'We have spoken enough,' the usurping leader said, and I have much to do. Do not try to break out with your soldiers, for you will be run through with the lances or brought down by the jezails of my foot-soldiers.'

Gaftar turned and rode off with his personal escort, harness jingling in the semi-darkness. Ogilvie felt the sharp tip of a lance bite into his back, and he turned, staring up at the horseman. First in English, then in Urdu, he asked, 'What now?'

The answer came in Urdu: 'For now, nothing but to wait.'

'Wait here?'

'Yes.'

'Where is Dewar Sahib?'

'Waiting also. You will see where, when the dawn comes over the mountain peaks. Now be silent, and wait, and all things will become clear.'

Ogilvie shrugged and looked around the circle of cavalrymen. They were incredibly hard-looking men, dark-skinned, hairy and very watchful; and they outnumbered his company by almost three to one. It was a fairly hopeless situation, as MacTrease also seemed to realise.

'Maybe the elephants'll come back, sir,' the colour-sergeant suggested, 'though I've a feeling they've made a bid for their permanent freedom this time!'

'So have I – and in any case we'd come off worse than the cavalry if they charged us.'

'Better to be trampled to death than . . .'

'Than what, Colour MacTrease?'

'Och, I don't know, sir – we can't tell what the dirty bastards have in store for us and so I'll say no more. In any event, sir, you know the Frontier as well as I do. But I'll say this: I'd sooner take a chance on a break-out, than wait the pleasure o' yon brown-faced –'

'Careful,' Ogilvie warned. 'We don't know how much English these men have. As to a break-out, the answer's no. Just look at those lances!'

MacTrease nodded. 'Aye, you're right, sir, of course. I wouldn't expect success. That wasn't what I meant!'

'I know. But there'll come a time when action could be

196

successful. As soon as I see a chance, I'll take it, you may rely on that, Colour MacTrease!'

* * *

During that long night there was full watchfulness inside Kalundabad, with few men other than those in sick quarters taking any sleep. Bingham was with his mountain guns, covering the gateway, first line of defence for the sick. Robin Stuart maintained his vigil on the south wall, with the Regimental Sergeant-Major. Subalterns were posted at intervals all the way round. The progress of James Ogilvie's sortie had been watched throughout; the surrounding of B Company had brought despondency, and Stuart had gone along to the convalescent tent for a word with Andrew Black, whose bout of cholera had not been severe and who was well on his way now to recovery, though still too weak to resume the command.

'What,' Black asked in a listless voice, 'were Captain Ogilvie's instructions?'

'There were none to cover his capture.'

'And in the case of other eventualities?'

'Also none – except that Bingham was to cover the gateway and open fire at his own discretion if a sizeable attack came.'

'That's all?' Black, his face white and thin, had a vague look about him in the flickering light from a storm lantern.

'His chief concern was for the sick, I think – '

'But you were not told to send men to his assistance if things went wrong?'

Stuart shook his head. 'No.'

'Then you must obey the spirit of such orders as Captain Ogilvie did give, Captain Stuart. You will act so as to protect the sick and keep the natives out of the city.'

'And leave B Company to it?'

'To what?' Black blinked up at him.

'To what looks to me like certain death, Captain Black.'

'You are melodramatic, Captain Stuart! However, you are

in charge now, and yours is the responsibility. I am a sick man and can do no more than offer advice.'

A look of contempt passed over Stuart's good-looking face as he left Black's quarters. Black's 'advice' had been very carefully put together so that it could not be quoted against him in the future, and its careful construction seemed to point to a lesser degree of sickness than Black himself claimed. Re-joining the Regimental Sergeant-Major at the south wall, Stuart made his decision.

'I'll not send out more men, Sar'nt-Major,' he said. 'To do that . . . it would only be to waste more lives.'

'Aye, sir. I believe that would be Captain Ogilvie's own wish.'

'It's not a decision I like, Sar'nt-Major.'

'Nor do any of us, sir, but it's the only one. We must consider the sick.' Cunningham's tone was heavy and sad: he and James Ogilvie had together bridged the gap that must of military necessity lie between warrant and commission, had bridged it and become good friends, good comrades-in-arms. Since the day James Ogilvie had joined the regiment at the depot in Invermore on Speyside, the Regimental Sergeant-Major had watched him grow from a Sandhurst-fresh second lieutenant to a captain in command of a company, from a youth to a man – watched, and done all he could to aid the young officer's progress. To Cunningham the name of Ogilvie of Corriecraig was synonymous with the name of the regiment itself. James Ogilvie's father, Sir Iain, had commanded the Royal Strathspeys as Colonel when Cunningham himself had been a junior N.C.O. Before Sir Iain, before Cunningham's own time, the grandfather had commanded. From its inception as a regiment of the line, it seemed, the 114th Highlanders had nurtured an Ogilvie – and now it began to look as though there would be no more. Cunningham had plenty of reason to know the ways of the Frontier tribes and of rebel leaders in particular . . .

He stiffened his shoulders. Sentiment and friendship must never intrude upon proper military decision. Young Captain Stuart was perfectly correct in the course he had decided upon, and he would have full support. Cunningham's vision blurred a little, and he thought bitter thoughts about Mr Hamish Dewar.

*　*　*

The Moon continued bright and cloud-free all through the night, spreading its light over all the area until it was paled by the rising dawn. Soon after Ogilvie's few words with Mac-Trease, two things had happened: firstly, the officer of the cavalry guard had ordered the prisoners to move, and they had been herded a matter of a hundred yards to their right, a manoeuvre designed simply to shift them clear of their surrendered arms. Secondly, the brilliance of the moon had shown them some work going on to the west, down towards the city gate but outside rifle range from the walls. A horde of tribesmen, forming a human chain, were moving bundles of collected brushwood, dried out by weeks of fierce sun, to build a pyramid-like structure around a tall pole set upright in the ground with a kind of totem surmounting it. As the night wore away, this pyramid grew and grew, broad based, high around the pole and its strange totem-figure; and it was not long before the British soldiers took in its eventual purpose: this was to be a bonfire, the signal for attack on the city as indicated by Gaftar Sahib earlier. But it was not until the more revealing light of dawn spread outward from the eastern hills that the full truth could be realised.

It was MacTrease who caught on first. 'Captain Ogilvie, sir! Didn't that native, Gaftar say something about a *woman's* death, sir?'

'Woman's death?' Ogilvie sounded puzzled.

'*Suttee*, sir! A Brahmin widow's death, sir! For Mr Dewar, sir! He's to die in the bonfire.'

Ogilvie stared in horror. 'God, no! What makes you say that, Colour-Sar'nt?'

MacTrease lifted an arm and pointed towards the pole. 'That thing at the top, sir, what we thought was a sort of totem. It's a corpse, sir – '

199

'*Mr Dewar?*'

'No, sir, not Mr Dewar. Just a corpse, sir. I can see it clearly. Look hard yourself, sir.'

Ogilvie was already doing so. He said, 'Yes, you're certainly right – about that.' He frowned, staring intently through narrowed eyes at the drooping corpse: there was a half-familiar look about the face, as of someone he had once met, someone forgotten. 'But I don't follow the rest of it.' He paused. 'That woman you questioned – did she –'

'She said nothing at all, sir, that Gaftar didn't say himself just after.' MacTrease spat on the ground. 'It was a waste of time, that! But, d'you see, sir, the native spoke of a signal – of Mr Dewar's death being itself the signal of a woman's death for him! It's what I say, sir, I am sure of it.'

'But the corpse –'

'The husband, sir, the one for whom the widow proclaims herself *suttee*, sir –'

'But it's sheer play-acting!'

'Which is what these people like, sir. A kind of symbolism –'

'But *suttee* was a Hindu custom – these people are not Hindus –'

'No, sir. They regard Hindus with contempt, sir. I spoke of symbolism. This is contempt for the Raj, sir – a contemptuous death, a Hindu woman's death, for a British officer, in full view of his whole regiment, sir!' MacTrease tugged at the neck-band of his khaki-drill tunic. 'It's made more pointed, sir, by the fact that *suttee* was abolished by British decree, sir, back in 1829. And it's bloody diabolical, sir!' The colour-sergeant was shaking with his emotion. 'With respect, sir. Mr Dewar's been God Almighty foolish, but he destroyed the guns, and he's not deserving of this, sir!'

'I know. Wait and see what happens, Colour-Sar'nt –'

'Captain Ogilvie, do you not –'

'That's enough, MacTrease. You know as well as I do, there's nothing anyone can do at this moment. And you may be wrong. We shall wait and see. Mr Dewar will not be let down if it's humanly possible to save him.'

He stared at MacTrease. After a few moments the N.C.O.s gaze fell away. 'Aye, well, sir. When you act, you'll have every man behind you, and that's a promise!'

* * *

Cunningham lowered his field-glasses. 'It's a corpse all right, Captain Stuart, sir, just as I thought. And been dead a fair while, I believe.'

'What's the idea, d'you suppose, Sar'nt-Major?'

Cunningham shrugged. 'That I can't say, sir, but the point of the bonfire is clear enough. They like nicely visible signals!'

'There's no movement yet.'

'No, sir, but that'll come the moment they light their beacon. Well, we're all ready!' Cunningham hitched at his Sam Browne belt.

'You're really convinced they'll attack?' Stuart asked.

'As convinced as I stand here, sir. They'll be wanting to finish us off as a point of honour, of revenge before the relief arrives, and if Mr Dewar was right, they'll have the word it's coming. They'll be believing they'll have it easy, too, sir, with the length of our sick list, which they'll be able to assess well enough.'

Stuart nodded. 'They won't like the guns, Sar'nt-Major. Well, you'd better pass the word quietly – we'll use no bugles yet. It's better if they're allowed to think we haven't tumbled to what they mean to do. Captain Bingham is to be ready to fire when the order's passed, all companies not detailed as sick quarter guard are to be alert along the walls and be ready to repel scaling-ladders and the like. All ammunition to be issued – all we have, and every man to be armed, including the medical details.'

'Very good, sir. Anything else, sir?'

Stuart raised an eyebrow. 'What have you in mind, Sar'nt-Major?'

'The pipes and drums, sir.'

'Pipers and drummers to be armed with the rest, and take their places along the wall.'

'Sir! With respect, sir. Just a few rifles . . . they'd not be missed until it comes to hand-to-hand fighting, sir.'

'You mean you want them to make music, Sar'nt-Major?' There was a hint of a smile in Stuart's eyes. 'To pipe us to Kingdom Come?'

The Regimental Sergeant-Major was far from smiling. 'Sir! It's important to give the men heart. We're a Scots regiment, sir, a *Highland* regiment. The pipes are our life's blood.'

Stuart blew out a long breath, and nodded his agreement. 'Have it your own way, then! My compliments to the Pipe-Major, and he's to muster the pipes and drums outside sick quarters, ready to march through the city.'

'Sir!' Cunningham's hand flew to the salute, and he turned about smartly, marching along the wall to the steps, left-right-left, back straight, shoulders square, pace-stick rigid and horizontal, Sam Browne as brightly shining as if it had just left the hands of his bearer in cantonments. Stuart looked after him with pride, respect, admiration, affection: if all the Regimental Sergeant-Majors of the British Army were fallen in on Horse Guards Parade in London, old Bosom Cunningham would still stand out as the best. As the deep-chested ramrod went down the steps, Stuart turned away; and as he did so, a lance-corporal called to him urgently.

'Sir! There's a party of natives making for the pile of brushwood, sir, carrying torches –'

Stuart ran towards the steps and shouted down. 'Sar'nt-Major . . . stand by now! They're about to light the bonfire.'

Cunningham glanced up. 'Sir!' He quickened his pace, began shouting at groups of men. Stuart went back to his own command position and looked down through one of the embrasures towards the advancing tribesmen and their smoking, flaming torches. His field-glasses picked out a familiar figure in the centre of the native torch-party, a figure with bound hands, being led along on the end of a loose rope and wearing the tartan of the Royal Strathspeys: Hamish Dewar, moving defiantly with an arrogant swing to his shoulders, and a look of contempt for his native escort on his face. For a moment Stuart was puzzled: but not for long. The intent was all too obvious and whatever the risks, whatever Ogilvie's orders had been, something now had to be done, and fast.

Stuart looked down upon the guns, grouped before the gateway, then shouted down urgently to the gunner captain.

NINETEEN

SINCE SHORTLY AFTER dawn, sound had been in the air — sound and movement. MacTrease stuffed his fingers in his ears. 'By God, sir,' he said, his face grey with strain, 'I can't stand the bloody tintinnabulations the bastards make!'

Silently, Ogilvie nodded, his own nerves stretched to breaking-point as he watched the corpse on its pole, the huge pile of brushwood waiting to lick clean the bones, and listened to the tinny music of the natives' bugles and trumpets. Gaftar's army was assembling now, making its dispositions for the climactic attack on the city and its besieged highlanders. Time passed painfully; helpless, Ogilvie and his company watched from inside the ring of the cavalry lances as, later in the morning, Hamish Dewar was hauled along on a rope's end. They watched as he was halted beside the waiting wood-stack. A few minutes after he had been halted, a runner came from the bonfire, where now Gaftar Sahib himself was sitting his horse, towards the herded, captive Scots.

This runner spoke to the officer in charge of the cavalry, who passed an order to his men. There was more movement then, movement of the prisoners themselves: the horses and the lances pressed in, shifting the Scots, willy-nilly, closer to the brushwood and the pole-held corpse. When they were within some twenty yards of what was to be Dewar's funeral pyre — for it seemed that MacTrease's forecast was likely to be proved correct — they were again halted, with the native cavalrymen holding the ring closely, so closely now that there was scarcely room for any man to move an arm. Gaftar, look-

204

ing down from horseback, gave Ogilvie a sneering smile and rode towards the circle.

'I think you understand now, do you not, Captain Sahib?'

'Understand what?'

'The course of events, my friend!'

Ogilvie said, 'I understand one thing, and that is, you'll not live long to boast in Dir of your vile – '

'Do not mislead yourself with false hopes, Captain Sahib! You believe your British Army will come in revenge, do you not?'

'I believe that, yes – '

'And well it may, but to what purpose?' Gaftar waved an arm around the great arena below the hills. 'Look, Captain Sahib, look at my own army – and then have second thoughts! Remember also that I have thrice as many men in Dir, and all well armed!'

Ogilvie was well enough aware of the massed force: infantry in solid blocks, regiment after regiment of eager natives, armed and jubilant, anticipating total victory; in support, the cavalry squadrons whose mounts were even now pawing the ground, almost human in their obvious keenness for swift running. Drawn up in the van of this army was the remnant of Gaftar's artillery: three heavy guns, with the action bullocks already yoked to the limbers. Thanks to Hamish Dewar, the artillery strength was little, but that little, Ogilvie knew too well, would go a long way towards the destruction of the 114th Highlanders inside Kalundabad . . .

He looked, as Gaftar rode superciliously away, towards Hamish Dewar. Dewar was standing straight, his head high, but his face was haunted and his whole body was trembling, while the set of his mouth indicated hard-clenched teeth. All the men were staring at him now: Ogilvie, looking away from what he could not currently help, studied the faces of his company. There was horror in many, hard anger in others. Ogilvie knew that not all the anger would be for the natives: Dewar had been all kinds of a fool, however brave, and soon they, as well as he, would suffer the results of his folly. Sick at heart, Ogilvie closed his eyes, trying to shut out horror while he could. He heard by his side the heavy breathing of Colour-Sergeant MacTrease, and a curious low muttering: he realised that MacTrease was saying a prayer, calling upon God for His urgent intervention. Then the prayer was cut off and Ogilvie heard MacTrease's voice, hoarse and high:

'They've fired the brushwood!'

Ogilvie opened his eyes. He saw the first lick of flame, heard the crackling as the tinder-dry wood caught. Smoke rose, spiralling high into the cloudless blue. Dewar was jerked forward on the end of his rope: he stumbled and fell. Men kicked at him as he lay on the ground, as he tried to climb back on his feet. There was a rising growl from the Scots, and an outward movement quickly halted by the sharp points of the lances.

'The bastards!' MacTrease's eyes were blazing. 'Oh, the bloody bastards!'

Dewar, back on his feet again, was dragged forward, pushed from behind by rusty, prodding bayonets. As his tormentors closed in towards the flaming bonfire, the rope was let go and he was held in a ring of bayonets, like the rest of the Scots in the ring of lances. The red light of the flames played over him. Looking past Dewar, past the billowing smoke, Ogilvie saw in the distance the Wolseley helmets along the top of the city walls, men watchful behind ready rifles, other men on the move behind them. He wondered what Robin Stuart would decide to do: his own orders had been clear, but in changing circumstances Stuart might well decide to ignore them and mount an attack.

As the flames licked upwards to the corpse at the head of the pole, Gaftar called for Dewar to be brought to him. The subaltern was pushed towards the native leader, to be held by the bayonets at the horse's side. Gaftar, imperious and upright, swept Dewar with his glance. 'You understand *suttee*, Lieutenant Sahib?'

Dewar said nothing.

'You will go to your death as did Brahmin and other high-caste Hindu widows, who immolated themselves at the cremations of their dead husbands, Lieutenant Sahib. An ancient custom among the Hindus, prevailing in India for two thousand years until stopped by the British. It is now to be started again by you, and your death shall be the signal for my army to attack the city.' Gaftar smiled, a strange light showing in his eyes. 'The Hindu women, the widows about to burn, used to cast their bodies on the flames shouting *satya, satya, satya* . . . which is to say in your tongue, truth. And in very truth, Lieutenant Sahib, the manner of your death, your dishonourable death as a woman, is a fitting one for a renegade who would fire and kill beneath a flag of truce,' Gaftar went on, in disregard of the actions of his own tribesmen in desecrating the English missionaries' flag of truce. He waved a hand towards the fire, towards the corpse now well alight at the head of the pole. 'Your companionship in death is also fitting, Lieutenant Sahib. The corpse that now burns is that of Jahangir Khan himself, the lickspittle of the British Raj, a traitor to his race. Are you ready to join him, Lieutenant Sahib?'

Still there was no answer from Dewar, who stood like a ramrod beside Gaftar's horse. Ogilvie stared up at the corpse of Jahangir Khan: he remembered his earlier half-recognition of a once known face. Now, as a result of Gaftar's words, that recognition was in full; the burning corpse he knew indeed to be that of Jahangir Khan. Earlier he had failed to connect the dead face with that of a man he had met, only the once, in circumstances that had been so different as to make the very difference an act of cruelty in itself: Jahangir Khan, at the great levée in the Murree garrison, a guest of Ogilvie's own father, had been imperious, haughty, handsome, richly turned out and bedecked with precious stones, a man of power and position who could not readily be correlated with the poor dead flesh, now burning away to extinction on the pole. Ogilvie's thoughts tumbled about in his brain. So Jahangir Khan was really dead: a long search was confirmed as ended. Was his death to signal the beginning of the end for the British along the Frontier, as Dewar's was to signal the attack upon the city behind? Gaftar's army was undefeated: victory bred its own support, its own aggrandisement.

Graftar was becoming impatient. 'Will you throw yourself voluntarily upon the flames, Lieutenant Sahib? Or must I order you to be thrown like carrion? I await your answer.'

Suddenly, Dewar's head jerked, striking forward and upward. Gathered saliva shot towards Gaftar, dribbled down his arm. In a loud voice Dewar spoke characteristically: 'You have my answer there, you swine. And may you rot in hell when the Raj catches you, and you hang in the civil jail at Nowshera, like a common thief!'

There was a cheer from the Scots behind him, but it was cut off short when once again the lance-points pressed cruelly into flesh that found no room to cringe away. A moment later Gaftar, his face twisted with fury, gave a hand signal. Close by, a bugle blew, a call that was taken up by others. Looking about him, Ogilvie saw the reaction in the native levies, a stiffening, a slight movement but a preparatory one. At any moment, the attack would begin, a great surge forward of men and horses, of rifles and scaling-ladders and rock-throwers and what was left of the guns. As the notes of the bugles died away, Ogilvie saw many pairs of dark-skinned hands reach for Hamish Dewar, and lift him off his feet, and sway his body backwards and forwards to gain momentum. His face was haggard, tortured in the red and yellow light, and his lips moved, but no words came. Sweat streamed down Ogilvie's face, soaking into his tunic-collar. Beside him, MacTrease was praying again, mumbling out his supplications almost incoherently.

Dewar's body was released at the height of the momentum; it shot forward in a rising arc, legs wide, bound hands close behind the back. It took the bonfire in a massive splutter of scattering sparks, hitting the burning remnant of the deposed native ruler's corpse: Dewar was almost at once lost to Ogilvie's sight, and imagination took over. The subaltern must have crashed through the thin crust of the flaming brushwood, must now be in process of cremation deep inside

208

where the fire would be at white heat. At least, it would have been a quick end.

Sweat poured from Ogilvie like rain, and he felt an uncontrollable shake in his body.

'Hold on, sir,' he heard MacTrease say. There's something happening round the other side, but I can't – ' The colour-sergeant broke off, then excitedly, grabbed Ogilvie's arm. 'Look, sir, look at the gates!'

Ogilvie lifted his head, then gave a gasp. From outside the city gateway there came a flash, followed closely by a puff of smoke that drifted on a light breeze, then a sharp crack. He had scarcely time to register the fact that Bingham's guns were in action before the explosion came, only a matter of yards to the right of the ring of native cavalry. There was a sharp crack and a rush of hot wind: earth and stones and rubble flew about and Gaftar went down in a heap on the ground. On the instant, the whole scene degenerated into the utmost confusion, with the attention of the horsemen now diverted towards their fallen lord and master.

Ogilvie heard MacTrease's urgent voice: *'Now, sir, now – take your chance, sir!'*

Ogilvie gave his head a shake as though to clear it. He looked around quickly, and took the offered chance. He reached out for the leg of one of the horsemen, and gave it a sudden tremendous jerk. The man came off his horse, looking mightily surprised but still holding on to his rifle. He smacked into the ground hard, flat on his back. Twisting his body away from Ogilvie, he was up in seconds, swinging his rifle-butt like a club as he came back on his feet, eyes harrowed and vicious above a heavy black beard. Desperately Ogilvie dodged the wild swings of the rifle, then went in with a fast crouching movement and managed to get his hands round the dismounted horseman's throat.

He squeezed with all his strength, squeezed murderously. Writhing, the native dropped his rifle, the better to tear at Ogilvie's strangling hands. At once, Ogilvie let go of the throat, brought his knee up hard into the man's groin, and grabbed the rifle from the ground. As the native let out a roar of pain, and doubled up, Ogilvie belted towards the funeral pyre. As he went other men followed, men who had already carried out their own personal attacks on their guards. Many rifles were taken before the horsemen could overcome their shock: and the Scots used these rifles well, bringing down a number of natives before Ogilvie had reached the fire. The heat was intense, insupportable: he could never fight through it, and in any case Dewar must be dead and burned already and he was wasting his time and effort . . . there was a roaring in his ears, his uniform began to smoulder, as did hair and eyebrows. Forced to retreat, he turned away and ran around the pyre. Above, the pole still carried the charred remains of Jahangir Khan, burning with a blue flame. As he ran he was dimly aware of more movement amongst the levies, of a rising sound of fear, and then he heard more explosions, the thunder of guns and the overhead whistle of shells. Then, suddenly, he was flat on his face on the bare ground.

For a moment he lay still, feeling he must have been hit by flying debris. Beneath him, something moved, and he struggled clear of a body. A voice said, 'For God's sake, James, why don't you look where you're putting your feet?'

'Hamish!'

'Yes,' Dewar said. 'It's me all right. Those bastards chucked me too bloody hard – I just skimmed the top and came down the other side. I –'

'Are you all right?'

'No. I think I've broken an arm. It hurts like bloody hell. D'you think you can untie my hands *carefully*, old man?' Dewar lifted his head a little, wincing with pain. 'What's going on – no one seems to be bothering about us, do they, and –'

'Bingham's brought his guns out,' Ogilvie said. 'Gaftar has other things to think about just now.' He fumbled at the ropes around Dewar's wrists. 'You've been lucky,' he said. 'I thought you were a goner, Hamish. We all did.'

Dewar grinned from a dead-white face. 'Not luck, just

bloody inefficiency. If those natives had been cricketers, they'd have bowled me better!'

* * *

'Sir!' Colour-Sergeant MacTrease came through the smoke clouds at the run, kilt swirling. 'By God, sir, you have Mr Dewar! Thank the Lord for that, sir!' He added, 'The natives are on the run from the guns, sir, and I believe the garrison's coming out. Do you not hear the pipes?'

Ogilvie listened. Faintly in the distance, he heard the wailing, accompanied by the beat of the drummers. The tune was 'Cock o' the North', traditional word that the 114th were attacking, marching into battle. His heart seemed to swell, and he felt a pricking behind his eyeballs that was not wholly due to the smoke. He asked, 'How are the rest of us, Colour-Sar'nt?'

'A company again, sir. We have a good few rifles among us, and we have a prisoner.'

'Who?'

MacTrease grinned like a devil with excellent news to give. 'Gaftar, sir. The wee bloody princeling himself – the bastard! He's in the midst of us, sir, and not liking it!'

'I'll bet! But keep the men in hand, Colour-Sar'nt –'

'I'll see to that, sir, as best I can, but I've no eyes in the back of my head, sir. If you understand me. Now, sir, can I give you a hand to bring Mr Dewar inside the lines as it were?'

Ogilvie nodded. 'Take it easy – he's broken an arm. All right, Hamish?'

'Yes, I can walk by myself. Just give me a hand on to my feet.'

They did so, then followed MacTrease's directions clear of the smoke. It was an astonishing scene that showed itself: the native levies were in much confusion, with men running here and there, shouting, and bugles and trumpets sounding out all over the place. From just outside the city walls Captain Bingham's mountain battery was pumping shells into

211

disorganised groups of cavalry and infantry; and from the gates the regiment, in sight now, was coming out behind the pipes and drums. It was a tiny force compared with Gaftar's still virtually undepleted army, a force of no more than four hundred men all told who could be advancing to extinction yet, once some kind of native leadership was re-established ... with this much in mind, Ogilvie turned to MacTrease. 'How is Gaftar?' he asked. 'Hurt?'

'No, sir. Just a fall from his horse, sir.'

'Fit to lead still?'

'Aye, sir, but so long as we have him –'

'That's the point, Colour-Sar'nt. We have to hang on to him, or he'll rally his troops, and then we're all done for. And *ipso facto*, when his levies know where he is, we're going to be the main target for attack.'

'Aye, sir, that's true, but he's the trump card for us to play when the attack comes, is he not, sir?'

'A hostage?'

'Exactly, sir! I'll be behind him with one of his own dirty bayonets, sir. The moment there's any trouble, sir, he gets a touch o' rust up his bottom. With your permission, sir.'

Ogilvie grinned. 'Permission granted, but only when I give the word. General Fettleworth will want a live leader rather than a dead one – and so will we, if we want him as a hostage.'

'I'll remember that, sir.' MacTrease clicked his teeth. 'It'll be a lesson to the bastards, sir, not to neglect the cleaning o' their bayonets. Rust can bring blood poisoning, sir, I'd not wonder!' Ogilvie, glancing sideways as they continued with all possible speed towards B Company, saw the keenly anticipatory look shining like a beacon in MacTrease's eyes. B Company had withdrawn with their prisoner – who, prudently, was being kept well out of sight of his followers – some distance from the funeral pyre, and were bunched together behind the outer cover of such of the men as had managed to seize rifles in the general confusion. There was a cheer as Ogilvie and MacTrease came in with Dewar, the square opening to let them through towards Gaftar Sahib.

212

Shells from Bingham's guns were coming dangerously close from time to time, but at least were having the effect, so far, of encouraging the native hordes to keep their distance. Gaftar was revealed lying on the ground beneath the bottom of one Private Forster, a big-built man who was taking his ease and clearly enjoying it.

'We appear to have changed roles, Gaftar Sahib,' Ogilvie said pleasantly.

'For a short time only –'

'Don't rely on it,' Ogilvie interrupted, wiping sweat from his forehead with the sleeve of his tunic. Grinning, he gestured to MacTrease. 'Prepare to take up your bayonet station, if you please, Colour-Sar'nt! Forster, let Gaftar Sahib get up, then take off your tunic.'

'Sir!' Forster scrambled to his feet and removed his tunic. 'What do I do with this, sir?'

'Wrap it round Gaftar Sahib's head. Tie it tightly by the arms.'

'Sir!' As Gaftar was lifted up, Forster made a good job of eclipsing the leader from sight of his army. MacTrease remained in rear of Gaftar Sahib, holding a bayonet with its point towards the native's rump.

'Now what, sir?' MacTrease asked.

'We make towards the gates, Colour-Sar'nt, and make contact with Captain Stuart. When we're fully re-armed with rifles, we'll join the main attack.'

'Will there be much hope of success, sir?'

Ogilvie shrugged. 'There's a chance. But our best hope lies in Gaftar Sahib. Are you ready, Colour-Sar'nt?'

'All ready, Captain Ogilvie, sir.'

'Right! March out at the double, Colour-Sar'nt – straight for the pipes and drums.'

MacTrease saluted, bawled the order and got on the move, keeping close behind Gaftar Sahib, who was guarded also by a private on either arm. The Scots ran as though being chased by the devil himself, the armed men on the flanks firing as they met groups of natives. The main part of the rebel army seemed to be concentrating away to their right; and, judging from the continuing panic and the wild, hither-and-thither dashes of the horsemen, they appeared currently to be in search of their leader. Ogilvie's running advance went on behind the cover of Bingham's exploding shells; and they seemed likely to be getting clear away with it when Ogilvie, looking round, saw a strong infantry formation cutting across from the right in an attempt to intercept. By this time, too, the native gunners had got the heavy artillery in action, and once again the city was under bombardment. Hoarsely Ogilvie encouraged the Scots on to greater speed: panting and gasping in the increasing heat of morning, they rushed on. One or two men fell headlong, to be grabbed on the run by their comrades and set back on their feet. Ogilvie saw the native infantry closing, then saw the flashes as they opened with their rifles. Men fell, clutching at throats and chests or going down with their heads running blood: a bullet zipped through Ogilvie's right sleeve, another through his helmet. His own few captured rifles were giving back a good answer, but they were not enough. Then, cutting across the sound of the guns, he heard the wailing of the pipes and for a moment he saw Pipe-Major Ross, marching straight and firm and taking no notice of the flying bullets: just for a moment, then Ross was overtaken by an avalanche of Highlanders, men who yelled out time-honoured war-cries and fired as they advanced on the native infantry. There was a lust for killing in the faces, a desire for revenge every bit as strong as that of Gaftar Sahib himself. They came on behind the steel of their bayonets, unstoppable: and the body of infantry broke, and turned away. Cheering came from the Highlanders, hoarse and victorious, as they charged after the fleeing rebels. Ogilvie cupped his hands round his mouth. 'Leave them!' he yelled. 'Back to the gates!' He turned as he felt a hand on his arm, and found Robin Stuart.

'They're on the run, James. Can't we finish the job?'

'With all that mob waiting? Don't be stupid, Robin. Get them back – and that's an order.' He waved a hand towards the centre of his own company. 'We've got Gaftar Sahib – I'll explain later. Have you a bugler?'

'Yes – '

'Then sound the Retreat at once.'

'But I tell you – '

'Get on with it, damn you!'

'Oh, all right!' Stuart called up his bugler and gave the order. The notes rang out, clear and strident over the confused battle sounds. The astonished, disappointed Scots slowed to a halt; belligerence glowed in their faces but they were taken in hand by the sergeants and corporals, and turned back. Ogilvie, cupping his hands again, roared out: 'To the gates, all of you! Back to the gates and into the city!' He waited until he had seen the order obeyed, then he moved his own company onward at the double with their vital prisoner. Coming up behind the mountain battery, he shouted at Bingham to cease fire, but the gunner captain took no notice. The guns crashed out again and again.

'Captain Bingham, you are to cease firing!'

'Don't be a bloody fool!' Bingham almost screamed at him, his face contorted. 'I'm firing my guns till we're over-run – '

'I tell you – '

'For God's sake, Ogilvie, use your eyes, can't you?' Bingham pointed. 'Look!'

Turning, Ogilvie felt suddenly cold in spite of the intense heat from the climbing sun, shining down on death and battle from a clear metallic sky. Through the smoke of the exploding shells a horde of men was pouring, horse and foot, apparently the whole of Gaftar's army advancing in an immense and powerful tidal wave. Almost in desperation, he looked around at what was left of his own small force: weary men, exhausted and wounded men in blood-stained uniforms, half of them without helmets, most of his own company without rifles – and, inside the walls, the very many sick; the sick whose last line of defence they were. Stiff-faced, he nodded at Bingham. 'Sorry!' he said. 'Carry on firing, and the best of luck!' He clapped the gunner captain on the shoulder, called an order to the Regimental Sergeant-Major who had at that moment appeared at his side. 'Form square, Sar'nt-Major. We'll fight here, and we'll fight to the last man. I want you to take personal charge of Gaftar Sahib, Sar'nt-Major – you and MacTrease. Take him inside the city and use him as a hostage to ensure proper treatment for the sick. You'll know what to do. You'll also report to the Colonel that Jahangir Khan is positively confirmed as dead and that his body was the one at the top of the pole. Quickly now, Sar'nt-Major –'

'Sir, I've no wish to leave you –'

'Orders, Sar'nt-Major! You've not much time. Don't waste what there is.' He held out his hand, and used the regiment's nickname: 'Goodbye, Bosom.'

'Goodbye, Captain Ogilvie. I'll be doing my best. Sir!'

'I know you will.' Ogilvie turned away, heard the Regimental Sergeant-Major passing the orders for forming square. He looked back towards the advancing hordes of tribesmen, saw pockets of them vanish in blood and flame and mangled flesh as Bingham's shells landed on target. Only those guns, gallant little pieces of almost toy artillery in such a situation, were slowing the native advance. That advance could not be held by the guns alone: within minutes now, the mob would be upon the Scots square, yelling, screaming, shooting and hacking with knives and the snaky, rusty bayonets. In his heart, Ogilvie knew that not a man could survive. It was to a large extent his own fault: he should never have made his sortie – but he had had to bring out Hamish Dewar. Or had he? Was any one man worth the sacrifice of a battalion?

A tumult of words flooded to Ogilvie's lips as he saw Dewar approaching: too many words, too many mixed emotions, for speech to prove adequate. He saw Dewar as through a mist, a mist of hatred, hatred that even now he must not give way to. He must cast no blame now, not even upon a cruel act of Providence that had sent Hamish Dewar to the Royal Strathspeys, sent him, it appeared, to wipe them out forever.

He met Dewar's eye. 'We fight to the last,' he said. 'You'll join the square, Hamish.'

'Of course. I just want a word, that's all. I want to say I'm sorry, James. Truly and deeply sorry. I've been a bit of a chump, I suppose. But I never thought it would turn out like this – ' He broke off suddenly, a puzzled look on his face as he stared around at the smoke and shell-bursts and the advancing tribesmen. He frowned, cocked his head a little towards the south. 'What's that, for God's sake?'

Ogilvie looked at him, then turned towards where Dewar was staring with his mouth half open. He could see nothing; but he heard a rhythmic thump, the distant but unmistakable thump of brass, and then what he believed to be a rattle of drums. He felt light-headed, felt like bursting into insane cackles of laughter as the sounds formed in his mind and began to make sense. It was military music, a regimental quickstep: *Do you ken John Peel at the break of day, Do you ken John Peel when he's far, far away . . . With his horse and his hounds in the morning . . .*

'It's our troops,' he said unsteadily. 'The Border Regiment, from Peshawar : . . it's Bloody Francis's relief column coming in!'

TWENTY

ROUNDING A SPUR of rock, Brigadier-General Fortescue saw
the walls and minarets of Kalundabad ahead in the distance,
white beneath the high sun. For some time past he and his
officers had heard the rumble of gunfire in the north; and
the word had been passed for all possible speed in the
advance. Now, through his field-glasses, he saw the splashes
of colour, the tartan of the 114th Highlanders.

'They're forming square,' he said, turning to his Chief of
Staff. Standing in his stirrups, he called across to the Colonel
of The Guides. 'Column of squadron,' he ordered. 'Fast as
you can! Then charge the main enemy force in line.' He
turned back to the Chief of Staff. 'Bring up the guns, Beech-
ing. They're to close the range a little, then wheel into line
and open in support of the Cavalry. Bugler?'

'Sir!'

'Sound the general advance.'

*　　*　　*

As the stirring notes of the bugles came clear and sharp
across the space between the city and the overwhelming
might of the advancing column, cheer after cheer rose from
the close-packed square and from the men left to guard the
city walls. Eyes became brighter, shoulders squarer. Now, the
tribesmen were going to get a taste, and more than a taste, of
their own medicine! The soldiers watched with full hearts as
The Guides and the men of Probyn's Horse thundered down
on the native concentration, watched as the heavy batteries

218

of the Madras Artillery opened in smoke and flame and thunder. Then, through the din and the acrid smell of the bombardment, came the onrush of infantry, men in khaki drill behind the Lee Enfields and the gleaming steel of the fixed bayonets. And as the shells crashed down and burst among them, Gaftar Sahib's hordes wavered and then ran, screaming, from the hooves and sabres and lances of the British cavalry that came in close behind the high explosive. They ran in complete confusion, seeming hardly to know where to go for safety: caught by the advancing infantry, they were spitted in their hundreds, like pigeons, on the English bayonets. Others were ridden into the ground by the mounted squadrons and decapitated by the slicing sabres or pinioned in agony by the lances. A long wail rose from them, from those that lived: a wail of anguish. The British infantry, men from Yorkshire and Lancashire, Derbyshire and the border lands of northern England, closed in at the run, hard and vengeful faces behind the steel and the bullets. From the first moment of Fortescue's order to engage, the issued was never in doubt. Before the noonday sun was over-head, Gaftar's army lay in ruins, with all his guns now smashed and useless and the fleeing remnants of his horse and foot — such as had escaped the pincer of Fortescue's column — being pursued to a surrender as they were herded like sheep towards the waiting rifles of the Sherwood Foresters, who had been detached to cut them off. Ogilvie, whose company had joined the relief force and had fought alongside them, was in no doubt that that day the flower of Gaftar's rebel army had withered and that this defeat would take the heart right out of the dissident movement in the capital of Dir.

* * *

'So you're Ogilvie. I know your father, of course. He'll have news to be proud of, when I'm able to send in a report.' Brigadier-General Fortescue, his uniform tunic dark with sweat, and the right sleeve in shreds from a sabre cut, leaned down from his horse and laid his left hand on Ogilvie's shoulder. 'Well done, Ogilvie – very well done indeed!'

'Thank you, sir – '

'You've had a hard time – I've had a word with your Sar'nt-Major, so I know the command had devolved upon you. I hear Jahangir's dead – do you confirm this?'

'Yes, sir.'

'Regrettable – very! Fortunately he has a reliable son.' Fortescue stared into the distance, frowning. 'How are things inside the city, Ogilvie?'

'Bad, sir – the Colonel and Major Hay are still very sick and – '

'Yes, I'm sorry about that, but medicos will do all they can, of course. Meanwhile I'll hold my column in camp outside the walls, but working parties will be sent in as required, in addition to the medical and nursing details. I'll see to it that all your men are rested while fresh men take over. Now – your full report, if you please, Ogilvie.'

As briefly as possible, Ogilvie informed Fortescue of past events, stressing the length of the sick list. The Brigadier-General listened intently; and that day he was as good as his word, relieving the 114th Highlanders of all duties and bringing out the sick to more sanitary conditions in his camp. Not until the sick had been made comfortable did he send for Ogilvie to come to his command tent and discuss among other matters the political issues and the capture of Gaftar Sahib. The rebel leader, he said, would be taken back to Peshawar when the column returned to cantonments.

'With his army defeated – which will much please General Fettleworth – and himself a prisoner, I don't expect further trouble. His support will melt fast now, we may be sure! I know you spoke of his having another large army in Dir, Ogilvie, but our Political Officers do not support this in their reports.'

'But isn't there a possibility of a rescue attempt, sir?'

Fortescue nodded. 'Of course there's a possibility, but I'm not unduly worried. However, because of that possibility, I

220

shall not delay here longer than is necessary to re-establish authority in the city. I'll get Gaftar away to safety as soon as possible, and leave a strong enough force here to conduct negotiations with Jahangir's successor.'

'And Gaftar Sahib himself, sir?'

'Will await General Fettleworth's pleasure – or more strictly, of course, Calcutta's. We'll have to take his damn tribesmen back as well – the prisoners. They'll be a confounded nuisance, but I can't leave them here to cause more trouble. They'll rot in jail for a while, then be packed off home again – sadder but wiser men, I would trust!' Fortescue blew out a long breath, then changed his tack. 'Your Mr Dewar,' he said abruptly. Tell me about him, Ogilvie. I've heard already about the flag of truce business, so don't be shy of including that.'

Ogilvie hesitated, guessing that Fortescue's informant would have been Andrew Black. He said, 'The flag of truce was unfortunate, sir – '

'Unfortunate, by God!'

'Sir, I think Mr Dewar acted entirely without thought – '

'No doubt! For an officer not to *think* is scarcely a recommendation, Ogilvie!'

'No, sir. But in the circumstances I think a Court Martial would be most unfortunate. Mr Dewar has acted with extreme courage, sir. Not only in his destruction of the guns, which saved a good many lives, but also on the march here – '

'You mean when he attacked a pocket of snipers when you were crossing the Panjkora. I've heard about that too.'

'From the Colonel, sir?'

'Yes. Also from your Sar'nt-Major.' Fortescue stretched out his legs and lay back on his camp stool, supporting his body against the tent-pole. 'Yes, he's acted as a man often enough, I'll grant! I gather he saved your Colonel's life on that occasion.'

'Yes, sir. I witnessed it myself.'

Fortescue gave him a sweeping look and pulled at the ends

of his moustache. 'More may well be heard of that – and I agree that a Court Martial might well be inappropriate. It's a problem for General Fettleworth rather than for me, of course – a dilemma, indeed – but there may be a way out.'

'Sir?'

Fortescue shrugged. 'I've brought news for Dewar – bad news certainly, but it could be turned to good account. Lord Taymouth's dead, so is –'

'Lord Taymouth, sir – Dewar's father?'

'I'm afraid so, Ogilvie. An accident that also carried off Dewar's elder brother – and many other people also. They were crossing the Pentland Firth, on a shooting trip to the Orkneys, and the ferry capsized in a gale. A bad business.' Fortescue shook his head, then went on, 'So Mr Dewar now becomes the Earl of Taymouth, which I'll wager is something he never expected . . . with all the responsibilities of that high position, and a large estate to administer!'

'Sir, you mean –'

'I mean,' Fortescue said, this time with a throaty chuckle, 'that this may be thought an appropriate moment for an heir to send in his papers . . . so that bygones can be left to be bygones. It might help, Ogilvie, if it were put to him tactfully that an officer who fails to think in a time of crisis is better off in honourable retirement – do you follow me?'

* * *

Four days later, with Lord Dornoch and Major Hay still sick but progressing towards full recovery, the Royal Strathspeys marched out southward for cantonments with a part of Fortescue's column, escorting their prisoners. They left their many dead behind them in their lonely plots beneath the high surround of the hills and they drew their sick along in the wagons of the medical column. The York and Lancaster Regiment had been left behind on garrison duty, together with a squadron of cavalry and two gun batteries, and were encamped outside the city until such time as the disease had

222

cleared away. The column marched proudly towards the Panjkora and the Malakand with the regimental colours and the guidons of the cavalry streaming out, and the sound of the pipes and drums in the van of the advance. During the long days of marching Ogilvie had many talks with Hamish Dewar: but found that it was not necessary to implement the suggestions of Brigadier-General Fortescue. The new Lord Taymouth, it seemed, had come to certain conclusions on his own by the time the column reached the Malakand.

'The old man,' he said in reference to his dead father, 'was always terribly keen on his land. The tenants, you know, the men who worked for him, the clan – all that sort of thing. It was his life. I dare say you understand.'

'Of course I do.'

Dewar, whose left arm was splinted and carried in a sling, marched for a while in silence. 'I've been thinking,' he said farther on. 'It's up to me now, to carry it all on. To take over.'

'You've done that already, haven't you, in a sense? You're the Earl, Hamish. Just as when the Monarch dies . . .'

'Yes, but for the Monarch it's automatic. In my case it isn't. I have the option – there's nothing to stop me being an *absentee* earl. The thing is, I'm not sure I want to be.'

Ogilvie said nothing.

'Of course, there's the regiment to consider too, and that's my difficulty. I have a responsibility there as well. I don't like to . . . well, duck out after one action. It would be letting the men down in a way, wouldn't it?'

'Oh, I dare say they'd get over it,' Ogilvie said with his tongue in his cheek.

Dewar looked at him sharply. 'What do you mean by that, James?'

'Oh . . . simply that it's up to you to get your priorities in order! Perhaps your tenants need you more, Hamish, than the regiment.'

'D'you think so?' Dewar sounded wholly serious. 'I don't know so much. The 114th are something of a family, after

223

all, and members of a family don't walk out on each other. You know how the men like titled officers in their regiments. It gives them an extra edge, socially, something to boast about. Besides, there's something else.'

'What else?'

'Well,' Dewar answered, sounding self-conscious now but at the same time mightily proud. 'I don't mind telling you, but I'd sooner it wasn't talked about yet.' He paused. 'The Colonel sent for me just before we marched out. Not a word about the flag of truce – I suppose he thought the one wigging was enough. He talked a lot about the Panjkora, and that business with the guns . . . '

'Go on?'

Dewar said, 'He's recommending me for the V.C. And I don't like the idea of depriving the regiment of that, you see.'

Ogilvie almost gasped: there was something grotesque about the award of the Victoria Cross to Hamish Dewar in all the circumstances, in all the results of his various acts of foolishness, even though two of his acts had undoubtedly merited it. Controlling himself Ogilvie said warmly, 'My dear chap, you have my congratulations. I'm delighted to hear it, I really am.'

Dewar gave a small cough. 'I understand you yourself verified to the Colonel . . . what I did.'

'I told him the facts, Hamish, that's all.'

'Well, that was decent of you, very decent. It makes my leaving the regiment even harder, even more of a let-down. I hope the men will understand.'

'Then you've decided?'

'Well, yes, I have really. In my heart, you know. For my father's sake.'

They marched on behind the pipes and drums, triumphantly yet sadly wailing, the wild Highland sounds echoing back off the rocky hillsides as the column came once again into the Malakand Pass. Ogilvie's head was in something of a whirl as, turning, he looked back on what was left of the regiment. So many dead in the name of the Raj, men who had died and been left behind far from their native glens and lochs and high mountains, sacrifices made to the balance of power along the North-West Frontier of India, men who had died that an Empire might live on, men who had died because a fanatic had stirred up the tribes to bloody rebellion against the Queen-Empress, men who had died because a stupid subaltern had been unable to control his innate hatred of other men, men with brown skins . . .

Ogilvie gave an involuntary sigh. It seemed not even to have crossed Hamish Dewar's self-centred mind that he had only narrowly escaped a Court Martial and total disgrace. He could well appreciate the dilemma that might have faced Bloody Francis, for if Dewar had not made his decision the right way, that Court Martial could have been inevitable, and would have made a most curious bedfellow for the Victoria Cross! Ogilvie stifled his sigh and said, 'I think you've decided wisely, Hamish.'

*   *   *

On a morning three months later Ogilvie stood looking down from his bedroom window in London's Eaton Square, where he and his mother were staying with friends for three nights before taking the train north from King's Cross to Corriecraig. Hamish and the widowed Countess of Taymouth were also staying with the Ogilvie's host and hostess, whose kindly view had been that brother officers would wish to be together. This morning, a great day, Ogilvie was wearing the full-dress uniform of the 114th Highlanders, The Queen's Own Royal Strathspeys. Once again, his head was in a whirl, and had seemingly been so ever since the day he had been sent for in Peshawar by Lieutenant-General Francis Fettleworth to be informed officially by the Commander of the First Division in person of sundry awards: the Victoria Cross to Lieutenant the Earl of Taymouth whose papers would shortly be going in; of the Distinguished Service Order to himself, Captain James Ogilvie; and of the Medal for Distinguished Conduct in the Field to Colour-Sergeant MacTrease, this latter being on Ogilvie's own recommendation and report. And informed further that Her Majesty, much excited by the news from Kalundabad, had commanded the personal appearance of all three recipients at a special investiture to be held in their honour at Buckingham Palace. From that time on, life had been a round of non-military duties: the social obligations had taken over. Levées, parties, balls, with himself and Hamish Dewar being lionised, objective of all the matrons in Peshawar, Nowshera and Murree with daughters for disposal. There had been one quiet interlude with his parents in Murree, but the quiet was only relative and inclined to be interspersed with more social demands, for the son of Sir Iain Ogilvie, General Officer Commanding the Northern Army, could not be allowed too much anonymity. After this, the P. & O. for home with a proud Lady Ogilvie, and more lionisation, with Hamish Dewar not especially backward in speaking of his deeds.

And then London, and wild scenes of enthusiasm upon disembarking at Tilbury; and similar scenes at St Pancras, where the boat train pulled in; and in the very streets, and outside the house in Eaton Square, and outside Wellington Barracks where Colour-Sergeant MacTrease was an honoured guest of the Sergeants' Mess: crowds and cheering, and enthusiastic bawling of Soldiers of the Queen, and waving of flags, and gasps from the young ladies strolling, beneath their parasols, with their chaperons or parents along Bond Street, and urchins grasping sleeves in Piccadilly – for the press had seen to it that the faces of Captain Ogilvie and Lieutenant Lord Taymouth were very well known to everyone in London; and London, which was proud of its soldiers and its Empire, had responded warmly to bravery and endeavour.

And now this morning, with the hands of his watch approaching ten-twenty-five.

A knock at his door, discreet, polite.

He turned from the window. 'Yes?'

A private soldier, detached from the regiment to act as his

servant whilst away from India, entered. 'Sir! The carriage is ready, sir!'

'And Lord Taymouth?'

'Going down now, sir.'

Ogilvie nodded. 'Thank you, Garrett.'

'Sir!' The man hesitated. 'The best o' luck, sir, when you meet Her Majesty.'

'Thank you again, Garrett,' Ogilvie said with a smile. He walked across the room, picked up his Highland bonnet bearing the distinctive hackle of the Royal Strathspey, looked at his reflection in a long mirror while Private Garrett ran a final brush over his tunic and tartan cloak and examined the sheath of his broadsword. The set of the kilt was perfect, should prove a joy to Her Majesty, who loved her highlandmen; the shoes shone with polish beneath white spats. The sun-browned face spoke of foreign service, of the long years of fighting on the North-West Frontier . . . with a frown of irritation with himself Ogilvie turned sharply away and left the room to be greeted in the hall by his mother and Lady Taymouth, and by his host, Lord Westringham. Waiting by the carriage, after the bowing flunkeys, he found Hamish Dewar, whose arm was still in a hero's sling. Dewar was silent for once, and his fingers were shaking a little.

'Nervous?' Ogilvie asked, smiling.

'Oh, a little, don't you know! Nothing much. I doubt if she's as . . . ferocious as people say.'

The ladies came down the steps: after them, Ogilvie and Dewar entered the carriage and the coachman got on the move. There was cheering from a group of workmen, and as later the carriage, taking the long way round, rolled along Piccadilly, gentlemen removed silk hats, and bowed, whilst the ladies on their arms smiled approvingly of valour. Valour! Ogilvie, remembering the newspaper placards and headlines, felt himself flushing in embarrassment. ROYAL WELCOME FOR HEROES' RETURN TO OUR ISLAND SHORES, they had said. GALLANT SOLDIERS OF THE QUEEN TO HAVE AUDIENCE OF HER MAJESTY AT THE PALACE WHERE SHE WILL BESTOW HER REWARDS FOR GLORIOUS VALOUR. And the horribly overwritten news story, sentimentalised out of all recognition by a sugary pen: HOW OUR SCOTTISH HEROES OF THE DAY SAVED THE PAX BRITANNICA IN THE SAVAGE ORIENT.

Along Piccadilly, and down the Haymarket and Cockspur Street to Admiralty Arch and the Mall. The Mall was packed all the way to the palace; police and soldiers of the Brigade of Guards lined the road. As the carriage came out from Admiralty Arch it was joined by a mounted escort of The Blues in shining breastplates and red-plumes flying over brightly-burnished helmets. The cheers continued all along the route, with Hamish Dewar, smiling, politely acknowledging them: he was, naturally, the principal hero. It was not every day that Her Majesty bestowed the Victoria Cross. Ogilvie looked across at the fresh green of the trees lining the Mall: so different from the grim brown-ness of the Frontier! It was a wonderful morning, fresh and bright with sun and a slight cool breeze to ruffle the leaves and bring a dapple to the roadway. Down to the gates of Buckingham Palace, the sweep into the forecourt past the saluting sentries and policemen, then out of the bright sunlight as they came beneath the palace itself. They were met by polite gentlemen in strange uniforms as a flunkey held open the carriage door: there were bows, salutes, handshakes from a bewildering collection of dignitaries, then they were led by a splendid-looking figure along a maze of passages and corridors until at last they emerged into a great ante-chamber to be met by no less a person than the Lord Chamberlain, the Marquess of Cholmondeley, who would present them to Her Majesty. Here, awaiting their arrival, they found Colour-Sergeant MacTrease.

Ogilvie greeted him warmly and with pleasure in a familiar face. 'How are you feeling, Colour-Sar'nt?'

'Sir! Poorly, sir. Just nerves. Waiting to see Her Majesty, sir, is worse than waiting for Gaftar Sahib to use his bloody guns, sir.'

Ogilvie coughed: the Marquess of Cholmondeley was looking faintly amused, but Her Majesty Queen Victoria would scarcely approve strong language. A moment later there was a gesture and a word of command from the Marquess: great doors were opened by footmen in knee-breeches. A long way off, it seemed, at the end of a red carpet, a small figure in black, with a white bun of hair drawn tightly back from a round face, was sitting regally upon a throne – the Queen-Empress waiting to receive her returned soldiers.

With Dewar and MacTrease, Ogilvie advanced upon the Queen. Dewar, as recipient of the highest honour of all, was first presented. Ogilvie was scarcely aware of the details of the ceremony: he could recall, later, his somewhat stumbling kneel so that Her Majesty could pin the cross of the Distinguished Service Order to his breast with its blue-edged red ribbon: he could recall the fact, but not the form, of Her Majesty's few words of congratulation and gratitude. He could recall Dewar's somewhat self-satisfied smirk, and Mac-Trease's terrible and unusual clumsiness that led him almost to fall physically upon the small, rotund figure of Her Majesty. And that was all.

What remained in his memory afterwards with vividness was the informal talk with the Queen once the ceremony was over. She sent everyone else away except for Lady Ogilvie and Lady Taymouth, saying she wished to talk privately with her soldiers. Coffee was brought, and biscuits and cake, and a very sweet sherry. MacTrease, when addressed, stammered himself into utter speechlessness: the Queen understood well enough. 'My soldiers,' she announced, 'are more accustomed to the field of battle than to drawing-room idleness. I am a fortunate woman that this is so. You have done splendidly, Colour-Sergeant MacTrease, and you are a credit to Scotland and the Empire. Now, tell me about *your* battles, Lord Taymouth.'

'Ma'am, I hesitate to bore you,' Dewar said with a nice self-deprecation. 'It was little enough.'

The Queen smiled, and laid the end of a fan upon Dewar's arm. 'So modest,' she said. 'So brave, and so modest. We shall allow Captain Ogilvie to tell us of your heroism, Lord Taymouth.'

The scraped-back white hair, the direct and challenging

eyes, the tight mouth were turned in Ogilvie's direction. He
moistened his lips. 'Ma'am,' he began in embarrassment at
having to talk in heroic terms of a soldier's duty. 'Mr – Lord
Taymouth – we were crossing the Panjkora River . . . ' He
stumbled on, recounting to Her Majesty what he was well
aware she must of necessity know already. The Queen
listened intently, darting an occasional glance towards Lady
Taymouth and Lady Ogilvie, who were also listening with
rapt attention. When he had finished the Queen turned
again to Hamish Dewar, her eyes unashamedly moist.

'So *brave*,' she said once again. 'Such a *leader*. Yet we
understand you have sent in your papers, Lord Taymouth,
or are about to do so?'

Dewar inclined his head humbly. 'Yes, Ma'am, with great
regret.'

'A pity, such a pity,' the Queen murmured. She paused,
looking at Dewar with much friendliness and concern. 'You
will not reconsider – perhaps as a personal favour to us?'

Ogilvie held his breath: the Queen could scarcely know
what she was asking!

'Ma'am, I really don't know what to say.' Dewar looked
helpless, saddened, and appealing. 'There is a conflict of
responsibilities, and I don't feel free to follow my own
inclinations. I hope you'll understand, Ma'am, and forgive.'

'Forgive, Lord Taymouth?' The Queen raised her eyebrows. 'Really there is nothing to forgive, since you are following your duty to succeed your dear father. Such a
tragedy. We are *deeply* sorry.'

'Thank you, Ma'am.' Dewar looked down at his feet: for
the first time Ogilvie, following the downcast eyes, realised
how big the feet were, very suitable for putting into things;
but there was no doubt about it, Hamish Dewar was doing
splendidly with Her Majesty. She assured Lady Taymouth
that she had a son to be proud of, a son to whom duty was
paramount; she enquired interestedly about the Taymouth
estates, part of which marched with her own royal lands at
Balmoral on Deeside: she enquired about his sporting
interests. Then, with a happy look in her eye, she made an

announcement. 'Lord Taymouth,' she said almost archly, tapping a black-shod foot, 'we have had words with our good Lord Wolseley. Since it is your intention to leave our army, we must see that you leave with a proper rank. You will be promoted Captain before your papers are accepted. As Captain the Earl of Taymouth you shall have not only rank in our peerage, but will also have the overt indication that you have served with honour and glory in our wonderful army.' There was quite a shake in the old Queen's voice and she gave every appearance of having an enormous lump in her throat. After that, her words with Ogilvie and his mother were perfunctory, consisting of an enquiry as to his father's health and a reminder that Sir Iain, when commanding the battalion years before and doing duty at Balmoral, had brought his family to afternoon tea in the castle, at which repast the young Ogilvie had rudely rejected a bun he considered stale; and a somewhat acid comment that Sir Iain, when *his* father had died, had remained with his regiment in preference to taking up his feudal duties on his estates. This was both contrary and unjust, and no doubt no one knew better than Her Majesty; but one did not argue with the Queen.

That night James Ogilvie attended another function, one of a very different character and, on the whole, more natural and enjoyable: a celebration in mufti with Colour-Sergeant MacTrease, just the two of them, Hamish Dewar having sped north to Taymouth Castle by an overnight train. The celebration was in Ogilvie's club, and MacTrease became rather the worse for drink.

'It's one way to promotion, sir,' he said, wiping the back of his hand across his mouth. 'Mind, I'd not grudge any good officer a bit o' luck in getting promotion, but yon Dewar, sir, with respect . . . och, I'll not say it in case they call it bloody treason! But there's not been a word said, sir, about that flag o' truce, or about him getting the battalion into the bloody muck in the first place – '

'Careful, Colour MacTrease. It's all in the past now, and it must stay buried.'

231

MacTrease took a gulp at his whisky. 'Aye, sir, you're right, o' course. But I lost many friends out there in Kalundabad, from the bloody filthy cholera as well as from bullets. That's what sticks in the throat, sir.' He took a long look around the room in which they were sitting: old, worn leather chairs, dark old wood, beautifully polished. Desiccated old retainers in stiff white shirts and black tails, waiting to do the gentlemen's bidding. Elderly inert figures laid at full stretch in the comfortable chairs, some younger ones laughing by a new-fangled bar across one corner. MacTrease once again wiped his mouth with his hand and said, 'Captain the Earl of Taymouth, Jesus wept! Och, it'll no' be long before yon lord's back in London, estates to look after or not! That's his life, sir, and I'll no' believe he's leaving the regiment from any sense of duty to his tenants – but just because once he'd seen the Frontier, sir, he made up his mind he didn't want ever to see it again!'

'If I were you, MacTrease, I'd keep that opinion to myself.'

MacTrease chuckled throatily. 'Awa' with ye, Captain Ogilvie, ye share it yersel'! Do you know something, Sir?'

'Well?'

'London's lost its savour, sir. Och, I've had a good time, but enough's enough.' He brooded over his glass, sadly.

'Why stay in London, then?'

'I'm not, sir. I'm awa' to Glasgow in the morning, to visit a sister. Then on to Invermore, where I'll drink whisky till the *Malabar's* ready to sail to Bombay. And I'll tell you another thing, Captain Ogilvie, sir, and it's this: I can't wait, sir, to be back with the regiment again!' He hiccupped, loudly.

Ogilvie smiled. 'It's the same with me, Colour MacTrease, just the same. I'm off to Corriecraig with my mother tomorrow night and I'll not miss London either.' He brought out his watch. 'Time I was off to bed,' he said.

'Then good luck, sir.' MacTrease raised his glass high. Ogilvie did likewise. 'Aye, luck,' MacTrease repeated sardonically, 'and a long life to enjoy it in!'

Ogilvie drained his glass. They left the club together, and in the street Ogilvie held out a hand. '*Au revoir*, Colour-Sar'nt. I'll see you aboard the *Malabar* for Bombay.'

Walking alone into the night, his thoughts went across the seas to the Indian sub-continent, to hot days on manoeuvres or in action or on parade, to lazy days in cantonments or in the cool hill-station air of Cherat or Simla; to sweating nights beneath the mosquito-nets, to great parties given by men who had done things with their lives – by colonels and generals and native rulers; to dancing, drinking, or riding out in the fresh air beneath the clustered low-slung stars. It was a better life than London had to offer, for all the green freshness of St James's Park and the Mall! Ogilvie wished Hamish Dewar all the luck in the world: he felt that MacTrease had been right and that it would indeed not be long before the newly-fledged Earl returned to London. He had the London drawing-room look: fleshy-faced men, men who would run to paunches in later life, often had. Dewar would like being lionised in the drawing-rooms of Mayfair and Belgravia. He would be able to make much of his brief military service, and the only flag of truce he would need to worry about would be that borne by the matronly mothers of the season's debutantes . . .

Ogilvie walked on, not hurrying swinging his cane, sniffing the summer-night air. Ahead of him an old man, who looked like an old soldier, cranked the handle of a barrel-organ. *Do ye ken John Peel with his coat so gay. Do ye ken John Peel when he's far, far away, With his horse and his hounds in the morning . . .*'

Coincidence! Memories crowded again. Ogilvie fumbled in his pocket, brought out a half-crown and dropped it in the old fellow's ready cap.

'Why, thankee, sir, thankee.' A finger lifted to the lined forehead. Before he was recognised, Ogilvie moved on. His thoughts were resting, jumbled. In his mind the audience with Her Majesty lingered still. The old Queen's farewell words to Hamish Dewar would be with him to the end of his days: 'You will be such a loss to our army,' the Queen had said solemnly, 'and *especially* to your own regiment. Had you remained in our service, you would have had such a *splendid* future.'

Like MacTrease, Ogilvie couldn't go back to India soon enough.

THE END

VICTORY AT SEBASTOPOL by VIVIAN STUART

Thousands had died during the harsh Crimean winter of 1854/55, but the besieged Russian naval base of Sebastopol was still holding out . . .

On May 22nd an allied squadron of fifteen thousand men was on its way to attack Kertch and Yenikale and force entry into the landlocked Sea of Azoff, in order to cut the enemy's vital supply route to Sebastopol. Commander Phillip Hazard of *HMS Huntress* had a gruelling, if not impossible, task ahead of him. For he had been ordered to sound and buoy a channel off the Cheska Bank to ensure safe passage for the Allied squadron. He knew he would have to face the treacherous silting sandbanks, the Russian gun batteries, and the dreaded floating bombs which could cause so much destruction. But what Phillip Hazard didn't know was that he'd have to face a court martial as well . . .

0 552 09869 8 – 40p

THE LOTUS AND THE WIND by JOHN MASTERS

It is 1881 and Britain and Russia face each other across the North West Frontier. The prize is that great jewel of Asia which Britain treasures and Russia covets – India – and in between lie the deserts of Afghanistan, Persia, Turkestan . . .

Under stigma of cowardice in action, a young Ghurka officer, Robin Savage, is sent as a spy to uncover a Russian plan of invasion. He follows the trail of a murdered agent thousands of miles over plains, mountains and lonely deserts where the merest whisper seems an intrusion . . . where only a man like Savage, whose strange affinity for solitude cuts him off from his fellow men, could ever feel at home . . .

0 552 09256 8 – 40p

BAMBOO AND BUSHIDO by A. G. ALLBURY

I heard a thin scream in Japanese.
I opened my eyes, my stomach churning, and half rose on to my elbows. There was a blinding, shuddering crash and a sheet of acrid flame, and the Rakuo Maru faltered, and then seemed to leap broken-backed out of the water. I tried to get to my knees, and a solid wall of green pounded me flat on to the deck. I lay there, flattened, helpless, as the giant sea boiled and hissed around me. I thought then, for one terrible moment, that we were plunging straight down into the boiling sea.
The deluge suddenly ceased and, spluttering and choking, I struggled to my feet. A sickly gleam was spreading across the sea; squatting on the horizon hung a half-grown moon. It looked indescribably evil.

0 552 10015 3 – 50p

HORNED PIGEON by GEORGE MILLAR, D.S.O., M.C.

George Millar was an army lieutenant fighting in North Africa when he was captured by German soldiers. Handed over to the Italians, he was taken to Italy and imprisoned in a concentration camp at Padula. Despite dysentery and hardship, George's courage and determination kept him from despair. His first planned escape failed by a hair's breadth and he was transferred to a punishment camp. After the Italian armistice he and some fellow-prisoners attempted a second break-out, but were foiled by the Germans. Next Millar was moved to a German camp near Munich. He made his third daring bid for freedom at night, from a fast-moving and closely-guarded train. As he jumped, he was shuddering with cold and fear of failing once again . . .

0 552 09901 5 – 60p

THE LAST DOGFIGHT by MARTIN CAIDIN

An island in the Pacific during the last months of World War II ...

Captain Mitch Ross was a veteran, the leader of the 441st Fighter Squadron. He had been badly wounded, bounced, shot at, set aflame – and survived. Flying inferior planes, he had destroyed many of the enemy. He was tough, skilled, a killer, a craftsman. Rumour had it he was charmed in the air ...

Lieutenant Senior Grade Shigura Tanimoto was the last member of an ancient *samurai* family, living by the code of the Bushido. Since the war began, he had shot down nineteen American fighter planes. Tanimoto treasured loyalty and devotion, honour and courage. Revered by his fellow pilots, he was their champion ...

Ross and Tanimoto had become living legends. And, as the end of the war approached, one of the young air aces challenged the other to a duel of honour in

THE LAST DOGFIGHT

0 552 09929 5 – 60p

PRIVATE NAVY by BAIRD EATHERLEY

H.M. Motor Launch 127 was built for war. Her Captain was a veteran, wearing the ribbon of the Victoria Cross. Her crew was a tough, battle-scarred group of men to whom war was no stranger ...

PRIVATE NAVY

And Captain and crew shared many things – the screaming shells of fighter cannons, the lethal threat of enemy submarines, and the knowledge that war was a dangerous business and that their lives were easily expendable ...

'As exciting and gripping a tale of unconventional war as has yet been told.'   – GUARDIAN JOURNAL

0 552 09932 5 – 50p

THE RAVI LANCERS by JOHN MASTERS

The Ravi Lancers are an anomaly: the private regiment of an Indian Prince, serving with the British. Their new commanding officer, Warren Bateman, is determined to mould the regiment into a first-class fighting force, although like all the best officers of the old Indian Army he is sympathetic to his men. They, though, owe their allegiance to Krishna Ram, the Rajah's heir and demi-god. It was Krishna's anglophile enthusiasm which brought the Lancers to the Western Front. But once there bitter conflict becomes inevitable. And in the Flanders mud and horror of 1914, the clash between Indian and English temperament and tradition becomes a private war between two men and their women that has tragic consequences.

0 552 09253 3 – 45p

They dropped from the air into the midst of the enemy defences . . . prepared to fight hand to hand as soon as their boots hit the ground. They were the 'paras' – all of them volunteers – reckless men with a reputation for incredible toughness, boldness, and bravado . . .

HUNTERS FROM THE SKY by CHARLES WHITING

And the men who started it all were the fanatical German paratroopers, the *Fallschirmjaeger*. In 1941 they captured Crete from the air, and achieved a staggering victory. At the same time they sowed the seeds of their own defeat – for their losses were so heavy that they could never again drop into battle in such large numbers . . .

Hunters from the Sky traces the extraordinary history of the German Parachute Regiment from 1940 to 1945.

0 552 09874 4 – 50p

A SELECTED LIST OF WAR BOOKS
APPEARING IN CORGI

All these books are available at your bookshop or newsagent ; or can be ordered direct from the publisher. Just tick the titles you want and fill in the form below.

CORGI BOOKS, Cash Sales Department, P.O. Box 11, Falmouth, Cornwall.
Please send cheque or postal order, no currency.

U.K. and Eire send 15p for first book plus 5p per copy for each additional book ordered to a maximum charge of 50p to cover the cost of postage and packing.

Overseas Customers and B.F.P.O. allow 20p for first book and 10p per copy for each additional book.

NAME (Block letters)...

ADDRESS ....

(NOV 75)..